THE MIDAS MURDERS

THE MIDAS MURDERS

PIETER ASPE

Translated by Brian Doyle

PEGASUS CRIME
NEW YORK LONDON

THE MIDAS MURDERS

Pegasus Crime is an Imprint of
Pegasus Books LLC
80 Broad Street, 5th Floor
New York, NY 10004

The translation of this book is funded by the Flemish Literature Fund
(Vlaams Fonds voor de Letteren - www.flemishliterature.be)

First Pegasus Books edition December 2013

Interior design by Maria Fernandez

Library of Congress Cataloging-in-Publication Data is available.

ISBN: 978-1-60598-487-2

10 9 8 7 6 5 4 3 2 1

Printed in the United States of America
Distributed by W. W. Norton & Company

For my daughters
Tessa and Mira

Let him who seeks continue seeking
  until he finds.
When he finds, he will become troubled.
  When he becomes troubled,
  he will be astonished,
  and he will rule over the All.

—*Gospel of Thomas*

The best of prophets of the Future is the Past.

—Byron

1

Adriaan Frenkel sipped at his cloudy, lukewarm cocktail. It tasted bitter. He pulled a face and tapped the glass with his signet ring.

"Waiter," he grunted.

The bartender put down his rag and looked the Dutchman up and down with a sneer.

"Sorry, friend, but there's no way I'm gonna drink this piss."

"Monsieur is not satisfied?"

Mario, thickset with Mediterranean features and traces of permanent stubble, glared in anticipation at the difficult customer.

"Non," the Dutchman responded self-consciously. "Je veux . . . eh . . . give me. . . ." His French had reached its limit. The bartender tossed the contents of the customer's glass into the sink with a gesture of disdain. Frenkel shrugged his shoulders in resignation. *So this is Belgium,* he thought, despondent.

Frenkel pointed to the bottles behind the bar. He felt like a 19th-century explorer forced to communicate with the natives by using sign language.

Mario's face lit up. He grabbed a clean glass with a victorious smile, mixed a gin and orange in the wink of an eye, and slid it across the bar.

"Jesus," Frenkel sipped and groaned. "What kind of garbage is this?"

Mario shrugged.

"Okay, I give up," Frenkel sighed. He handed back the glass and tellingly shook his head. "You give me bon, I pay," he added Tarzan-like.

"*Ah, ce n'est pas bon* . . . you don't like!" Mario grimaced childishly.

Frenkel was at the end of his tether. A friend had recommended the Villa Italiana as the best bar in Bruges. Hot drinks, hotter girls, he had bragged.

"I mean a bon, a check, for my boss," he said in desperation. Mario picked up the glass and held it to the light.

"Monsieur prefer *un bon whiskey,*" he said paternalistically.

"Yes, okay, whiskey," Frenkel dropped his head and almost gasped. It had been a lousy day. In the absence of female company, booze was the only alternative.

Mario turned and pointed at the bottles on the gantry.

"Yes," Frenkel cheered. "J&B if you've got it."

The bartender ran his finger along the line of bottles, ostentatiously passing over the J&B and hovering at the Chivas.

"Whatever. Chivas then," Frenkel growled.

"An excellent choice, monsieur," said Mario, winking as if they were best buddies.

He polished a glass and held it up to the shot tender. His gorilla grin was beginning to get on Frenkel's nerves. The barman fished an ice cube from the bucket and held it motionlessly above the glass.

Frenkel nodded and Mario dropped the ice in the whiskey with a splash. He repeated the ritual and awaited Frenkel's response.

"*Oui, oui,* another."

After four cubes, Frenkel gestured that it was enough. "Basta," he said cautiously under his breath.

Mario smiled like a Sicilian shepherd who had just selected the tastiest sheep from the flock. He crouched and produced a bottle of cola from the cooler.

A huddle of new clients made a loud entry. A couple of dolled-up bimbos took to the dance floor while their formally dressed partners settled on the empty barstools.

"Shame for the bon whiskey," said Mario as he poured the cola over the ice and Chivas.

Frenkel took a deep breath and tried to control himself. He hadn't ordered cola.

The hip-swaying tramps on the dance floor waved insistently in the direction of the bar. Mario turned up the volume. He knew his customers.

Frenkel nipped at his substantial whiskey-cola . . . then the obstinate beat of the turbocharged house music slammed his intestines against his diaphragm. He could have finished his Chivas in one gulp and paid the check, but instead he made his sullen way to the adjoining lounge. At least it would be quieter. He really didn't have much of a choice. Heads: counting sheep in a postmodern hotel room. Tails: more booze.

"Villa Mafia" won the toss. Adriaan Frenkel collapsed into one of the leather armchairs, worn out.

"Those Hollanders fall for it every time," said Mario to one of the other waiters, a pale and lanky imitation of Count Dracula.

"Needed a receipt for his work. It's always the same with that crowd," Mario whined. You could have cut his Bruges accent with a knife.

The pallid waiter smiled wearily. "Make sure he doesn't hear you. Hollanders are our best friggin' customers."

Mario shrugged his shoulders and tapped four glasses of beer.

"You're such a sourpuss, Jacques. Can't a person have a laugh now and then?"

He took a gulp at the gin and orange the "Hollander" had refused and scribbled 600 francs on Frenkel's check: 280 for the cocktail and 320 for the whiskey-cola.

Mr. Georges was a regular at Villa Italiana. When he walked in, a couple of waiters appeared from the shadows and helped him and his guest take off their coats.

"Is the lounge free, Jacques?" asked Mr. Georges, bossy but affable.

If Mario hadn't pissed around with the Hollander, Jacques could have answered in the affirmative.

"Just one customer, Mr. Georges, if I'm not mistaken. A tipsy tourist."

Mr. Georges grinned like a wide-mouthed frog with Cushing's syndrome. It took a few seconds for the various rolls of fat to resettle.

Jacques didn't budge an inch. Mr. Georges's bouts of laughter were legendary, and no one was ever sure if they were a sign of good news or bad.

"Okay, Jacques. No problem." His chubby hand vanished into his inside pocket and reappeared with a two-thousand-franc note.

"Make sure we're not disturbed, and bring us a bottle of bubbly, Ruinart 1983 *si c'est possible*."

"Consider it done, Mr. Georges," said a genuinely grateful Jacques. The pasty waiter had three children from his first marriage and needed a small fortune to pay for their upkeep.

Adriaan Frenkel saw the men arrive. A pair of elderly gentlemen wasn't exactly the kind of company he had been hoping for. He considered leaving, but the more-than-ample ration of Chivas had made him listless. When he looked up, the ceiling swirled like a carousel above his head.

He watched Jacques serve the champagne and ordered another whiskey-cola. If any girls showed up, he could always pretend he was married.

"*Ach, wunderbar,* Georg," he heard one of the men say as Jacques uncorked the champagne. The man who had just said "wunderbar, Georg" reminded him of a character played by Dirk Bogarde in some second-rate Visconti movie. The man deposited a black briefcase on the marble coffee table.

"Why not, *mein freund*. We have something"—he said it like *sumzing*—"to celebrate, *nein*?" said the other in horrendous German.

"Everything is going according to plan. Another couple of months and we'll have control of the entire market."

The German feigned a smile and raised his glass. "*Prost.*"

They guzzled the champagne like thirsty sheep. Half an hour later, the portly gentleman ordered a second bottle.

Frenkel, by contrast, didn't touch his second whiskey. He had settled comfortably into his lounge chair, the ceiling was no longer spinning, and he was still enjoying the buzz of the first.

"So . . . that other business has also been taken care of," he heard the German say.

The two men chatted freely, the volume of their conversation increasing by the minute. Frenkel had no trouble listening in.

"Dietrich, you know me. Everything has been taken care of."

"*Gut.* But in München they're asking questions. Consent to the project is not unanimous."

"*Ach, scheisse,* Dietrich. You have your doubts, that I understand. But wasn't this evening enough to convince you?"

"The board appreciates your efforts, Georg. I'll be sure to say so in my report, but. . . ."

"Trust me, Dietrich. There's a council meeting next month and it's on the agenda. The new Bürgermeister is a minor stumbling block. But all he can do is slow things down a little."

Dietrich Fiedle wasn't really impressed with Georges's response. The German had already guzzled four glasses of champagne, but the bubbles appeared to have had little effect as yet on his frosty tone.

"Don't forget that too many stumbling blocks could endanger the merger."

"You can reassure them in München that I'm a man who keeps his promises," Mr. Georges retorted assertively. "It'll all be in the bag by Easter. I don't understand what's panicking the Germans. We Flemish are men of our word. You should know that, surely."

The German looked around the lounge like a startled hawk. His eyes flickered in the direction of Frenkel, who was listening carelessly to their every word.

"Admit it, Dietrich. It was absolutely unnecessary to—"

Fiedle interrupted in mid-sentence. "That was a question of service, Georg. Consider it a foretaste of what's yet to come. Kindermann is soon to become the largest tour operator in Europe, and after the merger you'll be one of its senior managers. Don't ask questions, Georg, just enjoy your privileges."

Mr. Georges indulged himself with more champagne. Frenkel looked on as the costly nectar sloshed down the man's gullet past a plump array of double chins. "But I still don't understand why this had to happen this evening," he persisted.

"We could have saved the entire discussion for Zeebrugge on Monday."

Dietrich ran bony fingers through his slicked-back hair. The Belgian had no idea that he was a pawn in a game of which only a few were privy to the rules.

"Herr Leitner wants copies of the notarized deeds on his desk by tomorrow morning," he said adamantly. "Monday is too late."

The portly Belgian laughed. He wasn't about to get into a discussion on Leitner.

"In any case, Bruges is a handsome city, don't you think?"

Fiedle held his glass to the light as if he was looking for "impurities." "Very handsome," he admitted. "Shame most of the buildings are fake."

Mr. Georges almost choked, and Frenkel blinked.

"Don't exaggerate, Dietrich. The place attracts millions of tourists every year from all over the world. They love the atmosphere."

"They do indeed come for the atmosphere," said Fiedle superciliously. "That's precisely why Kindermann is prepared to invest three hundred million marks in the project. The customer is always right, after all; and if we give the consumer what he wants, we make a profit."

Frenkel was unaware of the scope of Fiedle's words. Mr. Georges filled the glasses. "What makes you say 'fake,' by the way?" he asked. "Bruges is medieval to the core."

The German raised his glass to his lips and drank like a bored swan. His angular adam's apple bounced up and down almost imperceptibly.

The way he said "Nein, Georg" made Adriaan Frenkel freeze.

"Only a handful of the monuments in Bruges are authentic," Fiedle continued condescendingly. "The rest is pure camouflage."

Mr. Georges straightened himself. The lines of rosacea on his cheeks glowed like smoldering filaments.

"That's bullshit," he snapped.

Fiedle threw back his head. "The city hall and the churches are real and the bell-tower is unique, but the rest is either neo-gothic or so radically restored that it's hardly worth looking at."

"Dietrich," Mr. Georges protested, spilling fifty francs' worth of champagne in the process.

"You don't believe me," said Fiedle arrogantly. The German took a gulp of champagne.

Frenkel followed his example with a sip of tepid whiskey-cola. He could have punched the Aryan bastard.

"Then I'll let you in on a major secret," Fiedle swaggered.

"No need, Dietrich, no need. I believe you, honestly. . . ." the portly Belgian tried to placate his guest. "Shall I order coffee?"

"Have you lost your mind?" the German roared.

"It's all good, Dietrich," said Mr. Georges. "Speak, I'm listening."

"First, another bottle of sekt," Fiedle snarled.

Adriaan Frenkel was captivated. It wasn't the first time he'd seen a respectable member of the *Master Race* undergo an abrupt metamorphosis. One minute they were paragons of reason and propriety, and the next they were beyond recognition.

Jacques reacted quickly to Mr. Georges's raised finger and scuttled into the cellar like an aging whippet.

Dietrich Fiedle waited stubbornly until Jacques returned with the third bottle of Ruinart. When Jacques had refilled the glasses, the German continued in a subdued voice.

Adriaan leaned carefully in their direction.

"My father was familiar with all of Bruges's artistic treasures. He had been charged. . . ."

As the conversation progressed, Frenkel could sense the blood throbbing in his veins. This was impossible. The son of *that* bastard! And in Bruges of all places!

He remained seated until the men got up to go. The third bottle of expensive champagne stood almost untouched on the table. Adriaan tossed back the remainder of his whiskey-cola and mechanically made his way to the bar. He had sobered up fast.

"Can I pay with Visa?" he asked.

"Pas de problème," said Mario with a straight face.

The bartender kept up the pretense. If they pay with a credit card, you can forget the tip.

Adriaan Frenkel signed the check and scurried to the toilet. A receipt for his boss was the last thing on his mind.

2

The first timid snowflakes started to swirl around six A.M.

By the time Gino Hilderson started work at eight-thirty, Bruges was sporting its most romantic outfit. He wove his solitary way through the empty snow-covered streets in his enclosed Piaggio motorized three-wheeler. When he reached the Fish Market, he tipped the first garbage can into the raised loader.

Halfway along Blinde Ezel Street, Gino automatically slowed down. At the beginning of the street, there was a bluestone post designed to keep out potential traffic, but a clever driver like himself could easily maneuver the Piaggio between the post and the side wall of the city hall. It saved him five valuable minutes.

In spite of its leisurely pace, the Piaggio still managed a tremendous skid in the snow when Gino hit the brakes. Two yards in front of him there was a man lying face-down on the cobblestones. Gino clambered out and slammed the Piaggio door with a muffled curse, but the man didn't move.

"Too much booze, friend. That's what you get." The man was wearing a chic camel-colored overcoat and had neatly polished shoes.

Gino forgot his initial irritation and looked the man over. It was a worrying sight. The well-dressed gentleman must have had a serious skinful.

Gino got to his knees and shook the man vigorously by the shoulder. "Hey, buddy," he whispered hoarsely. The man suddenly started to groan.

"Come, friend," said a relieved Gino. "Stand up. Wait, let me give you a hand."

Gino worked for the municipality and was sturdily built. He grabbed the man under his arms and dragged him to the wall of the city hall, just beneath the glass display cases with the wedding announcements.

"Feeling a little better?" he asked hopefully.

The man wasn't young. His face was deathly pale. Even his lips were without color. Gino leaned over him and sniffed, expecting alcohol.

"That's what you get, eh, bud," he said resignedly.

Dietrich Fiedle heard the alien voice through a hollow haze, as if he was under water, registering sounds from above. Gino stared at him, not sure what to do, chewing on a soggy cigarette butt. When the man slumped to one side, he noticed congealed blood on his head, above his left temple.

"Fuck," he said. "Gimme a sec, mate. I'll be right back." Gino took to his heels, hared diagonally across Burg Square, and turned into Breidel Street.

There were four public telephones on Market Square. Fortunately, one of them was in working order. The number he called rang six times.

"Hello! Is that 911?" he screamed when Jozef Demedts finally picked up. "There's a guy bleeding to death. You have to send someone right away."

Demedts carefully positioned his cigarette in a glass ashtray and picked up his ballpoint.

"Can I have your name, please?" he asked, unruffled.

"Gino Hilderson. The man's lying under the Bridge of Sighs in Blinde Ezel Street," Gino sputtered.

He wasn't aware that Demedts had transferred the call to the police and that a couple of ambulance men were already on their way to a waiting ambulance. Demedts had hit the alarm button when he heard Gino say "bleeding to death."

"Is the injured party still conscious?"

The duty police officer was listening in via a special emergency line. He contacted a patrol in the vicinity by radio.

"If you ask me, he's on his way out. If you don't get a move on, it'll be too late," Gino blared.

"Okay, Mr. Hilderson. Go back to the injured party and stay with him. Help is on its way."

Demedts broke the connection abruptly. The situation seemed serious enough to call in the emergency medical services.

Before going on duty, Dr. Arents of the Mobile Emergency Team had enjoyed a quickie in the supply room with an agile young nurse and was in the best of spirits. The call from Demedts wasn't about to change his mood. He and Ivan Dewilde raced to the garage. Arents felt like a young god. Unlike the poor buggers in white jackets wasting away in sterile hospital rooms, life had treated him kindly. He was young and healthy, and he earned a decent living.

In spite of the absence of traffic, Dewilde switched on the siren. The Renault Espace responded perfectly to the gas pedal and careered irresponsibly down the snow-covered drive.

To Gino Hilderson, the minutes seemed like hours. He stood poker-faced beside the victim. There were now no signs of life.

The police van appeared first, hurtling across Burg Square. Officer Bruynooghe directed his colleague to the designated location.

"I think he's snuffed it," Gino said to Bruynooghe.

Bruynooghe, short but robust, leaned over the victim. He was an experienced officer, twenty-two years on the force, and he could see right away that the street sweeper wasn't exaggerating. He wasted no time and rushed back to the van.

"Officer Bruynooghe here," he said into his radio. "The victim's unconscious, probably on his way out."

His voice was calm and relatively emotionless.

"There's an ugly wound above his left temple. Doesn't look like a fall," he added, throwing in some personal weight.

Duty officer Jean-Marie Vervenne looked at his watch. His shift was up in ten minutes. He considered the possibility of handing the case over to his relief on the next shift. On the other hand, Bruynooghe wasn't the bullshitting type. If criminal intent was involved, he might be regretting those ten minutes for a long time to come.

"Understood, Bruynooghe. I'm on my way."

The short-of-stature Bruynooghe grinned when his superior broke the connection.

The ambulance cut through the snow like a plow through a rain-drenched field. Jan Decoster held the first-aid box tightly to his chest. He braced himself. In wintry conditions like these, every second counted. Hypothermia could be fatal, even in a minor traffic accident. When they got there, Wim Defruydt parked the ambulance three or four feet from the victim. Decoster grabbed an extra thermal blanket before jumping out. His colleague crouched over the wounded man; when he couldn't find a pulse, he pulled him away from the wall. Decoster removed the thermal blanket from its plastic packaging and wrapped it around the elderly man. In the absence of a doctor, the ambulance man knew there was only one thing he could do. He followed the standard procedure, known as ABC in the business: Airways, Breathing, and Circulation. He cleared his airways, administered mouth-to-mouth, and tried to maintain blood circulation with heart massage.

In the meantime, Defruydt had fetched a saline drip from the ambulance and was ready with a tourniquet.

Gino Hilderson watched the scene unfold from a distance. A second siren suddenly interrupted the hush. A Renault Espace with the MET team turned onto Burg Square out of Breidel Street. Jean-Marie Vervenne arrived ten seconds later. The tracks left in the snow by the two vehicles were reminiscent of a Mondrian painting.

Decoster immediately made way for Arents, who knelt down at the victim's side. The doctor checked the man's vital functions and continued to administer heart massage. After a minute or two, he called Decoster back.

"Take over."

Decoster nodded. As far as he was concerned, the man was as dead as a dodo.

Arents threw open his bag, rummaged around between the sterile syringes for twenty seconds, and found what he was looking for.

The six-inch needle made Gino shiver. Arents emptied an ampoule of adrenaline, checked the syringe against the light of a streetlamp (still on because it was a dark, snowy day), leaned over the victim, marked the spot, and drove the needle through the dying German's sternum directly into his heart.

"I wouldn't complain if I were you," Versavel grinned. "You were the one who asked for more Sunday shifts."

Van In cleared his throat and lit a cigarette. The suit he was wearing looked like a crumpled rag.

"Which doesn't mean I have to clean up Vervenne's shit," he rasped. "I didn't sleep a wink last night. And Sundays are supposed to be quiet."

Versavel stroked his moustache and glared pityingly at Van In. The miffed commissioner crossed to the windowsill and poured himself a mug of coffee.

"Who commits murder on a Sunday morning, for Christ's sake?" Van In grouched.

"He was still alive when they took him to the hospital," said Versavel dryly. "But according to one of the ambulance men, his condition was critical. Subdural hematomas are often fatal in circumstances like that."

"Cut the crap, Guido."

"Fractured skull with internal bleeding. Sorry, Commissioner."

Versavel sat down at his desk and stretched his legs. In contrast to Van In, he was impeccably dressed.

"And a bloody German," Van In smirked. "A stroke of luck?"

Versavel refused to react. Everyone knew that Van In hated Germans.

"I'm afraid we're going to have to do something, Commissioner. What if detective Columbo calls and wants the whole story?"

He ducked instinctively when Van In aimed his half-empty mug of coffee at him.

"A waste of coffee," Van In growled.

Versavel sat upright.

"Has Vervenne written his report?" Van In asked.

"You know Vervenne. A page a day is too much for him. Anyway, I think he's still hanging around Burg Square."

"Jesus H. What are we getting so worked up about?"

"In that case, you can pour me a coffee as well," said Versavel, resigned.

"I hope Vervenne contacted the public prosecutor," said Van In after a minute. "If that German's on his way to Valhalla, they can take over the case."

"Aren't you curious?"

Van In shook his head. Versavel knew he was faking it.

"Motive might be interesting," Versavel fished. "It can't have been money. The victim had eight hundred marks and three credit cards in his pocket."

"Eighty thousand marks would have been better," Van In responded sarcastically.

Versavel held the mug of steaming coffee to his nose and inhaled the aroma. He was used to the commissioner's moods.

It had started to snow again. It was five after nine and the cars on the street still had their headlights on.

"We've got four officers checking out the neighborhood," said Versavel, tossing another hook.

"Are you expecting results? Last time I looked, nobody lived on Burg Square." Van In got to his feet, yawned, and walked to the window. His vision locked on to a plump snowflake swirling slowly to the ground.

"The janitor at city hall said he heard a muffled noise around two-thirty."

"Did he *see* anything?" Van In lost track of the snowflake and searched for another.

"What do you think? He only got out of bed when he heard the sirens."

"Not much help then." Van In started to see double from staring at the snow. He turned, refilled his mug, and tossed in a couple of sugars.

Versavel ostentatiously patted his flat, muscular belly.

"You win, Versavel. Imagine if everyone looked like Mister Universe. What would you do then, kiddo?"

"Would you really like to know?" Versavel sneered.

"Jesus H. Aren't we subtle today!"

Versavel grinned. The commissioner was coming around, albeit slowly. "Some have perfect bodies, others have to use their brains," Versavel quipped.

That settled it.

"Less of the sweet talk, Guido. Call Vervenne and tell him we're taking over. If we sit around and do nothing, I'll have the chief on my case in the morning."

"At your command, Commissioner."

"Did Vervenne have photos taken?" Van In asked as they got into the hospital elevator.

"I called Leo," Versavel smiled. "With a bit of luck, we'll see him in the cafeteria."

"Arrogant punk. You knew I would come, didn't you?"

Versavel wisely held his tongue.

"I presume the bloodwork is ready. You don't trudge through the snow in the middle of the night if you've been to the movies. It wouldn't surprise me if our Jerry friend had enjoyed a night on the town."

The nurse sharing the elevator pulled a doubtful face.

"Intoxication isn't a reason to kill someone," said Versavel in a neutral tone. He wanted to add that the commissioner would have been long dead had that been the case.

Intensive Care at Saint Jan's was full. Eight nurses and two doctors were doing their best, but they were a poor match for the usual deadly toll claimed by the weekend traffic.

"Police, ma'am," said Van In, American style, to the dolled-up receptionist at the counter.

"Good morning, gentlemen." Her tone was sprightly and civil. "What can I do for you?"

Versavel hoped Van In would respond to her vague question with equal civility. He saw the commissioner hesitate.

"Might we have a word with the doctor on duty?" he asked.

The girl raised her eyebrows as if Van In had asked for an appointment with God the Father.

"The doctor responsible for the Medical Emergency Team," Van In added, for clarification.

"Doctor Arents," said Versavel.

"And tell him it's urgent."

Medical staff, and doctors in particular, needed to be treated with caution. "Urgent" was a word they usually reserved for themselves. Versavel expected trouble.

The receptionist took a deep breath. Van In enjoyed the sight of her bosom swelling beneath her thin white apron. She stiffened and gritted her teeth. She had recently graduated with a Master's in medicine and had spent the last six months applying for jobs. This was the best she could find. She was overworked and frustrated, and she barely earned enough to live on her own.

"Doctor Arents was called away fifteen minutes ago," she said with a chiseled smile. "If you'll excuse me, gentlemen." The receptionist turned and sat down at her computer. She opened a medical file, flattened a crumpled page, and started to type.

"Do me a favor, sweetheart." Van In's voice had dropped an octave. Even Versavel was taken aback. "I'm investigating an attempted murder. The victim's name is Fiedle and I know Arents was the first to attend to him."

His "sweetheart" didn't appear to be the least bit impressed. She straightened her back and started to tap the keyboard like an irate harpy.

"Tell me, sweetheart, I'm curious. Are you on a monthly contract?" Her fingers stopped, hovered above the keys, and she glared at the police officers in a rage. "Thing is . . . if you don't get Arents's ass here in five, you'll be picking up your groceries next month at the Salvation Army store."

Versavel stroked his moustache to camouflage an emerging smile. Van In could be seriously blunt if it wasn't his day.

The girl looked at them like a deer that had just lost its fawn.

"If you put it like that," she said, her voice wavering.

Her slender fingers reached for the telephone. Van In wallowed in the Bruce Willis effect and lit a defiant cigarette.

"Doctor Arents just got back," she admitted reluctantly. "If the gentlemen don't mind waiting, he'll be ready in a moment. I'll take you to him."

Arents was wearing an expensive Italian suit under his white coat. Versavel couldn't take his eyes off him.

"Doctor Arents. Assistant Commissioner Van In. This is my colleague Guido Versavel."

They shook hands.

"A pleasure," said Arents coolly. He had a nine-hour shift in front of him, and a police interrogation wasn't exactly the kind of intermezzo he'd been looking forward to. Versavel stepped back and enjoyed Doctor Adonis.

"It's about Dietrich Fiedle, the German tourist—"

"He's in the OR as we speak," Arents wearily interrupted. "The man's in very bad shape. He won't be receiving visitors for a while."

"Of course, Doctor." Van In was deliberately submissive. "Questioning the victim was the last thing on my mind. I presume he's in a coma."

Versavel lifted his hand to his mouth and pretended to root around in his moustache. The commissioner was laying it on a little too thick for his liking.

"I'm afraid I can't comment, Commissioner," Arents snapped.

"*Professional confidentiality,*" Versavel sniggered.

"You said a moment ago that he was in bad shape," Van In gently insisted.

"His condition is critical," Arents admitted. He had lost interest in the cat-and-mouse game. "What do you want me to do, for Christ's sake? Half an hour ago, I gave someone from the police permission to take a photo. Even if the surgery is a success, Mr. Fiedle will be 'incommunicado' for at least a couple of weeks."

Van In straightened his back and dumped his cigarette in a plant pot. Arents hadn't said a word about it. He presumed the good doctor wasn't quite the macho man he pretended to be.

"I'm only interested in his personal possessions," said Van In nonchalantly. "We all have our job to do, Doctor, I understand that. You take care of sick people; I'm trying to close a case."

Arents nodded. He suddenly didn't appear as flashy as before.

"How can I be of assistance, Commissioner?"

The question proved once and for all that most doctors rarely listen. Van In had already told him what he wanted.

"I would appreciate the chance to take a look through Fiedle's personal effects," Van In repeated.

This time he deliberately left out the word "doctor."

"That shouldn't be a problem," said Arents in a starchy tone. "Myriam, will you show the gentlemen what they're looking for?" The receptionist nodded pointedly.

"I'll be in Emergency if you need me."

Versavel noticed an exchange of looks between Arents and Myriam. Arents was straight. Shame, he thought.

3

"Pity they don't serve Duvel," Leo Vanmaele barked when he caught sight of Van In and Versavel heading toward the cafeteria bar.

"Hoi, Leo," Van In chortled. "I'll have to settle for a cappuccino."

Leo shifted his hefty Nikon invitingly out of the way.

"Didn't Versavel tell you I'd be waiting?"

"God's ways are mysterious, and so are Versavel's," Van In mocked.

Sergeant Versavel winked at Vanmaele.

"What can I get you, gentlemen?"

The heavily made-up lady behind the bar looked Van In indifferently up and down.

"Three cappuccinos, please."

He fished a couple of hundred-franc notes from his wallet.

"That'll be two hundred and ten," she snorted contemptuously.

In addition to the two hundreds, Van In only had a two-thousand-franc note. It was the last of his cash, and he didn't fancy breaking it for change. So he rummaged nervously in his trouser pocket. He was the only customer, so the counter-woman was patient with him.

"Guido, do you have a spare ten francs?"

Versavel reacted quickly. The commissioner's financial problems were the stuff of legend. It wasn't the first time he'd had to pitch in. "Put your money away. It's on me. I owe you for yesterday."

Van In didn't protest when Versavel handed him the tray with the cappuccinos and conjured a thousand-franc note from his inside pocket. The painted bird of paradise gave Versavel his change, and he left a couple of twenty-franc coins on the counter.

"It wasn't easy getting the photos," said Leo, pointing to his camera. "Don't expect the best of quality. Those doctors really believe photos can damage a patient's health." He raised the cappuccino to his nose and greedily inhaled the aroma of hot coffee through the layer of cool cream.

"I'm happy with reasonable," said Van In, putting the photographer's mind at rest. "As long as I have them by seven."

"No problem. Anything for you, Van In. Even a Sunday evening in the darkroom. I'll deliver them tomorrow in person, no less."

"Sorry, but when I said seven, I meant seven P.M. I need the photos tonight, Leo."

Versavel concentrated on his cappuccino. He knew what was coming: Leo gets worked up, Van In makes it worse. Thank God I'm a morning person, he thought to himself.

"Why not make it *six* P.M., Commissioner?" Leo leaned threateningly across the table, his feet dangling six inches above the floor. "Next time, Mr. Big Shot should order Polaroids!"

"You don't expect me to sketch the bloody German by hand, do you?" Van In snapped indignantly. "My artistic talents might not be the best, but it would save a lot of time, you can be sure of that."

"With your dick as a pencil, right?" Leo sneered. "Save that for the assistant public prosecutor."

Ouch. Van In was speechless. Even Leo was taken aback at himself. He stirred angrily at his cappuccino.

"Have you seen *this* photo?" Versavel asked in a well-intentioned effort to break the unpleasant silence. He produced a brown envelope from his inside pocket, opened it, and emptied its contents on the table: a key ring, a beige calf's-leather wallet, and a museum ticket. Versavel opened the wallet and removed a sepia-tinted photograph.

"This was among Fiedle's personal belongings," said Van In by way of information. "I'm not quite sure if we should be showing evidence like this to a low-grade official."

"Cut the bellyaching," Leo groused.

"What do you think of the photo?" Versavel persisted.

Leo furrowed his brow. The sergeant had stirred his professional interest. "What am I supposed to see?" he said after a bit.

"Sergeant Versavel wants to know if anything in the photo catches your eye, a detail, something that doesn't quite square, *quelque chose de suspect*. Jesus H. We're in the middle of an investigation, Leo."

"I see an old-fashioned photo of Michelangelo's *Madonna*."

"Look closer, good friend," Van In smirked. "Use a magnifying glass if need be, but have a good look."

"It looks at least forty years old," he said hesitatingly. "Excellent quality, but the light could be better."

"The light could be better," Van In roared. "Did you hear that, Guido? The light could be better."

A man with a mobile drip got up and moved closer.

"Take another look, Leo, and this time forget the light."

Leo stuck his finger in his ear and pulled an indignant face.

"The vegetation, Leo."

"Is there something wrong with it?"

"The statue's outside, Leo . . . see the hills in the background?"

"So what?" He examined the photo again. "Remarkable. Do you want an analysis?"

Van In heaved a sigh of relief. "If that's not too much to ask," he groaned.

"I'll need a couple of days, Pieter."

"Monday's fine."

Checkmate, thought Versavel.

Leo arrived back at the station at four-thirty that afternoon. He took the elevator to the third floor, beaming from ear to ear and whistling the opening bars of *The Barber of Seville*.

Van In was in his shirtsleeves, at his desk, chain-smoking. He had had copies made in the hospital of Fiedle's passport and the photo of the *Madonna* and had faxed them to the *Bundeskriminalamt*—Germany's Federal Criminal Police. Waiting for their response was getting on his nerves.

Versavel had turned the thermostat to the highest setting and opened one of the pivoting windows. Even the hardy ficus plant had trouble with the smoke in room 204, shedding a nicotine-stained leaf every hour.

"Am I on time, or am I on time?" Leo blared.

He posed in the doorway like a blushing Apollo, a bulging envelope under his arm. When no one answered his rhetorical question, he hopped inside.

"The door, Leo," said Van In without looking up.

"Sorry, Commissioner. I didn't know you were allergic to fresh air." Leo took a seat near the window and handed Versavel the envelope. "Herr Fiedle doesn't look too hot, but he's still quite recognizable in spite of the head bandage."

Versavel examined the enlargements and compared them with the German's passport photo.

"You're sure we're talking about the same guy?"

Leo's face pleaded innocence. "The passport photo's more than thirty years old."

"Give them here." Van In stubbed out a half-smoked cigarette and demanded the envelope with an impatient gesture. Versavel pitched the whole shebang across the office like a Frisbee.

Fiedle looked like a living skeleton. His pointed nose dominated his hollow face, and his bushy eyebrows stood out against the whiter-than-white head bandage.

"You have to account for the circumstances," said Van In philosophically. In the air he waved the fax that he had received from Arents half an hour earlier. "Fiedle had a blood-alcohol level of 2.8. No wonder he looks like death warmed over."

"You look the same after six Duvels," Leo mocked. "And your passport photo is only five years old."

Versavel left them to bicker. He fired up his brand-new word processor and opened the file named "Fiedle." The screen flickered ominously, and Versavel couldn't help thinking about his trusty old typewriter. Those had been the days.

Bruges nightlife was limited to a handful of notorious cafés and bars. Van In presumed that the German had visited one of them before the encounter on Blinde Ezel Street. The 2.8 blood-alcohol count seemed to point in that direction, unless he'd tied one on in his hotel room before heading out for a walk in the snow.

Two officers were still checking the hotel registers. They hadn't managed to locate Fiedle's hotel yet.

At seven-fifteen, Van In and Leo Vanmaele left Versavel to get better acquainted with his word processor and headed out.

"Page me if there's news on the hotel," Van In shouted as he closed the door behind him. His spirits had lifted.

Armed with the photos, the two men went bar-hopping on the Egg Market. Most of the proprietors knew Van In and were happy to cooperate, or at least pretended to be. Waiters and regulars examined the photos, but no one recognized the German. Almost every café cost them a Duvel. At one-thirty they ordered their sixth in the Vuurmolen, an after-hours bar on Kraan Square. The place was packed, and hard rock music was slowly but surely ruining the expensive speakers.

Leo ordered a double toasted sandwich; Van In finished his Duvel and switched to coffee.

"Hard to keep up, eh?" Leo scoffed between bites.

Van In grudgingly sipped the hot but bitter concoction.

"Christ pulled the same face when they offered him a sponge soaked in vinegar," Leo grinned.

"I remember it like yesterday," said Van In, stony-faced. "You were on the left and you died of thirst."

"Very spiritual, Pieter. You'll be lying next, before the cock crows a third time."

Van In glanced at his watch. "Jesus H. Two-fifteen."

"Tired?"

"Of course not," Van In snapped. "Finish your sandwich. Whiskey-cola in the Villa. My treat."

"Your treat!" Leo grinned. "The entire force knows that you get your meds in the Villa for free."

"Shout it from the rooftops. My guess is you're not planning to cough up for that dog food you're guzzling either. The double portion is a giveaway."

Leo took a final serious bite and shrugged his shoulders. "We'll see when the bill comes."

Although Van In looked like a dredged-up vagrant, the bouncer at the Villa let him in with a friendly smile. An indignant young American couple—he in expensive Levis, she in $140 Nikes—watched them go inside. Jean-Luc, the bouncer, had shown them the door.

The Villa was alive and swinging. After midnight the place was usually packed to the doors. Hot chicks writhed on the dance floor, playing with the dazzling laser beams. From a distance, and in the constantly changing light, they looked irresistible. Their miniskirts left nothing to the imagination, and the promised land rippled under their tight tops. The majority were over thirty and divorced. Van In was familiar with the genre. An overblown title or a nonchalantly flaunted bundle of banknotes was enough to get them on their backs.

"Hello, Mario," Van In yelled, and the bartender read his lips. Mario gave him a thumbs-up and automatically grabbed a pair of long drink glasses. He leaned over and shouted something into the ear of a balding forty-something customer. The mature yuppie took his girlfriend by the arm and hey, presto, a couple of empty barstools.

Van In thanked him with a wink, sat down, and slumped over the bar. He was tired. His ankles were swollen, and he had pins and needles in his calves.

Mario didn't spare the Glenfiddich. One bottle of cola was enough to fill the glasses to the brim.

"It's been a while, Commissioner," he bellowed. "And your luck's in. Véronique's here. Want me to call her over?"

Van In sensed Leo's disapproving glare burning a hole in his left cheek. *The booze isn't the only thing that's free*, he could hear him think.

"Not today," Van In roared. "We're here on business."

Mario grimaced. "Nothing serious, eh?"

Van In showed Mario the photos. "Do you recognize him?"

He stared the bartender in the eye when he asked the question. Even seasoned liars can sometimes give themselves away with an evasive glance or an overly glib answer.

"Wait a minute," Mario shouted. "Can't be. . . . Surely. . . . Isn't that . . . nah. Sorry, Commissioner. A stranger to me. Gimme a sec. I'll ask Jacques."

Mario disappeared without troubling himself with the half-wit dandy who had been trying to order a fresh margarita for the last two and a half minutes.

"Bingo," Leo roared when the bartender vanished behind the back of the bar. "Our friend's heading in the wrong direction. That's Jacques over there." He pointed to a table near the dance floor. Van In barely reacted. The whiskey was struggling with the Duvels. He felt nauseous.

"It never fails to amaze me," Leo raved, "that the last address is always the right address. If you're looking for a report, it's guaranteed to be at the bottom of the pile."

Van In nodded. All the shouting made his ears ring, and he was doing his best to fight the fuzziness filling his head.

"I should call it Vanmaele's law," Leo roared.

Van In nodded once again. But he wasn't quite sure what connected Leo's last two statements.

After five minutes or so, Mario reappeared with Patrick, alias the Gigolo. Patrick was forty, slim, tanned. He had been running the Villa for the best part of six years and he knew the tricks of the trade. In principle, the world of after-hours bars and private clubs tended to be frequented by two types of cop: the ones who did their job, and the ones you could sweeten up. Van In was the proverbial exception to the rule. The commissioner didn't like to be pigeonholed. The Gigolo was on his guard.

"Bonsoir, Pieter."

He extended a cheerful hand. A fortune in gold chains dangled from his wrist.

Van In tapped his ear. The Gigolo understood immediately.

"Let's go to my office. There's less noise." Leo saw the Gigolo beckon with his head. He hadn't heard what the man had said. The words had wriggled through the elated jumble of groggy dancers grinding to the perverse beat.

Van In knew the way. He had been there more than once.

The padded door absorbed ninety of the decibels. The Gigolo's office was furnished like a Greek temple, complete with Corinthian columns and salacious chaises longues. The white marble fluoresced blue in the indirect UV light. A fountain splashed in the corner. The tasteless thing, three shell-shaped basins piled on top of one another, was crowned with a plaster replica of the *Venus de Milo*.

"Tell me, Pieter. What can I do for you?"

The Gigolo settled unashamedly into one of the chaises longues. Van In followed his example, and Leo perched on the arm like a leprechaun. His short legs didn't quite reach the mosaic floor.

"I'm looking for a man," said Van In with difficulty. His tongue was acting up, and the Gigolo knew what that meant.

"That's strange," he answered lightheartedly. "You're usually looking for a woman."

"This man," said Van In. He took the photos from the envelope and handed them to Vanmaele. Leo played go-between without protest. A good slap in the face was what the Gigolo deserved, he thought.

"What makes you think I would know this old man?" asked the Gigolo after looking at the photos a couple of times.

"It's important," Van In insisted. "Believe me. If someone here can identify the man, I promise—"

The sentence was interrupted by a rattling coughing fit. Leo jumped to his feet and helped Van In stand up. The commissioner wasn't a pretty sight.

"I'd be happy to help you, my friend," said the Gigolo with a note of pity. "But I just got back from Jamaica. And even if I had been here. . . ."

Van In recovered and sat down on the edge of the chaise longue.

"Jesus H.," he wheezed. "I'm not asking if *you* recognize him. I want permission to talk to your staff. Mario had his doubts, but perhaps Jacques can identify him."

The Gigolo gulped at his whiskey like a true American, greedily and without enjoying it.

"Listen here, Pieter. The place is packed. Leave the photos with me and I'll get everyone to have a look after we close."

"Much appreciated, Patrick," said Van In, peering at the Gigolo like a dazed reveler.

Leo followed the conversation with growing amazement. He couldn't understand why Van In was letting the guy walk all over him. He took a swig of his drink out of pure frustration. It tasted like stale cough syrup.

"Do we have a deal, Pieter?" The Gigolo fidgeted with a golden scuba diver on a chain dangling around his neck. "If Véronique had been here. . . ." He deliberately cut his sentence short.

"I thought she *was* here," Van In said.

"Not tonight," the Gigolo lied.

"You expecting her?" Van In reached for his glass. His hand shook. Leo gave him a dig in the ribs. He had known Van In for more than twenty years, and it hurt to see his friend let himself down like this.

"She'll be here on Wednesday," the Gigolo dawdled. "I can ask her to wait for you."

Van In retched and lay back in his chaise longue. His eyes started to turn in their sockets like a pair of revolving lights, and his left leg suddenly went into a spasm.

"I think we should go, Pieter." Leo got to his feet and shook Van In by the shoulders. The Gigolo nodded and came to take a closer look.

"He's not a well man. Maybe he ate something?"

"Just give me a hand," Leo snarled. "He needs air. Fresh air," he added bad-temperedly.

The two men helped Van In to his feet. He seemed in a daze and didn't put up a struggle. The walk to the padded door took forever. Van In felt like he was walking on a conveyor belt, his legs like those of a comatose spider, his head still resting on the chaise longue.

It took Leo and the Gigolo a full five minutes to work their way through the heaving masses. Jacques lent a hand when they got close to the exit. The Gigolo slipped quietly out of the picture.

"Have a good day, gentlemen." The anemic waiter made no effort to disguise the derision in his voice.

"Have you lost it completely?" Leo snorted when Van In leaned against a wall and slumped into the snow. "You'll catch your death if you're not careful."

Van In scooped up a handful of snow and rubbed it into his face.

"You're smashed. Don't expect me to sympathize," Leo snapped.

"The fucking . . . ," Van In shuddered. "The fucker spiked my drink."

"Of course he did," said Vanmaele sarcastically. "They spiked your cola with whiskey."

Van In started to cough and retch. He took off his jacket and shirt and tossed snow on his chest like a child burying himself in sand on the beach.

"Are you all right, buddy?" A well-dressed gentleman had stopped out of curiosity. "Shall I call an ambulance?"

"Mind your own business," Vanmaele snapped.

"Your friend looks as if he needs one," the obliging stranger insisted.

Leo Vanmaele was known for his gentle character and his preference for the stoic approach, but the Duvels he had consumed with too much haste had awakened the Mr. Hyde in him.

"Is he on drugs or something?" the concerned passerby added. "Times have changed, haven't they? He's no spring chicken, either. You only get to see the young guys on TV, but you can't believe everything they show you on—"

"Listen, friend." Leo filled his lungs. "If you don't cut the crap and fuck off out of here, I'll have you arrested for disturbing the peace."

He fumbled in his inside pocket and produced his ID.

"Crime Squad."

The threat sounded serious.

The talkative Samaritan took a quick look at the card and scuttled off like a novice skater.

Leo Vanmaele looked at the card and grinned. He had shown the man a supermarket loyalty card by accident.

4

Van In called in sick the following morning. His tongue was swollen and there was a cartload of grit under his eyelids. A lump of raw flesh seemed to be thriving in his throat, and it hurt to swallow. Even a twenty-minute shower barely helped ease the pain in his bones. His joints grated like ungreased hinges. He felt as if he'd slept with a block of lead on his chest; he still found it hard to breathe now.

Van In prodded the most sensitive part of his body with his finger, just beneath his breastbone. The pain almost drove him insane.

His reflection in the mirror was like a crumpled shadow. The only advantage of his still-murky vision was that he didn't pay much attention to the expanding rolls of fat under his chin and around his middle.

The first cup of coffee tasted like diluted heating oil. The obligatory cigarette that usually accompanied the grimy brew caused a dry coughing fit.

Nothing can spoil my day now, he decided as he hawked, *nothing at all.*

Van In saw the mail dropping through the letterbox and went to pick it up with the speed of an almost-empty balloon. The Invest Bank logo on one of the envelopes didn't bode well. He poured himself a second cup of coffee. The warm liquid dissolved fifty percent of the lump of flesh in his throat.

"Cancer? Who said cancer?" he muttered under his breath.

He lit a second cigarette as he tore open the letter from the bank. It had taken him two days to recover from the tax bill he'd received the month before, but this letter from Invest Bank defied imagination.

"Jesus H.," he groaned. "This is the end." When Van In got worked up about something, he always wanted to do ten things at once. He headed to the kitchen, letter in hand, unplugged the coffee machine, and checked the collar of his shirt, which he had tossed without thinking on the kitchen table. The caffeine started to work on his intestines and he had to make a run for it. He read the letter a second time on the toilet.

This can't wait another day, he thought to himself defiantly. *It's time to show those pen-pushers what Van In is made of.* The collar of the shirt on the kitchen table was soiled and greasy, but he put it on anyway. His other shirts were worse: creased and festering in the laundry basket. A palm full of cheap aftershave was enough to camouflage the smell of stale armpits.

His best suit, of summer weight, was a little tight, but it looked respectable enough.

Invest Bank headquarters was a five-minute walk from the Vette Vispoort, a 15th-century city gate that opened onto the cul-de-sac where Van In lived. He shivered. He refused to wear his winter coat, because it didn't match his summer suit.

Fortunately the sun was shining, which made him feel ten degrees or so less ridiculous. But to try to avoid embarrassment, he still took a detour to avoid the busy Sint-Jacob Street.

Invest Bank had moved to a handsomely restored guildhall three years earlier. The façade was magnificent. But what lay behind the façade had been adapted by a consortium of highly paid architects to the functional needs of a modern bank and looked like a sleek bomb shelter, the kind in which the average clerk would feel perfectly at home.

The sliding doors opened automatically, welcoming Van In into the building. The dry heat of the sophisticated air-conditioning system grabbed him by the throat. Banks used this tried-and-tested tactic to daze their customers as they came in.

Four of the six counter positions were unattended. Van In had a choice between a balding amateur triathlon runner and a recently flunked-out economics student. The clerks shared one thing in common: neither bothered to look up at him. Van In chose the girl.

"Can I have a word with Mr. Lonneville? My name's Van In, Assistant Commissioner Pieter Van In."

She was wearing a modest jersey blouse and, he presumed, a Wonderbra.

"Sorry, Mr. Van In, but Mr. Lonneville isn't available right now. Do you have an appointment?"

"No. It's a personal matter. I would appreciate it if you could inform Mr. Lonneville that Pieter Van In wishes to speak to him."

He tried to sound unruffled yet intimidating.

Geertrui Vaes—the name on her uninspired pin—put down her pen and sized Van In up like a meat inspector sizing up a suspicious carcass.

"It's extremely urgent, Miss Vaes. I've known Mr. Lonneville for years," he lied with conviction.

She smiled routinely and fiddled with her earring. He could see that she was wavering.

"One moment, Mr. Van In."

She got to her feet with evident reluctance and disappeared through a door at the back. The modest blouse squared perfectly with the picture Van In had formed of her. Geertrui Vaes was wearing a pair of dirty-gray slacks with elastic foot straps. She had the silhouette of a cello and the moves of a Naomi Campbell adept.

Van In straightened his tie and checked his reflection in the mirrored glass that separated the counter from the outside world. The triathlon runner yawned unashamedly and—for want of customers—polished his expensive glasses.

"Mr. Lonneville will see you immediately," said Miss Vaes on her return. "Please come this way."

She pushed a button and unlocked the counter door. When Van In pushed against it, the lock mechanism flipped back to red. Clearly irked, she pushed the button a second time. Van In slipped inside like a thief and the door locked automatically behind him. Geertrui Vaes led him to a small waiting room and pointed to a chair.

"Take a seat, Mr. Van In. The manager will be with you shortly."

The smell of a name-brand cleaning product filled the waiting room. A couple of well-thumbed copies of the *Financial Times* had been left on a side table. This was apparently the reception area for those who couldn't keep up with their payments. Van In was convinced that cognac and chocolate cookies were being served in an adjacent room.

Lonneville kept him waiting for a good twenty minutes. In the distance, Bruges's carillon struck ten-fifteen.

The door suddenly flew open. An arrogant blond creature gestured that he was next and directed him to Humbert Lonneville's office. The man had excellent taste. Her legs were almost as beautiful as Hannelore's.

"Good morning, Mr. Van In. Take a seat. What can I do for you?" Lonneville rattled, routinely affable.

Van In settled into an expensive chair. Lonneville smiled benignly. He was forty-five, clean-shaven and completely impersonal. Banks love sophisticated machines, and the blond secretary also appeared to be part of the same strategy.

"So, Mr. Van In."

"Do you mind if I smoke?"

Lonneville glanced in horror at the recently painted ceiling. "I'd rather you didn't, Mr. Van In. But if you absolutely must." Van In nodded. His opening move had been ill chosen. He had fucked up.

"I presume you're familiar with my dossier."

Lonneville folded his hands and rested them dramatically on the edge of his desk.

"Eh . . . I'm afraid not, Mr. Van In."

Jackal. You know damn well why I'm here, Van In thought to himself. People in positions of power love to play cat-and-mouse games. The victim has to explain his own miserable situation. He was familiar with the technique from his police work.

"I'm five months behind with my mortgage payments, and I received this letter this morning."

Lonneville took the letter and quickly ran his eyes over it.

"Five months," he said nonchalantly. "Surely not a problem for a man in your position."

He referred unashamedly to the more-than-ample monthly salary that was surely paid to an assistant police commissioner.

"I still can't pay. I need more time."

Lonneville sighed like a schoolteacher realizing that his best pupil had managed to get half the questions wrong.

"Is that so, Mr. Van In? Of course, it doesn't make the problem any simpler. If you ask me, the letter is crystal-clear."

"I need more time," Van In repeatedly obstinately. "Or a bridging loan."

"More time, Commissioner? Five months is more than a bank can allow itself. Demands are usually sent out after three months."

"That's why I want a bridging loan, or a second mortgage. I don't care which, as long as you keep your hands off my house."

Lonneville seemed aggrieved. His red cheeks were a perfect reflection of Van In's financial straits.

Van In jumped when a printer in the room next door suddenly whirred into action. The dividing door was ajar, and he caught sight of a skinny man with a hefty dossier under his arm. He looked familiar.

"So you need more time. Did you have a deadline in mind?" Lonneville sneered. "Is there someone who might act as a guarantor? Family? Friends?"

Lonneville pushed back his chair and rested his head against the leather headrest. According to Desmond Morris, this was a sign that the bank manager was distancing himself and considered the conversation pointless.

"The house is too important to me. My problem is temporary. Surely you can understand that?"

"I understand you perfectly, Mr. Van In. But a bank isn't a charity. Without an additional guarantor, I'm afraid I'm going to have to disappoint you."

Van In ran his fingers nervously through his hair. He didn't have to feign the lump in his throat. "I love that house, for Christ's sake," he rasped. "I'll be back on my feet within a year and the mortgage is 75% paid. I don't understand why you can't extend me some credit."

"A year deferment!" Lonneville brayed. "You can't be serious! You have until April 1, Commissioner."

The date had already been fixed before Van In set foot in the man's office. Lonneville liked to give the impression that he sympathized, but this two-week stay of execution was the best he could do.

"And what if I don't pay?"

Lonneville's expression turned to ice. "Then the house you love so much will be put up for public auction. I'm told it's a magnificent edifice," he added, just to rub it in. "I can imagine there will be no shortage of interested buyers."

Suppressed rage swirled in his head like a vortex of water disappearing into a drain. Van In saw himself punching the scheming bank rat in the face.

"I've had enough, Mr. Lonneville." He got to his feet, took a step forward, and placed both hands on the edge of Lonneville's desk. The bank manager pressed his head deeper into the back of his chair.

"Commissioner Van In. . . ." he protested nervously.

"Just one more question, Lonneville."

The manager searched in vain for the alarm button. A pathetic smile took its place. "Yes, Commissioner?"

"Are you a relative of Scrooge?"

"Scrooge?" Lonneville echoed.

"Forget it," Van In snarled. "People who work for banks have to be able to count, but reading doesn't appear to be on the program."

"Commissioner," Lonneville sputtered indignantly.

"Have a nice day," Van In hissed.

He tossed back his head and marched to the door, dignity intact.

"And before I forget," he said with the door handle in his hand. "Touch my house, and you're a dead man."

Lonneville gasped for air. The transformation of his rosy complexion would have made a chameleon jealous. "Is that a death threat?" he asked in shock.

"Feel free to register a complaint with the police. I'll take a look at it in due course."

The blond freak jumped when he slammed the door behind him.

"Comfort him, sweetheart," said Van In scathingly. "What else are secretaries for?"

Van In trudged sullenly along Steen Street. Industrious shopkeepers had competently cleared the snow. The local authority had also kept its end of the bargain. After every snowfall, grit trucks scattered tons of salt over the roads. "Commerce" in Bruges appeared to be something of a sacred cow. Farmers who spread a couple of hectoliters of fertilizer on their land once in a while were considered the real polluters.

He thought about turning back and making his way to the courthouse. He had to get rid of his misery somewhere, and Hannelore certainly wouldn't refuse him. Or would she? They hadn't seen each other for a while, not after their last blazing row.

He stopped outside C&A, unable to make up his mind.

"Jesus H.," he muttered. "Am I a man or a mouse? Lonneville gave me two weeks. It's time I solved my own problems."

A couple of grunge fans turned their heads as they passed.

"Hallucinations, granddad?" the grungier of the two mocked.

Van In looked at them with disdain and stuck out his tongue. They each responded with a raised middle finger. It was a comical picture, and none of the few passersby paid it much attention. Van In smiled and thought back to his own youth. Hippie or grunge, rebels were always better than an army of brainwashed careerists. He fished a cigarette from his trouser pocket and enjoyed a shot of nicotine. After the smoking ban in the bank, he had almost forgotten that smoking in public was still allowed, for the time being at least, just like making obscene gestures at innocent citizens.

The artificial absence of snow and a fan of budding sunbeams created a misleading impression of an early spring. A number of fervent shop-window droolers braved the weather coatless. A typical example of the deception of being. Van In could feel the cold cut to the bone. He turned up his collar and picked up the pace without knowing precisely where he was going.

On the edge of Zand Square, Van In realized that the guys at work would have presumed he was on official sick leave when he didn't show up that morning. The police station was too close for comfort. If he continued in the same direction, some promotion-horny tattletale would be sure to spot him. It made no sense to go back to Market Square, so he ducked under the awning of the nearest café terrace. The warmth of the gas burners took him by surprise. A young couple with a baby huddled in the corner. The waiter brought a bottle warmed up in the microwave for the baby. The young couple asked for a menu and gave the impression that they planned to order something. The waiter made himself scarce.

A respectable gentleman sitting near the door savored his favorite monastery beer. Van In looked for a place far from the couple with the hungry baby.

"What can I get you?" asked the waiter, bordering on the impolite.

In the course of the day, Van In drank just little enough to avoid getting stewed and having to stagger home, and just enough to be able to cope with confronting Hannelore. It was the only way to suppress the inferiority complex that seemed to have embedded itself in his genes. He had tried alternative methods, but none of them worked and he had given up the fight years ago. He had managed to conceal his pathological shyness from the outside world, more or less, but intimates knew that Van In tended to avoid problems when the opportunity arose and preferred to withdraw into a corner and sulk. As far as he himself was concerned, the planned confrontation with Hannelore was a courageous initiative.

He waited for her outside the brand-new, exorbitantly costly courthouse near the Kruispoort, another of Bruges's surviving medieval city gates. She finished work at around six-thirty most days; today was, fortunately, no exception.

In the parking lot, she had the appearance of a transparent nymph in a dark primeval forest. She was wearing a tight gray ankle-length skirt and a short leather jacket with padded shoulders. The transparency was the result of a set of headlamps from someone's car ruthlessly penetrating the lower part of her skirt, exposing the contours of her well-trained legs with exceptional clarity.

"Hello, Pieter. It's been a while."

He walked to meet her and kissed her chastely on the forehead.

"Everything okay?" he inquired sheepishly.

"Were you expecting a lecture?" she jested. He didn't dare put his arm around her shoulder.

"I took a day off today, and I thought to myself. . . ."

"A day off sick, you mean." Her eyes flashed mischievously.

"A day off sick, then," he admitted reluctantly.

"I had Guido on the line this morning," she said apologetically. "Of course, he couldn't have known that you would be fit enough to spend the afternoon haunting the courthouse parking lot."

She unlocked the passenger side of her Renault Twingo and let him get in.

"You'll catch your death," she said with concern.

Van In was blue from the cold. His thin cotton suit stuck to his body like a frozen sheet. Hannelore started the engine and cranked up the heater.

"It only takes a couple of minutes," she said.

"Are you still mad at me?" he asked, trembling.

"Of course not, Pieter. Actually, I'm happy to see you. I have a bunch of things to tell you, and when I couldn't reach you at home or at the office. . . ."

Jesus, he looked like shit. She leaned toward him, threw her arm over his shoulder, and pressed her cool lips against his mouth.

"That's what I call a real kiss," she grinned when Van In's stuffed-up nose forced him to prematurely interrupt the embrace. "Feeling better?"

Van In nodded. The carillon bells chimed in unison in his head. Hannelore checked the heating vent and swished the melting layer of snow away with the central windshield wiper. She caught sight of Examining Magistrate Joris Creytens in her rearview mirror, gaping in the direction of the Twingo. The tight-fisted magistrate was carrying a leather briefcase, cracked and dog-eared.

"That's not his style," she scowled. Van In hadn't a clue what she was talking about.

"Take a discreet look behind you. Do you recognize him?"

Van In saw Creytens scraping the windshield of his dilapidated Mercedes with a plastic spatula. "Creytens, alias the Miser," he sneered. "Stingier than his shadow. Of course I know him."

Hannelore laughed heartily at his remark, and Van In was happy to have her next to him.

"Starting to thaw a little?" she inquired.

"Slowly but surely. I'll call for help if it gets too hot."

Hannelore usually ignored his feeble allusions, but this time it didn't seem to bother her. She rewarded him with a kiss. "Want a smoke?"

"Sure." He had run out of cigarettes hours earlier.

"So you're not angry?" he whined like a spoiled husband.

Hannelore took a puff of his cigarette and carefully shifted the Twingo into first.

"I *was* angry, Pieter Van In, and you know it good and well. You were completely loaded when you appeared at my parents' place at Christmas."

The cigarette tasted bitter. He had rehearsed the scene over and over in his head.

"But that was three months ago," she added reproachfully.

"Eleven weeks," said Van In, on his high horse.

She ignored his nit-picking correction. "And you're probably wondering what my folks thought about you snoring on the sofa."

"Did I snore?"

"You shook the house," she exaggerated. "My dad had to turn the TV up, and even then he had trouble following his favorite soap. But my mother took a liking to you."

"Really?"

"Mother likes just about everybody," she teased.

"Don't kid around with me, Hanne."

"Your wish is my command, sir."

"Hanne!"

"Fine. Plans for tonight?"

Van In took an irate drag on his cigarette and shook his head.

"Excellent, because—"

"You've got a bunch of things to tell me," he finished for her.

"Praise the Lord. Van In awakes."

She narrowly missed a couple of cyclists on Lange Street who were unashamedly taking up half the road. One of them shook his fist in rage.

"I assume you don't have much worth eating in that castle of yours, Pieter Van In."

He only had five hundred francs in his pocket, and the way she was looking at him didn't bode well.

"Look at the birds in the sky. They don't plant or harvest, and yet. . . ."

"What about the Greek in Ezel Street?" she suggested enthusiastically. "And don't worry, it's on me. Or did I misread the hint?"

Van In straightened his stiff spine and took another cigarette without asking.

"A date?" she asked.

He loved Hannelore but hated capitulating without putting up a fight. An icy silence filled the Twingo.

"Okay," she said lightheartedly. "For the last time: *Ego te absolvo.* Or don't you believe in female priests?"

Van In tried to control himself, but when she elbowed him hard in the ribs he could no longer contain his laughter.

"Finally," she sighed. "I thought you'd never give in."

"On one condition," he grinned. "That we finish with a nightcap at my place."

5

At the Greek, they had flambéed filet of lamb with greens and cream sauce . . . divine. Niko, the owner, treated them to a table near the fire. Van In could hear the sound of crunching car wheels outside and presumed it had started to snow again. The atmosphere was perfect.

They enjoyed every bite of the juicy roasted meat, and Hannelore made sure the carafes of house wine kept on coming.

"I wanted to have a word about the murder on Blinde Ezel Street," she said between gulps.

"Murder?"

He divided the last four slices of meat between their plates. Hannelore promptly returned a slice.

"Did Fiedle snuff it?" he asked.

"He succumbed to his injuries this morning. The public prosecutor appointed Examining Magistrate Creytens to the case; but when I heard you were the investigator, I was curious. That's why I tried to call you earlier."

"There are stiff penalties attached to bribing a police official," Van In teased. "But for a portion of baklava, you can have the lot."

"If I were in your shoes, I wouldn't be too cheerful, Pieter Van In. The magistrate was furious when he heard you couldn't be reached today. He handed the case over to the Federal Police without taking a breath."

"So much the better. And he did the right thing. I'll be grateful until the day I die."

"I don't get you, Pieter. You rarely get the chance to investigate a murder, and all you can say is 'so much the better'?"

"The German was still alive when we started the investigation. And who says he was murdered? The man was drunk as a skunk. It was snowing; the streets were icy. Maybe he just slipped," Van In responded matter-of-factly. "Anyway, I've got more than enough on my plate."

"There you go again. The perpetual underdog."

He ignored the sarcasm and popped the last chunk of lamb into his mouth.

"I've heard they appointed a certain commissioner Croos to head up the investigation," she continued nonchalantly.

The maneuver had the desired effect. Van In almost choked.

"Wilfried Croos?"

"Do you know him?"

"You bet I know him." Van In reacted like a schoolgirl to a bee-sting. "Everyone knows the dumbest commissioner in the Northern Hemisphere."

"Mmm, I wouldn't call him dumb," said Hannelore, straightening her face and hiding it behind a glassful of wine. "Macho and arrogant, perhaps, but dumb?"

"So you find the asshole attractive," Van In snorted. "Do you know what they call him? 'Bull's-Eye' Croos. Even his mother-in-law isn't safe."

Hannelore tried not to laugh. "I know you too well, Pieter Van In. Let's cut the crap."

Van In grinned like a kid watching the postman hit the saddle of his bike the wrong way.

"Order the baklava," he said provocatively. "And spill the beans."

"The public prosecutor's insisting on an in-depth investigation. Turns out Herr Fiedle was a prominent businessman."

"There we go again," Van In cursed. "The Kraut gets preferential treatment. I wonder if the public prosecutor would be putting on the same amount of pressure if Fiedle had been Moroccan. You can tell him from me that I'm not going to lose any sleep over a dead German."

"Pieter, behave yourself," she chided.

A couple of diners stared at them indignantly from another table. Niko, the Greek, whose Dutch was excellent, stood behind the bar and grinned. The SS had taken his father hostage during the Second World War and executed him in cold blood. He didn't give a shit what the other customers thought about Pieter's remarks.

"Didn't you know that Germany's most famous son was actually an Austrian?" said Van In at the top of his voice, intentionally.

The couple at the table beside them laughed heartily, although they had appeared as indignant as the rest moments earlier.

"Have you heard the one about the two Germans ordering a couple of martinis on a terrace in London after the war?"

Van In was on a roll now. Half the restaurant pricked up its ears.

"To avoid drawing attention to themselves, they order in English. The waiter nods and asks: 'Dry?' 'Nein: zwei,' the Krauts answer in unison."

While Hannelore thought the punch line was actually quite funny, she still did her best not to laugh. "That's no way to conduct a conversation," she said, unamused.

"Come on, Hanne. It was a joke!"

"That's what you always say, Pieter Van In."

Niko appeared with a generous portion of baklava. "On the house," he smiled.

"Fiedle worked for Kindermann," Hannelore began after they each took a bite, "one of the biggest tour operators in Europe. He was staying at the Duc de Bourgogne, a hotel on Huidenvetters Square. Croos had his men go through Fiedle's suite, and they found some unusual photos."

She leaned forward and fished a gray-brown envelope marked "Ministry of Justice" out of her handbag.

Michelangelo's Madonna, he wanted to say.

"What do you think?" Hannelore spread out about a dozen photos on the table.

"A German with a penchant for the polders. So he likes the Belgian lowlands. Should I find that suspicious?"

Van In clearly recognized the characteristic silhouette of a Flemish farmhouse and the street lamps along the motorway. The motorway in question connects the port of Zeebrugge with the hinterland, cutting through the protected landscape like a carbonized rattlesnake.

"So?" she asked, curious to hear what he had to say.

Van In examined the photos. They were recent and seemed to be perfectly innocent.

"To be honest, Hanne, I can't see the connection. If you ask me, they're just souvenirs."

"What about this one?" She produced a yellowing monochrome photo from her handbag.

"Aha, the *Madonna*. Did you also find that in his hotel room?"

"You know good and well where it came from," she growled.

Van In plunged his fork into the baklava once more, and Hannelore waited patiently until his mouth was empty again.

"So Croos has the file and everything in it?"

"Creytens insisted," she whispered. "A good thing Leo made a couple of copies on the side. Croos is protecting this file as if his life depends on it. And I don't like it."

"Correct me if I'm wrong, but did the public prosecutor happen to ask you to keep an eye on Creytens?"

Hannelore nervously fumbled a cigarette from the pack. She was on the verge of blushing.

"You have the right to remain silent, of course," Van In grinned when she didn't answer his question. "But as I said earlier: everyone wins if the Federal Police take over."

Hannelore filled her glass and summoned the waiter. Leading Van In down the garden path was proving to be trickier than she'd expected.

"A coffee and another portion of baklava," she said, slightly irked.

The Greek smiled and scuttled toward the kitchen.

"There's apparently something wrong with the vegetation in the background," she hinted.

Van In ran the photo between his thumb and his forefinger. "Is that so?" he asked naïvely.

Hannelore took the photo and shook her head. "I can see the cogs turning, Pieter."

"Then stop beating around the bush, Hannelore."

She gulped. Sometimes he caught her off guard. "I had lunch with Leo," she confessed. "He'd spent the entire morning trying to reach you, just like I had. He told me you'd had questions about the landscape in the background of the photo."

"Of course he did," said Van In resignedly. "I presume the photo's no longer part of the official file."

"Exactly. It's been removed." She seemed to take it for granted that he would spontaneously draw the correct conclusion. "Specialists have identified the vegetation in the meantime."

"That was fast," Van In observed sarcastically. "And what's the verdict?"

"Stop pissing about, Pieter."

Van In summoned the waiter and ordered a fresh carafe of wine.

"According to the experts," she said, "it's pokeweed."

"A very suspicious plant," Van In smiled derisively. Tears filled his eyes when Hannelore suddenly pinched his nostrils. "Ouch, that hurts . . . Jesus!"

The guests in the restaurant were getting their money's worth. Niko turned up the bouzouki music a tickle louder.

"*Ego te absolvo*," he groaned when she refused to let go.

"Be happy it was just your nose," Hannelore hissed. She let go, and he massaged his molested nostrils.

"Say a hundred Our Fathers," she said sternly. Van In pulled back when she threatened to pinch him a second time.

"I'll never laugh at pokeweed again," he promised, half-serious. "Talk to me. I'm all ears."

Hannelore grabbed his fork and nibbled at the sweet baklava. "Pokeweed only grows in the Southern Hemisphere," she breezed.

"And Michelangelo's *Madonna*—"

"Has never been sighted in the Southern Hemisphere, to my knowledge," said Hannelore self-assuredly.

Van In stuffed the last piece of baklava into his mouth. "So the question is: why would Creytens remove the photo from the file?"

"Precisely. That's what I wanted to discuss with you this evening. Exchange thoughts. . . ."

Van In furrowed his brow and tried to think clearly. Not an easy task after a liter of house jug.

"What do we know about Creytens?"

"Creytens is tainted," Hannelore whispered. "The public prosecutor's had his suspicions for quite a while."

Under normal circumstances, magistrates never gossip about their colleagues.

"So you have to keep an eye on him," Van In said.

Hannelore bit her bottom lip. She had sworn secrecy.

"Don't forget that judges are unimpeachable," said Van In. "They might dole out the dumbest sentences all their lives, but they remain honorable citizens deserving of our respect."

"Don't overdo it, Pieter," she sighed.

"Okay, so Creytens is a corrupt bollocks who manipulates files and withholds evidence. What do you want me to do about it?"

"I admit that we—"

"Jesus H. Even if we find truckloads of kiddie porn in his study, he's still a free man," Van In retorted. "When you're talking power, examining magistrates are right up there next to God. In the context of an investigation, he can take whatever measures he sees fit."

"You're right, Pieter. We need to be realistic."

Van In divided the remaining contents of the carafe between their glasses.

"I presume you're not planning to sleep at home tonight?" he inquired unexpectedly. He was much less reserved when he had alcohol in his blood.

Hannelore looked down, but not out of prudery. "If you'll light your fire and put on *Carmina Burana*."

"I still have a bottle of Cadre Noir in the fridge."

"Were those the bubbles you served with the shrimp in October?"

Van In closed his eyes. He was picturing her coming into the bedroom with the ice-cold glasses and the steaming shrimp.

"An unforgettable evening," he whispered.

He kicked off a shoe and searched longingly under the table for her calf.

6

WHEN VAN IN APPEARED NONE too early at the station on Tuesday morning, it seemed as if all hell had broken loose. Officers raced nervously along the corridors like blue shadows on accelerated film. But he was indifferent to the chaos. He had spent that night in heaven. Disguised as Dante, he had ascended through the spheres, and he had to admit that Hannelore was a much better guide than Beatrice.

"What's this? World War Three?" he asked an inspector as he raced past.

The man looked at him incredulously and continued on his way, shaking his head.

"Pfft," Van In sighed. "Cheerful Charlies everywhere this morning."

"Hey, Commissioner Van In."

Pieter turned his head. He could pick Versavel's voice out of a thousand.

"Guido! A normal person at last! What the fuck is going on?"

Versavel walked toward him with a spring in his step. In contrast to the others, he seemed his usual relaxed self. Van In envied him for it.

"So you haven't heard."

"Heard what?" Van In asked, pulling an innocent face.

"Some crazy terrorist blew up the statue of Guido Gezelle last night."

"You're kidding me."

"Scouts' honor, Commissioner."

"Why wasn't I informed?"

Van In had forgotten that he had disconnected his phone the night before.

"Bleyaert sent a patrol to your place at eight. He said there was some kind of problem with your phone."

"Bullshit," Van In muttered. "Who's in charge?"

Versavel stroked his moustache and pointed to the clock on the wall. "Starting at nine, you!" he said, gloating slightly.

"Jesus H."

"You really don't have a clue, do you?" Versavel repeated.

"What the fuck do you want? A declaration in duplicate?" Van In barked.

He regretted his words immediately. Versavel deserved better.

"Sorry, Guido."

"You're forgiven," Versavel grinned, unflappable as ever.

"You certainly know how to wake a person up in a hurry," Van In growled as they made their way into room 204.

"You're not the only one who's awake all of a sudden," said Versavel. "Half the city's on its head. Chief Commissioner Carton has had the mayor on the line three times, no less, and the city council is meeting this evening for an emergency consultation."

"Was there much damage?"

"It's not as bad as it sounds. According to Bleyaert, the statue fell on its back and broke into three pieces."

"Are there witnesses?"

"Take a guess."

"Sorry. Stupid question."

Slow down on the apologies, Versavel wanted to say, but he held his tongue. Van In sat down behind his desk and lit a cigarette.

"Is there coffee?"

Versavel shook his head and walked over to the windowsill. He shoveled five scoops of coffee into the filter and filled the water reservoir.

"My first bomb," Van In mused in the tone of a mother hugging her baby. "That I should live to see the day."

"Your first *what*?" Versavel perched on the windowsill and folded his arms.

"My first bomb." Van In stared at the sergeant questioningly.

"What about 1967?"

"I was still in school in 1967, Guido." Van In thought back to the Golden Sixties, the glory years of unbridled freedom.

"But you lived in Bruges, didn't you?"

"Jesus H. You mean the bomb attack on the courthouse on Burg Square."

"The very one," Versavel nodded. He made his way to his desk and fetched a couple of mugs and a Tupperware box with sugar cubes from the top drawer. "Not a single window survived and they never found the culprits. The public prosecutor interrogated half the province. The press cried shame, which was pretty unusual in those days."

"Now you're front-page news if you ask an asylum-seeker for his papers," Van In smirked.

Versavel carefully shook the coffee grounds into the waste-paper basket and filled the mugs.

"Do me a favor, Commissioner: don't start on the asylum-seekers. We'll be reading about it in the papers next. Headline: police discover evidence that Muslim fundamentalists blew up Gezelle because of a poem he wrote a hundred years ago."

"Who else can you blame?" asked Van In with a deadpan face. "The communists are gone, and the Africans are butchering each other."

"And the unemployed are probably too lazy to knock a bomb together," Versavel snorted.

"So who's left?"

"The employers!"

Versavel held out one of the mugs. "One lump?"

"Two, Guido. You know I'm watching my figure."

Versavel ignored the feeble remark and gave Van In the Tupperware box. "According to Carton, the mayor's main worry is the impact of the bombing."

"You mean he's scared shitless he'll lose a bunch of tourists."

"Everyone knows that business isn't exactly booming at the moment. No one can afford another bad season," said Versavel.

"The self-employed are always complaining. If their turnover is down five percent, they're screaming blue murder. They'll be selling Gezelle statues in three pieces next week, mark my words."

"Mayor Moens apparently doesn't share your opinion," said Versavel matter-of-factly. "Don't forget that the business community put him where he is."

"Did Carton tell you all this?" asked Van In, amused.

Versavel sipped his coffee, unruffled. He was long used to the commissioner's sarcasm. "Moens wants a discreet investigation, come what may," he said resolutely.

"If they spotted a man-eating shark off the coast of Zeebrugge, he'd still try to keep it under wraps," Van In scoffed.

"The politicians are calling it an 'incident.' For the time being, at least."

Versavel stroked his moustache. Van In was always going to be an awkward customer, he thought to himself.

"Has anyone claimed responsibility?" Van In asked.

"Not so far."

"Even better," Van In sighed. He got to his feet, walked to the windowsill, and poured himself a second mug of coffee.

"They'll probably pin it on a bunch of schoolkids."

Van In sniffed and imitated a tearful voice: "Mommy, I flunked my Dutch exam, so I stuck a bomb under Guido Gezelle."

"It might have been vandals," said Versavel.

"Vandals, my ass," Van In grunted.

"That's what the Federal Police are saying, their working hypothesis."

"Ditto Croos, I suppose," Van In flared up. "Don't they have enough on their plate with the dead Hun?"

"The bomb attack is for us, Commissioner. Moens is insisting that we handle the investigation."

"Is that a fact?"

Versavel's words seemed to calm Van In. The sergeant stood at the window and did some abdominal exercises on the sly.

"Did you visit the scene?"

Versavel turned and shook his head. "Bomb disposal has just arrived. I'm expecting more details any minute."

"So why do you think they chose Gezelle?" asked Van In out of the blue. "If I was given the chance to blow up a statue, I'd pick someone else."

"Surely not Michelangelo's *Madonna*?"

Van In froze. The photo of the *Madonna* with the pokeweed in the background had been following him around in his mind since the day before.

"Shit. Why didn't I think of that earlier? Two statues in the same number of days. That can't be a coincidence."

"No such thing, Commissioner."

"Exactly. It's high time we checked out the scene of the crime."

Van In gulped down the remains of his coffee, lurched energetically toward the coat stand, and put on his jacket.

"Let's go," he said impatiently.

As the two descended the stairs, Versavel couldn't stop himself from teasing his boss a little.

"Everything hunky-dory with the pretty Hannelore?"

Van In gave him a withering look.

"Or did you have a visit from your elderly auntie from Oostende last night?"

Van In slowed down and held out a threatening finger. "I happen to know that you go to see the Chippendales of a Thursday," he said affably. "A little birdie told me where you keep the tickets in your jacket. If I were you, I'd mind my words, Versavel, buddy."

"Sorry, Commissioner. If I'd known you wanted to join me, I'd have ordered two tickets."

"Laugh. Go ahead," Van In snapped.

"At your command, Commissioner."

A couple of young junior officers climbing the stairs pretended not to have heard the conversation.

"Is that Van In?" whispered the younger of the two when they had disappeared from view.

"Think so," the other whispered.

"Is it true that he's a bit. . . ?" The younger man tapped his temple with his forefinger.

"So they say," said the other timidly.

"And Versavel?" He made another knowing gesture, a flap of the hand.

"One hundred percent," the older of the two nodded resolutely.

7

THE ONCE-IMPOSING BRONZE STATUE OF Guido Gezelle was in a sorry state. The largest chunk had landed on a Mazda parked in the wrong place at the wrong time. The Japanese tin can had taken the culture shock badly. The car's roof was no more than a couple of inches above its wheels.

"Poor Guido."

"Sorry?"

"Not *you*, Versavel. Look at the poor statue. Our greatest poet, smashed to smithereens."

"There's no need to be condescending," Versavel snorted. "Get rid of iconoclasts? A pointless endeavor. But Guido's work will endure forever."

"Bravo, Sergeant. But that kind of verse is a little too amateur for my taste."

"At least I respect the man," Versavel sulked. "I love Gezelle, heart and soul."

"I can picture it."

"Priests had their feelings, even back then," said Versavel proudly. "Nobody would bat an eyelid nowadays."

"And bishops?" Van In smirked. Versavel sucked the cold winter air into his lungs, still indignant.

"I've many, many an hour with you been living and been loving, and never has an hour with you been for one instant irking.

"I've many, many a flower to you elected and devoted, and like a bee with you, with you the honey from it looted." *

Versavel recited the poem in a warm baritone voice. Van In had to admit that the languid, gentle West Flemish tones moved him.

"I didn't know you were such a fan," he said with undisguised admiration.

Versavel looked up at the leaden sky. *Snow does strange things to a person,* he thought to himself pensively.

"Gezelle was a monument," he mused. "And now the monument's in pieces."

The police had hermetically sealed Guido Gezelle Square. In spite of its being mid-March, tourists had gathered behind the barriers and had elbowed their way to the front like privileged spectators.

"Thank God we don't have to put up with mosquitoes in the winter," Van In growled as he weaved his way through the stubborn, chattering mini-mob, Versavel in his wake.

One of the officers inside the cordon fortunately caught sight of them, saluted, and pulled back the barrier to let them in.

---

* From Guido Gezelle's *Dien Avond en die Rooze* (The Evening and the Rose). Translated by Christine d'Haen.

Leo Vanmaele also caught sight of them and scurried in their direction on his short legs.

"No rest for the wicked, eh?" he chirped. The public prosecutor's diminutive expert was almost always in a good mood. "The guy who runs the Gezelle Inn right over there is serving up free coffee with cognac," he said with a twinkle in his eye.

Van In took a look around. Everyone else seemed to be hard at work. He had no reason not to accept the offer of a French coffee.

"So, tell me what you know," he said in a jovial tone. "If we hang around here, we'll just get cold."

In less than thirty seconds, the three men were buddied up to the nearby bar.

"Did no one else hear about the French coffee?" asked Van In, smelling a rat. Apart from the usual locals, the pub was empty.

"Surely you don't think I'd pass on valuable information like that to just anybody," Leo Vanmaele chuckled. "If the bomb squad gets to hear about it, our friendly barkeeper here will be cleaned out in no time, eh, Ronald?"

The manager of the Gezelle Inn, a wiry bloke in his forties, gave Leo a friendly slap on the back. "You know Leo. Always in for a joke." His voice resounded through the bar. Ronald spent his free time in a local gym. His voice and his chest capacity were in perfect harmony.

"We know Leo, all right," Van In concurred.

Vanmaele was clearly having a whale of a time. "But I can always rely on you to walk right *in*to it, eh, Van *In*?" he said, rubbing his hands together.

"You've had your fun, Vanmaele."

Leo grinned like a runaway chimpanzee. "Don't panic, Pieter. I'll take care of the cognac," he assured him.

"Just the coffee for me," Versavel shouted to the athletic barkeeper's chiseled back.

"Cookie with that, or fudge?"

Ronald stopped for a second, but even Leo didn't laugh at the tasteless allusion.

"Make it a cappuccino," said Versavel, ever the sport.

They found a table by the window. The bomb squad still had plenty to keep them busy. There wasn't a war on, so there was no need to rush.

Was Ronald trying to redeem himself, or was he always so generous? The ample snifters of cognac almost sloshed over the rim, and the aroma of the cappuccino was close to authentic.

"Semtex is in fashion," said Leo. "Lieutenant Grammens heads the bomb squad, and we're both certain it was Semtex."

Leo almost burned his tongue on the coffee.

"A professional job?" asked Van In.

"Maybe," Leo answered cautiously.

He tried to soothe his singed tongue with a swig of cognac, which wasn't exactly smart of him.

"Some water?" Van In asked when he saw the tortured expression on Vanmaele's face.

"Or a Duvel?" Versavel sneered.

A hefty top-loader and a tow truck arrived outside at the same time. Six laborers consulted one another on how to tackle the job. The foreman stared with envy through the window of the Gezelle Inn, but Ronald deliberately ignored him.

"According to Lieutenant Grammens, the bomber didn't set out to destroy the statue. He rolled the explosives into a long sausage and stuffed it between the pedestal and the foot."

"So it *was* professional," Versavel concluded.

"Or someone who knew absolutely nothing about explosives," Leo suggested.

"How much does that thing weigh?"

"No idea," said Leo.

"If the car hadn't been there, the statue would have smashed to smithereens," said Van In. "In other words, whether the culprit wanted to destroy the statue or just knock it over is irrelevant. Is there news from the door-to-door?"

"Everyone in the neighborhood heard the bang." Versavel had checked before they left the station. "Four teams questioned residents within a half-mile radius, but they didn't come up with much. And not a single eyewitness."

"Miracles are rare," Van In sighed.

"But the bomber carefully timed the explosion," Versavel continued unperturbed. "At three in the morning, Bruges is about as busy as the top of Mount Everest."

"*Bruges la Morte*," said Leo theatrically. "Yesterday somebody snuffs a German and last night some crazy guy blows up Gezelle? Bruges is alive and kicking, if you ask me."

"Has Croos made any progress in the Fiedle case?" Van In asked, out of the blue.

"I suspect you know more than I do," Leo grinned.

Both Van In and Versavel stared at the portly court expert in bewilderment.

"Didn't Hannelore whisper anything in your ear last night?" said Leo, feigning innocence.

"Not you too, Leo!"

"But she called me yesterday," Vanmaele protested. "She insisted on talking to you, so I figured. . . ."

Versavel buried his nose in his half-empty coffee, his shoulders shuddering from bottled-up laughter. Van In blushed, and Leo stared at the pair in confusion.

"Sergeant Versavel just threw away his ticket to the Chippendales," Van In growled.

"Sorry, Pieter, but I'm afraid you've lost me."

"Never mind," said Van In with a wave of the hand. "Ignore Versavel. When the police reports start to pour in later, he'll be singing a different tune."

"Excellent image, Commissioner, honestly. But beware of hidden agendas," Versavel retorted.

"All I wanted to know was whether Hannelore had talked to you about the Fiedle case," said Leo, shaking his head.

"No, Leo, she didn't. We went to bed early."

Vanmaele pigheadedly stirred the dregs of his coffee. "Timperman promised we'd have the results of the autopsy by tomorrow," he said apologetically. "I thought you knew."

Van In took a healthy mouthful of cognac. "We haven't been talking work much," he said flatly.

"This Fiedle guy seems to be pretty big." Leo tried desperately to neutralize the tension.

"According to Commissioner Croos, he is, or rather was, one of the bigwigs at Kindermann's. You've heard of them: the tour operator with a heart for your wallet."

"Old news," Van In drawled. Vanmaele stopped stirring and emptied his cup.

"According to insiders, Kindermann has control of forty-five percent of the tourist sector in Europe," Versavel offered.

"Good thing I never travel with Rhine monkeys," Van In grouched.

"Last time I was on holiday in Lanzarote, there was a rumor doing the rounds that Kindermann had bought up the neighboring island, Fuerteventura—or most of it, at least," said Versavel.

"That wouldn't surprise me," Van In pitched eagerly in. "Fifty or sixty years ago they made a pact with the devil, and all for a bit of *Lebensraum*."

"Let's not get distracted," said Leo in despair.

He made circles with his hands like a pope greeting the masses. If Van In got on his German hobbyhorse, they would be stuck here for the rest of the day.

"The affair has created a serious fuss in Germany. ZDF broadcast a three-minute piece on it yesterday."

"Creytens will piss his pants," Van In jeered. "And he might even enjoy it."

As he vented his gall about the investigating magistrate, a fleeting image flashed through his head. Just as he was about to figure out what it was, all three men were shaken by the piercing sound of grating metal. Van In tried to concentrate, but the image had vanished, just like a dream right before you wake.

A heavy-duty crane was carefully lifting the largest chunk of the statue: the poet's head and torso. The flattened Mazda squeaked like a skidding steam train. The tow truck swung immediately into action and hauled the wreckage away.

The six laborers, clearly on the local authority payroll or there wouldn't have been so many of them, followed the colossus with resigned interest.

Four other "civil servants" had positioned themselves in the back of the ten-tonner. They were responsible for loosening the chains.

"So when can I expect your report, Leo?" Van In inquired as the statue, or what was left of it, was finally secured in the back of the truck.

"On the bomb?"

"What did you say?" Van In's thoughts were elsewhere.

"Do you want a report about the bomb, or a report about my findings?"

"What findings?"

"About the bomb, then," Leo sighed.

"Of course, idiot."

"That depends on the bomb squad," Leo retorted. "Lieutenant Grammens told me the tests could take a couple of days."

"That's open to interpretation, Leo. Don't forget you're dealing with professional soldiers."

"Two days, Pieter," said the diminutive court expert resolutely. "And that's a promise."

"Good, two days. Otherwise. . . ."

"A crate of Duvel," Leo brayed.

"Two," Van In insisted impassively.

Leo Vanmaele accepted the verdict without complaint. He had won a bet only the week before. It only seemed fair to let Van In win now and again. But he wasn't certain he was going to lose. Grammens was the conscientious type. With a bit of luck, the military boys might just manage to sort out their paperwork in two days.

"Excellent," Van In beamed.

The diversion helped him forget the misery surrounding the potentially imminent auction of his house, albeit only for a while.

"I'm afraid there isn't much more we can do for the time being," he said when Ronald didn't give the impression he was planning to refill the glasses.

"Guido, will you collect the reports from the door-to-door? Then we can conclude the first phase of the investigation."

Versavel emptied his cup and wiped an imaginary smear of cream from his moustache. "Life is a battle standard," he lamented. "Torn by days both good and bad, stained, let slip almost, valiantly borne forward."

"Over and out, Sergeant. Save the poetical outpourings for your new word processor. I'll stop by this afternoon to check on your progress."

"At your command, Commissioner." Versavel jumped to attention and saluted. Ronald gaped at both policemen with a mixture of amazement and disbelief. *Is that why I pay taxes?* he wondered.

Leo shrugged his shoulders. He knew the pair. It was time they came up with something more original.

Van In spent ten minutes or so walking around Guido Gezelle Square, as if he wanted to give the onlookers the impression that the police were particularly concerned about the case. He let the cutting, frosty cold penetrate to the very fibers of his body and enjoyed the pain.

Van In hated bureaucracy. He had had his bellyful of the grind and the Kafka-esque treadmill. Suffering seemed to him an attractive alternative. But the real fun only came when he screwed up big-time.

Middle-aged men often get philosophical, he mused. Hannelore had done her best the night before, no question, but the euphoria had been short-lived and the memory fleeting. He felt old and past it. His life was a mess. The intelligent investigative work his superiors had congratulated him on only eight months earlier now seemed so trivial. Perhaps there was solace to be found in the fact that they were still dumber than he was, and still weren't aware of it.

Van In ambled along the Dyver Canal under a line of pruned and pared trees. The sound of the snow crunching under his feet was pleasingly familiar.

He knew that the Villa didn't open its doors until seven, but he walked automatically in that direction. When he crossed Burg Square, it suddenly dawned on him that he was about to do something stupid.

Van In increased his pace. The prestigious square was immaculate. The private parking lot belonging to the mayor and his council was full of cars. He recognized Decorte's gaudy

BMW and Mayor Moens's more modest Honda. The white-washed city hall stood out in sharp relief against the dark snow-filled sky. Leaden light engulfed the adjacent gothic Basilica of the Holy Blood like an ominous toxic cloud. There was a storm brewing above the city, but all Van In could think about was the Villa's lissome wenches. There wasn't a tourist to be seen on the square, and that in itself was creepy. Burg Square without a crowd was as unreal as a pop concert without decibels.

The Villa was closed, as he had expected. It made no sense to knock, so he found the nearest telephone box and punched in the nightclub's number. It rang for more than two minutes.

"Allo, Villa Italiana," a stifled voice said. Van In exulted in silence.

"Hello, Jacques." He recognized the voice of the longest-serving waiter. Jacques had been born in Limburg, on the other side of the country, and in spite of more than fifteen years in West Flanders he could barely conceal his Limburg accent.

"Commissioner Van In here. Is Véronique there?"

Silence. Under normal circumstances, Jacques would already have bitten the caller's head off.

"Not at the moment, Commissioner. She's gone shopping."

"In Bruges?"

Jacques had to think. He had no idea where she was. "I guess so."

"So you're expecting her back."

"Véronique has the evening shift," he said, hoping Van In would be satisfied.

"Tell me, Jacques, what do you get up to in that place so early?"

The waiter was taken aback. This cop wasn't so easily fobbed off.

"We're organizing an erotic karaoke competition for tonight. The technical guys are installing the sound system."

"So you're expecting a bunch of horny men?" Van In snapped.

"Why else would our Véronique be on duty?"

The "our" sounded possessive, too possessive. Van in didn't laugh and there was a painful silence. Jacques gulped.

"Do you mind if I stop by?"

"The show begins at eight, Commissioner. Everyone is welcome."

"I mean now," Van In insisted. "I have to work tonight and if Véronique's on duty, there's a good chance she'll show up early."

"We're closed, Commissioner. Try to understand my position."

"Come on, Jacques. Don't turn it into a question of conscience. It's just a favor. I know for a fact that Patrick won't mind. He still owes me one."

The waiter was torn.

"Jesus H." Van In wasn't in the mood to piss around any longer. "Let's agree on the following," he suggested high-handedly: "mix me a stiff drink and make sure the door's ajar. I'll be there in two minutes."

Jacques registered the dry click as Van In slammed down the receiver. He stared at the phone in disbelief and poked nervously at his ear.

"Mario," he yelled. "Whiskey sour for Commissioner Van In."

The bartender put down his screwdriver and made his way obediently to the bar.

Van In arrived two minutes later, puffing and panting like a punctured bellows. Jacques welcomed him with a thin smile and dutifully locked the door behind him.

"It could be hours before she gets back," he said resignedly.

"No problem. I'll wait."

Van In wheezed as he slumped onto a barstool and gulped at his whiskey sour. Jacques kept him company like a slimy chaperone.

With the exception of a skinny Moroccan in threadbare overalls, Van In couldn't see the "technical guys" Jacques had mentioned on the phone.

"You know I can't drink this rotgut, Jacques," Van In complained when his glass was all but empty.

"You asked for a stiff drink, Commissioner," said the poker-faced waiter.

"When I said stiff, I meant three measures of J&B and a splash of Coke for the color. Do me a favor and call Mario."

Jacques didn't protest. He didn't even ask himself how the commissioner could know Mario was on duty.

"Mario!"

The skinny Moroccan sitting at a table next to the dance floor barely looked up.

"Mario!" Jacques made his way to the lounge and yelled again. No answer.

"Yo, Mario," said Van In, delighted to finally see him.

The short bartender puffed, slammed the cellar door behind him, and dragged a crate of Coke behind the bar.

"Always hard at work," said Van In.

Mario wiped a couple of beads of sweat from his brow. He had only managed four hours' sleep and he didn't feel good at all.

"Everyone has to earn his living, eh, Commissioner?"

"There you are. Jesus! Here I am screaming myself hoarse and his lordship's in the cellar." Jacques was visibly upset, but the bartender didn't pay the least attention.

"Whiskey-cola, Commissioner?"

"Please," said Van In.

Mario knew the recipe. Why the commissioner had ordered a whiskey sour was a mystery to him.

"Everything tip-top?"

"Excellent," said Van In. The whiskey-cola tasted incredible.

"We solved the murdered-German case this morning," Van In said. "The killer's already behind bars."

"Congratulations. Who says the police can't do their job?" Mario laughed.

Jacques had turned pale and tried desperately to attract the bartender's attention.

"Excellent news, eh?" Mario said.

"Thanks to you guys," Van In beamed.

"Goodness. Mister Patrick will be happy to hear it," said Mario, relieved.

Jacques was on the verge of a heart attack.

"You guys are in the clear, naturally," Van In reassured his company. "The German was on his way from his hotel when someone flattened him."

"Thank God he wasn't on his way from here," said Mario, filling the icebox with Coke.

"He was here, of course," Van In guessed. "But that was much earlier in the evening."

"They came in at about eleven," Mario let slip thoughtlessly. For a bartender, eleven was indeed early.

"Exactly," said Van In. "Tallies perfectly with our witness statement."

"So that Hollander fessed up after all?" asked Mario naïvely.

Van In took a serious gulp of whiskey-cola and fished his cigarettes from his pocket. "The investigation's still under wraps," he whispered. He took advantage of the dramatic silence to light a cigarette.

Mario grabbed his dishcloth and stared to polish glasses with his usual thoroughness.

Jacques was flushing hot and cold.

Mario continued: "He was a total weirdo, that's for sure. First he ordered a fancy cocktail, then he wanted a whiskey-cola. And now that you mention it, the Hollander left and the other two. . . ."

Jacques turned away. His only comfort: bar work was easy to come by in Bruges.

"That other guy was the one who started the ball rolling," Van In bluffed.

A bad move, it seemed. Even Mario found the description a bit vague. A primitive alarm bell went off in the back of his head.

"Ah, that other German," said Mario, feigning surprise.

He looked at Jacques and realized Van In had taken him for a ride.

"They spoke German the whole time," he said awkwardly. "But we get so many tourists in here."

Van In realized his prey was trying to escape.

"Hollanders, Germans," Mario sighed. "You can't tell the difference after a while."

"Was the Dutch guy a regular?" asked Van In casually.

Mario was happy that the commissioner was interested in the Dutchman. At least he hadn't leaked Mr. Georges's identity. The Gigolo would appreciate that.

"Had you ever seen him before?" Mario asked Jacques, trying to pass the conversation over to his colleague.

"Absolutely not," the anemic waiter answered. He cursed the idiot bartender to hell and back. "Didn't look too savvy." The lack of response forced him to continue. "Even left his bank card in the restroom."

"That happens a lot here, I guess," said Van In innocently.

"You're telling me, Commissioner."

"But."

Mario held a glass up to the light and raised his finger. "If we find a card, we always turn it in right away."

"That's true," Van In conceded ostentatiously. "When it comes to bank cards, the Villa has an impeccable reputation."

Jacques realized that the battle was lost and withdrew with dignity to the lounge.

"One more question, Mario."

It was a gamble, but Van In sensed it was worth the risk.

"You didn't happen to see the man's name, did you?"

Mario stopped polishing. His exceptionally small brain was spinning hell for leather.

"Let me think."

He rubbed the stubble on his chin with the palm of his hand.

"It sounded Dutch, that much I remember," he said after a moment. "Andriessen or something. Wait. Adriaansen. That was it. Adriaansen, I'm sure of it."

"Well done, Mario," Van In cheered, overdoing the elation. "Mr. Patrick sure knows how to pick his staff, I have to admit. You're a credit to him. What a memory, man."

"What do you expect, Commissioner? The trickiest customers are hard to forget."

Mario blushed, grabbed a glass, and started to polish with enthusiasm.

"Another whiskey-cola, Commissioner?"

"If you insist," said Van In contentedly.

Van In cursed when the thing in his pocket started to beep. Mario recognized the sound and automatically handed him a wireless telephone. Van In punched in the station's number.

"Hello. Van In here."

"A moment, I'll transfer you."

The switchboard operator made no effort to hide his malicious delight. After a couple of bars of *Eine Kleine Nachtmusik*, the call was transferred, and Van In recognized Carton's low humming voice.

"Where the hell are you, Van In?" The chief commissioner didn't expect an answer. "There's an emergency meeting of the mayor's council this evening, and they want a report from the police."

Van In held the receiver a distance from his ear. Carton sounded exceptionally agitated.

"I would appreciate your presence at the meeting, Van In. You're supposed to be leading the investigation, aren't you?" Carton hated having to speak in public.

"No problem, sir," he said, self-assured. "I'll conclude my inquiries at once."

"The meeting's at the city hall at eight," said Carton. "If I were you, I'd go home, shower, and put on a suit."

"A plain tie or flowers, sir?"

"And drink a couple of pots of black coffee," Carton added as a parting shot. "I can smell your breath over the phone."

"I'll take care of it, sir."

Carton hated meetings as much as Van In did, but his rank allowed him the privilege of throwing his subordinate to the lions.

Véronique had her own key to the Villa. She made her appearance just as Van In was savoring his last whiskey-cola. She had carrier bags in each hand emblazoned with the logos of some very exclusive boutiques. A pale late-twenties assistant followed in her wake with the rest of her purchases. She immediately recognized Van In's well-rounded silhouette.

He barely moved when she ruffled his hair with her ice-cold fingers. He recognized her perfume, a mixture of musk and sandalwood. She stuck her nose in his ear, and it was proved to Van In then and there that there was nothing amiss with his hormone balance. Mario discreetly withdrew to let Véronique do her thing.

"Quelle surprise, Pierrot," she cooed.

Van In submitted willingly to a shower of kisses. Remorse was for later. Véronique's coy companion withdrew into a shaded corner. Véronique glanced back at him playfully. "Go and unpack, Xavier. I'll see you later."

The young man nodded submissively and assembled the various bags and boxes under his arms.

"He's so sweet," she giggled.

As Xavier stumbled up the stairs, Véronique settled on Van In's lap and sipped at his ice-cold whiskey-cola. Her fur coat barely concealed her pert bosom.

"It's been more than two weeks," she pouted.

"Seventeen days," said Van In, and those were the last meaningful words to pass his lips for some time. Véronique lured him into the Gigolo's room. As the fur coat slipped from her shoulders, Van In realized that he was about to do something he had never done before: write a dud check.

8

THE MAYOR'S COUNCIL HAD ASSEMBLED in a small antechamber next to the mayor's office. In contrast to what many believed, the city hall's magnificent Gothic chambers were only used for official occasions and weddings. The council chamber was cozier and easier to heat. The oak floor muffled the yackety-yack, and the Gobelin tapestries added a sense of intimacy.

"The situation is exceptionally serious."

Mayor Moens opened the meeting in stereotypical fashion. He had only been in the job for six weeks after his surprise win in the last elections, and this unexpected crisis pissed him off. If he made any mistakes, the opposition would drive him like a lamb to the slaughter. Nor was he expecting any support from the Socialists, with whom his party had formed a coalition. They had eighteen years of experience in office behind them. If things got skewed out of whack, they would dump the blame on his party in a heartbeat. Things weren't exactly hunky-dory within his own Christian Democrat party either. The influential local business community had been on the verge of withdrawing their support prior to the elections. The least quarrel with them could result in a political landslide.

"The bomb attack on the statue of Guido Gezelle was clearly the work of extremists. Their goal was also clear. They wanted to strike Bruges where it hurts, its most vital activity: tourism."

Moens gasped for air and took some water. His council barely reacted. Like the mayor, many of them were also new to the job.

"That's why I invited Chief Commissioner Carton and Assistant Commissioner Van In to join us this evening. They can help us take the appropriate measures."

The councillor in charge of Finances—an old-timer—muttered disapprovingly.

"If anyone has anything to say, then let him speak up," Moens barked.

Fernand Penninck, an appropriate name for a councillor in charge of Finances, took off his glasses and rubbed the sides of his nose with the tips of his fingers. Moens was a fellow party member and Penninck didn't want to get in his way in a crisis. But he had just missed the mayor's job himself by a hair's breadth as the business community's candidate. Penninck felt morally obliged to voice his dissatisfaction.

"I think we should work out our own measures," he said in an affable tone. "The police don't decide, they implement. De Kee's policies are a thing of the past."

Laughter filled the room. Everyone remembered the previous chief commissioner and his political shenanigans.

"It's a question of advice," Moens defended himself ineptly.

Penninck was a brilliant lawyer. If he had wanted to start a debate, Moens would have been dead in the water.

"Respected colleagues," he said. "I agree with the mayor as long as the police limit themselves to advice and we make the decisions."

Moens heaved a silent sigh of relief. Penninck had demonstrated loyalty. In a crisis, harmony was more important than venting shallow criticism. The other Christian Democrat councillors got the hint and bit their lips.

"We have to protect tourism whatever the cost," Moens resumed, a little more self-assured.

"Aren't we jumping the gun here, Pierre?"

Albert Cleynwerk, councillor for Monuments and Urban Renewal, made no attempt to hide his skepticism. The bearded Socialist was close to retirement and felt no obligation to grant Moens a honeymoon period.

The mayor didn't move a muscle, but his inner uncertainty churned like a pan of boiling milk.

"No one has claimed the attack, and we have no reason to believe that fresh attacks are on the way," Cleynwerk stated dryly.

"Perhaps someone just hates Guido Gezelle," said Marie-Jeanne Derycke, wading unexpectedly into the discussion. The handsomely coiffed head of the city's Records Office took evident pleasure in her intervention. It was the first time she had spoken at a meeting. But no one paid the slightest attention to her observation.

"If you ask me, we shouldn't be taking the situation too lightly. Vandals use spray paint, not bombs. If extremists are responsible, then it's clear to me that they're out to undermine the tourist industry. What other options do we have? We don't have embassies, or an airport, or an immigrant problem. The monuments are the Bruges Achilles' heel." Councillor

Penninck's brief apology drew a murmur of approval. "We have to face reality . . . unless colleague Cleynwerk knows more than he's willing to admit."

Cleynwerk had taken his seat. He scratched his sandy beard and said nothing.

"The tourist season begins in a couple of months," Moens continued. "I hope this is a once-only incident, but if we're dealing with extremists they'll probably strike again before Easter."

"When is Easter this year?"

Councillor Dewilde's question was completely irrelevant, but Moens checked the date nonetheless.

"April 16," he said affably. Moens wasn't planning to antagonize Dewilde with a condescending answer.

Dewilde, an aerodynamic copy of the Michelin man, produced a leather-bound pocket calendar. "That obliges us to have our monuments guarded day and night," he said with the air of a future statesman.

Dewilde had given up his job as a teacher at a technical school three months earlier. He had graduated from high school with a diploma in mechanics and owed his success in politics to his father, a thriving contractor.

"Do you have any idea what that means?" asked Penninck wearily. "Bruges has a *lot* of monuments!"

"Call in all the police personnel on the payroll and bob's your uncle," Cleynwerk sneered. "There's never a problem when the Brits are playing Club Brugge, is there?"

"Or we could drum up some neighborhood watch groups. I know plenty of people here in Bruges who would be happy to contribute free of charge," Marie-Jeanne Derycke suggested enthusiastically. She beamed like a bashful schoolgirl, quite a feat for a woman on the wrong side of two hundred pounds.

Penninck sighed—but, unlike the mayor, not in silence.

"Do you think my suggestion is ridiculous, Councillor? I wonder if you would have the same reaction if the suggestion had been formulated by a male colleague." She was clearly enjoying the moment.

Penninck didn't want to give the impression that he was sick to the back teeth of her inflated feminism. He smiled graciously, like a pharaoh who'd just been told that the architect working on his pyramid had passed away.

Marie-Jeanne Derycke interpreted the smile as an admission of defeat and folded her arms manfully.

"And if that doesn't work, we can always call in the paratroopers," said councillor Suzanne Dewit of Social Services, her tongue firmly in her cheek.

The two women hated each other with a vengeance. Marie-Jeanne was fifty-five, big-boned, and none too bright. Dewit was thirty-two, elegant, and a German philology graduate. She had picked up a mere 476 votes and owed her seat entirely to the fact that the Socialists had insisted on fronting a woman, determined not to tarnish their image as a woman-friendly party.

"Ladies, gentlemen, please. This isn't the time or the place," Moens intervened.

Dewit grinned arrogantly and Derycke lit a cigarette in a huff. She only did it to annoy Dewit . . . the bitch hated cigarette smoke.

"Has the investigation produced any results?" asked Cleynwerk, in an effort to get the discussion back on a respectable track.

"Correct me if I'm wrong, but isn't that why the mayor invited the commissioners?" asked Marc Decorte dryly. The councillor for Tourism had spent most of the meeting playing with his ballpoint, which he now set aside with a dramatic gesture.

Chief Commissioner Carton and Van In found the city's fathers and mothers in a dense haze of gray-blue smoke. With the exception of Dewit, everyone had followed Derycke's example. The crystal chandeliers were covered in a layer of brown nicotine, to which the previous administration had also made a serious contribution.

Van In inspected the rabble and hoped the bullshit would be kept to a minimum. He liked to compare politicians with psychopaths: they both killed without a motive, the latter people, the former time.

On the mayor's invitation, Carton took a seat at the head of the table. Van In was obliged to sit beside him.

Moens cleared his throat, and silence filled the chamber.

"Assistant Commissioner Van In, Head of Bruges's Special Investigations Unit, will now bring us up to speed on his inquiry into the bomb attack."

It sounded terrible. The inexperienced mayor used uppercase letters when he spoke, typical of a cautious politician trying not to step on anyone's toes. Moens folded his arms on his belly, peered over the heads of the assembled councillors, and took his seat like a Tibetan lama with a winning lottery ticket in his pocket.

Van In created a dramatic silence by staring passively into space. Carton treated him to a bad-tempered kick under the table.

"Honorable Mayor, Respected Councillors," he said reluctantly.

Van In wasn't aware that he too was speaking in capital letters.

"Today's incident is a concern for all of us. We're not used to terrorism here in Bruges."

Everyone listened with bated breath. Van In couldn't understand why, since he had yet to say anything that might warrant their apprehension.

"I will be contacting the National Security people tomorrow for a list of extremist groups who might be capable of such an attack. I'm also expecting a report from the bomb-disposal unit in a couple of days. My assistant is coordinating the investigation in and around the scene of the attack."

"Ridiculous," Cleynwerk snorted. "Any one of us could make up that sort of crap."

"Mister Cleynwerk," Moens intervened solicitously. "At least let the commissioner finish."

Van In thanked the mayor with a friendly nod.

"In cooperation with the appropriate services, we've put together an inventory of important monuments in the city. The Federal Police have agreed to cooperate, and the Army has provided expert personnel. The plan is to check important buildings for explosives as frequently as possible."

"But our respected colleague Penninck claimed only a moment ago that Bruges had so many valuable buildings that efficient police surveillance wasn't a viable proposition," councillor Dewilde whined.

Penninck rolled his Parker fountain pen between his thumb and forefinger, clearly irked. Moens had neglected to bring him up to date on police strategy. Now that sucker Dewilde had made him appear like a complete idiot.

"We're talking a selection of monuments, you understand," Carton intervened, coming to the aid of the councillor for Finance.

Penninck had supported Carton's application for chief commissioner without condition. Carton had no other option than to step up to the line for him.

"All the buildings with an electronic alarm system are secure and are not included on the list. The Army will be checking them before they close their doors in the evening."

Carton tried to make his reasoning sound convincing. He knew good and well that every alarm system had its weaknesses. Most had been designed to keep out burglars, not terrorists. Someone intent on planting a bomb didn't need to break in.

"This allows us to scratch all the museums, the city hall, the Belfort, and a number of churches off the list," said Carton.

"Is there anything else worth blowing up?" Derycke scoffed. She puffed a vigorous cloud of smoke in Dewit's direction. "And if they plant a car bomb on Market Square, you'll still be looking for it years from now," she added sarcastically.

Jesus H., Van In grumbled inwardly, *what gave the blond bimbo that idea?* He didn't fancy the idea of having to listen to a series of disaster scenarios late into the night. Of course the police were powerless, but try selling that to the ladies and gentlemen of the mayor's council.

As Van In had feared, the discussion was rekindled and finally degenerated into a mud-slinging match. At the end of his tether, Moens called in the booze, bottles of Straffe Hendrik—Bruges's strongest beer—and jenever. The generous servings of alcohol prematurely drained his councillors. They fell silent at one-fifteen, like a car engine with sugar in the carburetor. The situation was indeed worrying, so they agreed to the measures formulated by the commissioner and resigned themselves to the fact that little more could be done for the time being.

When everyone was about to leave, Van In noticed the mayor whispering something in Carton's ear. The chief commissioner hung back and out of necessity he did the same.

The city hall janitor, an unobtrusive man in a navy blue suit, waited docilely at the door, his keys jingling very discreetly.

"Go on up, Antoine," said Moens. "I'll call when we're done. It shouldn't take long," he added enthusiastically.

The man nodded and shambled resignedly down the corridor. But he didn't go upstairs. His wife had been asleep for more than an hour and there was nothing worth watching on the box. A recently opened Straffe Hendrik in the kitchen was more inviting.

The mayor's office was located at the rear of the city hall. It was a spacious room, a combination of an office and a sitting room. Visitors were treated to a magnificent view of the classically structured garden and the canals. The mayor owned his own motorboat, and a jetty had been provided.

"Take a seat, gentlemen," said Moens in a formal tone. He pointed to the red velvet lounge suite. A handsome desk in walnut veneer monopolized attention in the middle of the room.

"Cognac or whiskey?"

Moens deliberately didn't offer beer; otherwise he would have had to bother the janitor.

Carton opted for cognac. Moens and Van In chose whiskey. When all three had taken a polite sip, Moens made his way to his desk.

Dzing.

Van In recognized the sound of a spring-loaded latch, and that suggested a secret compartment.

"I received this letter at home this morning," said Moens glumly. He handed Carton a pale yellow envelope.

"I didn't want to start a panic," he said apologetically. Both Carton and Van In knew the real reason: Moens didn't trust half his councillors.

"This is an explicit threat," Moens said before putting on his reading glasses, "another attack. And next time we shouldn't expect another 'firecracker.' It says 'Bruges will tremble.' 'Les touristes should stay at home this year. . . . Le phénomène has already been observed in Turkey and Egypt.'"

Moens poured a good mouthful of whiskey down his throat while Carton explored the letter. He wasn't a fast reader.

"On top of that, they're threatening to liquidate me if I don't cooperate," Moens sighed.

"What does that mean, for Christ's sake?" Van In responded incredulously. "Cooperate? With what?"

"They don't say."

Moens had started to pace up and down. Carton peered over his glasses and asked himself why the mayor had given him the letter to read and then blabbed its contents.

"I don't think we should be too concerned, not for the moment at least," said Van In resolutely.

Moens stopped in his tracks and Carton grabbed his forehead.

"I mean . . . you're not in danger as long as they haven't made known their demands," Van In explained in response to the perplexed expression on the mayor's face.

"Is the letter signed?" Van In continued.

Carton took off his glasses and handed Van In the sheet of paper.

"Terrorists usually leave a signature," said Van In after reading the letter. "Call me old-fashioned, but your average bomber doesn't usually have a laser printer in his arsenal."

Moens nodded enthusiastically. So it was true what they said about Van In and his Sherlock nose.

"And why the French?"

Van In held the letter up to the light to check the watermark.

"This is the work of either a crazy person or a bunch of hot-headed Walloons," he said flatly.

The mayor sat down and gaped at him open-mouthed. Carton folded his arms over his belly and leaned backward. "So the watermark is French."

Van In folded the letter, making sure not to rub over the paper. "Do you have a plastic bag?" He carefully picked up the envelope by one of its corners.

Moens jumped to his feet and rummaged around in his desk. "Will a shopping bag do?"

They could immediately tell where the mayor bought his fish. Van In slipped the letter and the envelope into the bag with the greatest of care.

"I'll know by tomorrow if there's a useable fingerprint, at least if the mayor has no objection to my involving the technical boys at the judicial police lab."

"Can you guarantee the necessary discretion, Van In?" asked Moens, still clearly unsettled.

"Leo Vanmaele is a good friend. I'd even trust him with my love letters," said Van In nonchalantly.

Moens refreshed his whiskey and greedily emptied the glass.

The mayor is scared, Van In thought to himself.

"Fine, Commissioner, but on the condition that the contents of the letter are not leaked."

Moens shouldn't have repeated his condition. Van In had the impression he was shaking.

"What made you think of Walloons, Commissioner?" asked Carton out of the blue.

The crafty old dog sensed instinctively that Van In knew more than he wanted to share.

Van In lit a cigarette, self-assured and without asking permission. He filled his lungs and fired straight ahead.

"Everyone knows that the Walloon community is having a hard time. Advances in federalization are hurting them. They're afraid the Flemish are going to split social security. That would cost them more than a hundred billion, money they simply don't have. Belgium must be the only country in the world that never turned its ethnic issues into bloodshed; but if the Flemish stop the flow of money and the Walloons begin to feel the pinch, it wouldn't surprise me if certain extremists resorted to violence. The letter refers explicitly to Turkey and Egypt, where terrorists have been trying to intimidate tourists. Bruges is the most visited city in Flanders. And why do you think they chose Gezelle as their first target?"

"Jesus," Moens muttered. "Do you think . . . ?"

"Your analysis is alarming to say the least, Van In," Carton interrupted. "But I have to admit that such a scenario does sound plausible."

Van In relished the compliment. He had invented the entire theory on the spot.

"State Security should have more news for us tomorrow. If there's an anti-Flemish movement at work, that's where we need to concentrate our efforts."

"Excellent idea, Commissioner," said Moens enthusiastically.

"In the meantime, I suggest we place the mayor under around-the-clock surveillance."

"Excellent, Van In."

"But there's one more problem."

Carton and Moens were all ears, like children listening to a fairytale.

"Does it make sense to involve the other police services, or do we prefer to go it alone?"

Carton flushed hot and cold. Van In was playing with fire.

"I promised the Federal and judicial police that we would cooperate," said the chief commissioner with a tone of caution.

"Of course we'll cooperate; but if we can force a breakthrough in the investigation, we're not obliged to inform them right away. Wouldn't it be good if we managed to solve the case ourselves?"

The decision was made. As mayor, Moens was also in charge of the Bruges police.

"Good, Van In. We'll do it your way," said Moens boldly. "You've got a week."

"I'll do my best, sir." Van In emptied his glass in a single gulp. Moens might have been a mediocre politician, but he certainly knew his whiskey.

9

Van In appeared at the police station on Hauwer Street a good forty-five minutes late, having enjoyed a refreshing night's sleep. Nobody looked at the clock.

"Good morning," said Versavel; "you look good." They were in the hallway outside their office; Versavel had just made copies of a couple of police reports.

The commissioner was wearing an old-fashioned pinstriped suit under a crumpled gabardine overcoat. His tie was loud, to say the least. A ridiculous fedora defied gravity on his head. The sergeant saluted informally and tried to keep a straight face.

The commissioner proclaimed: "May I introduce secret agent Van In?"

Versavel asked himself if Van In was being serious. Van In didn't wait for an answer. He twirled on the spot and threw open his gabardine like an experienced runway model.

"Lead us not into temptation," Versavel groaned. He brushed his moustache and treated Van In to a wolf whistle. Van In stepped back instinctively.

"Keep your hands to yourself, or I'll cuff you," he threatened.

Versavel got the picture.

One of the officers the duo had bumped into on the stairs the previous day discreetly withdrew into his room. So it was true: Van In had a screw loose.

Versavel spotted the young officer peering through a crack in the door.

"Showtime," he grinned, throwing his arm around his boss's shoulder.

"Parumpumpumpum, pumpum, pumpum, parum-pumpum. . . ."

Van In willingly let Versavel take the lead as they danced to the melody of the world's most famous waltz.

"You're a bloody good dancer, Commissioner," Versavel chuckled. "Would you like my report as we dance?"

"Never mind, Guido. Before you know it, they'll be thinking we're a little . . . er."

"That *you're* a little. . . ." Versavel protested. "Everybody knows that I'm perfectly normal."

When Van In caught sight of the young officer, he turned and gazed longingly into Versavel's eyes.

"Your place or mine?" he asked in a hoarse baritone voice.

The voyeur had been joined in the meantime by a couple of colleagues.

"We're practicing for carnival," Van In roared. "Obligatory dance lessons for anyone caught staring for more than ten seconds, starting right now."

The curious faces disappeared as if by magic. Van In laughed loud and hard. Versavel was concerned.

"You look cheerful this morning, Commissioner."

Van In straightened his shirt and checked the position of his tie.

"I had a reasonably good day yesterday," he smirked. "Police work doesn't have to be boring by definition."

Versavel politely cleared his throat. "Did Véronique give you the special treatment?"

He sounded disapproving, and that was his intention.

Van In froze. He knew the sergeant would go through fire and water for Hannelore.

"The scrag called you half an hour ago," said Versavel, clearly irked. "She forgot to tell you something yesterday." He couldn't understand why Van In would drink cheap spumante when he had the best of champagne at home.

"Are you trying to say something, Sergeant?"

"Should I be, Commissioner?"

Van In pushed open the door of room 204 with his shoulder.

"The flesh is weak, Guido. I don't have to tell you that," he muttered. "Is there coffee?"

"I made a fresh pot at eight."

Versavel glanced knowingly at his watch.

"I said we would get back to her this afternoon," said the sergeant as he poured his boss a cup.

"Excellent," Van In snapped. "And don't forget the key to her chastity belt."

Versavel handed his boss the coffee and sat down at his desk, his head held high. Van In hadn't been on form for a couple of weeks. His depressions had been more frequent than an average northern European weather system. There was no point in getting his back up any further.

"Did the people at city hall have anything to say?"

Van In shrugged his shoulders indifferently. The thought of Véronique made him horny. What was he to do? His body reacted to the bitch like a hungry baby to a juicy breast.

"They were on the verge of declaring martial law," he sneered. "Did the door-to-door come up with anything?"

Versavel pursed his lips. "Shall I read you the reports?" he said in a tone that didn't bode well.

"Leave it. I assume everyone heard the explosion and went back to sleep."

"How did you guess? The people who called wanted us to file complaints."

"Of course," Van In hooted. "As if we've got nothing better to do."

"*Do* we have something better to do?" Versavel jested. "Take Depuydt, for example. He calls us almost every evening at nine fifty-five. The poor bastard lives next door to the Octopus, that piano bar on Wool Street."

Van In carefully placed his cup on his desk. He had been trying for more than twenty-four hours to recover the fleeting impression that had crossed his mind in the Gezelle Inn—and suddenly there it was, the skinny guy in Lonneville's office, clear as the nose on his face.

"The piano music is driving him mad, but we're not allowed to intervene. Depuydt's tried just about everything: official noise-abatement measurements, angry letters to the press; he even complained to a justice of the peace," Versavel chattered. "If it was up to me, I'd close the place down. There's an ambulance at the door every other night. Food poisoning. Jeez. I don't want to think about it."

Van In was only half listening.

"Depuydt, did you say? Surely not Philippe Depuydt?"

"That's the man. Know him?"

"I went to school with a Philippe Depuydt. Is he roughly my age?"

"I think so. If you want, I can get his address."

"Don't bother, Guido. It's not that important."

Versavel made his way to the windowsill and poured another cup of coffee.

"Apropos, is Carton here?"

Van In held out his cup and Versavel obliged with coffee and sugar. He himself was satisfied with a drop of skimmed milk.

"You know as well as I do that Carton can't handle the drink. And don't try to tell me that you two didn't touch a drop last night," Versavel laughed.

"So he's not here."

"I'm not expecting him before eleven."

"Good."

Van In sipped his coffee and lit a cigarette. The combination of caffeine and nicotine did him good. The old Van In was slowly beginning to surface.

"I want you to check something for me, Guido."

Versavel sat on the edge of his desk. In contrast to many of the other officers, his back was perfectly straight.

"Take a look at the hotel submissions for the last week. I'm looking for a Hollander."

Van In took out his notebook and read the description he had received from Mario.

"Probably a businessman, forty-five give or take, tall, thin, gray hair, trendy dresser. Goes by the name of Adriaans or Adriaansen."

"Okay," Versavel beamed. "Just my type."

"And a German," Van In continued, unruffled. "Sixty-five, portly and bald."

"Yuck," Versavel groaned.

"No sun without shadow," said Van In philosophically.

Versavel noted the descriptions. He was happy to see Van In back in action.

"So I'm guessing this has nothing to do with the bomb," he ventured.

"You guessed right, Guido. But what I'm about to say has everything to do with it."

Versavel held his pen at the ready. Mixing two cases together doubled the excitement.

"I want the mayor put under twenty-four-hour surveillance. Pick a couple of reliable men and keep it plainclothes."

Versavel pulled a face that would have made Till Eulenspiegel jealous. This was right up his alley.

The State Security Services were called in to deal with all sorts of odd jobs, but in reality they had little if any legal jurisdiction. Some politicians complained that they were redundant, others saw them as a necessary evil. State Security's primary task was to gather information. The service had half a million files covering every imaginable form of subversive behavior: from citizens who happened to attend a single meeting of a radical left-wing organization, to the CCC—Communist Combatant Cells—and its big guns, the Brabant Killers, and the French revolutionary *Action Directe*. It was remarkable that the files in the first category often contained more pages than the files on the serious bad guys.

With these thoughts in mind, Van In punched in the number of the Belgian Secret Service for the third time. The line had been busy on the previous two attempts. A telephone operator picked up just as he was lighting a cigarette. She quickly switched to broken Dutch when she realized the caller was a "Flamand."

Van In introduced himself and couldn't believe his ears when the bilingual operator immediately transferred him to the office of director Bostoen, one of the mandarins at State Security.

"Good afternoon, sir. Assistant Commissioner Van In, Bruges Police, head of Special Investigations." Van In shuddered at having to spout such official bullshit. "I'm calling about a recent bomb attack." He provided a brief report of events. "The perpetrators didn't leave a signature, and I was wondering if—"

"We've been informed," Bostoen interrupted high-handedly.

Van In was so taken aback by the abrupt tone that he didn't quite know what to say.

"Has the statue of Flanders's greatest poet been badly damaged?"

It was hard to tell whether Bostoen was being facetious or not. One thing was sure: he was having a difficult time disguising his West Flemish accent.

"It could have been worse," said Van In in a neutral tone.

Bostoen put on his glasses and leafed through the file on his desk. He had studied it in detail the day before. The faded letters *MWR* were inscribed on the front of the pale green folder.

"Good to hear," he said after a moment.

Van In tried to picture Bostoen in his mind. He could smell his arrogant self-assurance over the phone. He had to be a lawyer.

"And you had set your thoughts on some extremist organization?"

"Everything seems to be pointing in that direction," Van In responded cautiously.

"Hmm, you may be on to something," said Bostoen. "I have vague memories of a file on the Mouvement Wallon Révolutionnaire, but it's all a long time ago."

Van In had a pen at the ready and waited patiently. Bostoen apparently had all the time in the world.

"They distributed pamphlets for a couple of years, and the Service tried to pin half a dozen arson attacks on them. Their manifesto stated that they were intent on fighting Flemish imperialism with whatever means it took and that they weren't afraid of doing things the hard way."

"Sounds promising," said Van In, raising his level of enthusiasm a tone.

"But there's a problem. The MWR was disbanded in 1980," said Bostoen with a hint of regret. "Which doesn't prevent a bunch of hotheads picking up where it left off, of course."

Van In eagerly noted the details.

"I can have the file delivered to you if it helps."

"I would be more than grateful, Mr. Bostoen."

Van In put down his pen and lit another cigarette. Bostoen heard the click of his lighter, but withheld comment.

"I'll send a note to the archives right away," he said. "With a little luck the file should be in Bruges the day after tomorrow," he added condescendingly.

"Excellent," said Van In. "And thanks for being so cooperative."

"My pleasure, Commissioner."

Bostoen hung up, hauled himself to his feet, and hobbled to the mini-refrigerator in which he kept his medication.

Van In immediately punched in the number of the forensics laboratory.

"I was just about to call you," Vanmaele chirped. "Timperman faxed Fiedle's autopsy report half an hour ago."

Professor Timperman was a living legend in forensic circles. The unassuming pathologist/anatomist had a considerable reputation both at home and abroad, and his students idolized him.

"So what's the news?" Van In insisted. He knew Vanmaele liked to test his patience.

"Just a sec," Vanmaele chuckled. "Nothing we didn't know already in terms of the cause of death. Fiedle succumbed to a subdural hematoma. The massive hemorrhage killed him."

"Spare me the details, Leo."

"Okay. What about his liver, then?"

"Leo!"

"His stomach contents? Timperman discovered traces of *trigla lucerna* and *stizostedion lucioperca*."

"What was that?"

"Tub gurnard and zander."

"Sounds like fish."

"Correct."

"Is that it?"

"Yep," said Leo dryly.

"So Fiedle liked fish."

"Bouillabaisse, Pieter. Tub gurnard and zander are typically used in fish soup, Mediterranean style."

"That's really going to help us," Van In sighed. "Anything else useful?"

Leo hesitated. "Creytens has taken personal charge of the investigation, and Croos is as silent as—"

"A tub gurner," Van In interrupted tersely.

"Timperman also found a shred of tissue under the nail of Fiedle's right forefinger," said Leo.

If Creytens got wind of the fact that Vanmaele had copied the autopsy, Leo could look forward to a lifetime cleaning the corridors at the courthouse.

"Now, that's what I wanted to hear," said Van In, upbeat. "Have the report sent over. I owe you a Duvel."

"Shall I add it to the rest of the Duvels you owe me, or were you thinking of having it delivered too?" Leo sneered.

"Come and get it yourself. I'm at home this evening. And say hello to Creytens. Cheers, Leo."

Van In sat for a couple of seconds with the receiver in his hand. The tissue under Fiedle's fingernail was potential evidence that the German might have been murdered, the first so far. A simple fall now appeared to be out of the question.

It was beginning to look as if whoever did it had wanted it to look like an accident, and that of course made it all the more intriguing.

Van In broke the connection, waited for the tone, and punched in the number of the bomb-disposal squad. A friendly career soldier transferred him four times, but Lieutenant Grammens appeared to be untraceable. Van In didn't feel that he had the right to insist on being transferred to the canteen.

Versavel marched in at three-thirty. He was a sorry sight, covered in snow, and his moustache made him look like a walrus with a head cold.

"I think we're in luck," he said, bursting with enthusiasm.

Versavel hung his coat neatly on the coat rack and rubbed the ice from his moustache.

"According to hotel submissions, sixty-eight Dutch visitors spent last weekend in Bruges. One of them went by the name of Adriaan Frenkel, and the description's a perfect match."

"Mario must have thought that Frenkel was a Dutch first name," Van In nodded. "I'm listening. . . ."

"Do you mind if I finish, Commissioner? Frenkel had reserved a room until Tuesday, but left on Sunday morning in a bit of a hurry."

"Is that so," said Van In.

"And he paid for the entire reservation without batting an eyelid," said Versavel with a flourish.

"Then Frenkel's our man. Do we have an address?"

Versavel patted his breast pocket.

"Good, I'll contact our Dutch colleagues later."

"Is that wise, Commissioner?"

Van In clenched his fist and thumped his desk. "Jesus H. Christ. Every time we have our prey by the short-and-curlies, those dickheads from the public prosecutor's office run off with all the glory."

Versavel had long given up worrying about such matters. "Shall I type up the report?" he asked obligingly.

"Do that, Guido. But you don't have to dispatch it today," he said with a wink.

"I also paid a quick visit to the Duc de Bourgogne. According to the receptionist, Fiedle's room was booked by fax."

He consulted his notebook.

"A company by the name of Kindermann, Wagnerstrasse 45 in Munich."

"For one or two?"

"One. Fiedle was the only German in the hotel." Versavel scooped an ample amount of coffee into the filter and added some water to let it swell.

Van In got to his feet, stretched, and walked over to the window. It was snowing so heavily, the grit trucks were having a hard time staying on top of it. Bruges was slowly acquiring a rolling skyline.

"Either Mario's lying, or Fiedle must have run into another German on Saturday night," he said.

Versavel slowly poured boiling water into the filter. "Maybe that was why she called," he said in passing.

"Called?"

"The whore," said Versavel.

"Mario was at least telling the truth when it came to the Hollander," said Van In evasively.

"Don't make me laugh, Commissioner." He poured two mugs of coffee. "You know Mario, don't you? He gives you a perfect description of Frenkel, who probably has nothing to do with anything, but he's vague about the company Fiedle kept that night."

"I'm not sure, Guido."

Van In took a sip of the piping hot coffee and relaxed into his chair. Then he rubbed his chest like he was in pain.

"Is something wrong?" Versavel asked.

"Sorry, Guido. I'm not feeling my best today."

"We're all getting older," Versavel jested.

Van In barely reacted. This clearly wasn't one of his depressions, Versavel concluded. He knew the commissioner too well for that.

A sudden scurry of officers in the corridor made Van In look up for a second.

"Five o'clock," said Van In cynically. "Rats deserting a sinking ship."

Versavel wisely held his tongue.

"And you, Guido?"

"Did Merlin ever desert King Arthur?"

Van In smiled. Versavel was well-read and liked to show it.

"Thanks, Guido. You're an angel."

The pain suddenly hit home with a vengeance. Van In was sitting in an enormous bleak chamber, surrounded by people bidding greedily against one another. He looked on as an arrogant bailiff and four musclemen emptied his house. Blood pumped in irregular spurts through his aorta, and a swarm of aggressive fruit flies danced in front of his eyes. Then someone switched the light out.

"Jesus, Van In." Versavel's shout sounded muffled, as if a heavy curtain was hanging between them. Van In was flat on the floor. He had banged his head against a filing cabinet on the way down. Versavel reacted in a fraction of a second. He called the incident room and held a towel under the tap.

Van In could hear Versavel running back and forth, and he opened his eyes. To his relief, the pain was ebbing away. Four or five unfamiliar faces hovered above him, hideous faces, the type you see in horror movies. He recognized the smell of Versavel's aftershave. The sergeant didn't look happy at all.

The chill of the wet towel refreshed him, and he tried to sit up.

"Are you okay? Do you want me to call a doctor?"

Van In felt the cold of the floor penetrate his jacket on its way to his back. He shivered. Why was he lying on the ground? "No, leave it. I'm feeling better already." He leaned on his elbow for support. "Did I fall? Help me get up, someone."

Four obliging officers lifted him from the floor like a sack of potatoes.

"Thanks." His vision was clearing, but his chest creaked as if a truck had driven over it.

"I still think we should call an ambulance," one of the officers whispered in a broad Bruges accent.

"It's his heart. My father-in-law collapsed like that last week."

Versavel hesitated. He knew Van In hated doctors and hospitals. "Let's give him a moment," he said.

Van In grabbed his wrist and held it like a vise. "No ambulance, Guido. Everything is under control."

Versavel was faced with a dilemma. He wasn't happy, but the begging expression in Van In's watery eyes finally won the day. "Okay, gents. Thanks for the assistance. The commissioner's feeling better. I'll take care of things from here."

The officer who had said that his father-in-law had collapsed in much the same way the week before tried to describe the symptoms of a heart attack as best he could. The other officers left the room one by one.

"I think it was that coffee of yours, Guido. Too strong, too much." Van In smiled gratefully.

Versavel helped him into a chair. The commissioner grinned like a spoiled Alzheimer's patient.

"Coffee, sex, and excitement. I said it already, Pieter. You're getting a bit too old for that kind of cocktail."

Versavel rarely used first names with the commissioner, but hearing it gave Van In a warm feeling. He suddenly understood the difference between being a man's man and being gay.

"Not in that order, Guido," Van In groaned. "Please don't let me die from coffee."

"What about tobacco then?" asked Versavel cynically. "If I were you, I'd start paying attention to the warnings on those cigarette packs."

"You're right, Guido. Sex is extremely dangerous for a man of my years. Especially when a whore is involved," he jibed.

"Blowhard. I said tobacco."

"After the sex, Guido. Always after the sex."

"Birdbrain. You're as obstinate as a castrated pit bull."

"Give me two minutes and I'll be chasing your tail."

Versavel heaved a deep sigh of relief and held the towel under the tap. Van In was slowly getting his color back, and for some strange reason that made him happy.

10

Versavel booked out a car and took Van In home. He ignored his friend's protests and installed him on the couch with a blanket. He then lit the fire and forced him to take a Bromo-Seltzer.

"Try to get some rest," he said, doing his best to sound strict. "I'll do some reading."

Van In gave in and closed his eyes. He was gasping for a cigarette, but with Versavel on his case it would be the same as asking for strychnine. He heard the sergeant turn the pages of his book at regular intervals. He tried to relax, counted backwards from 100 to 1, but when that didn't work he turned on his side and did his imitation of a mineworker clearing his lungs.

Versavel slammed his book shut and looked at Van In, compassion written all over his face.

"There's a drop of whiskey in the refrigerator, Guido. My vocal cords are like glue sticks."

Versavel stared pensively into the flames. What harm could a drop of whiskey do? Doctors approved of it, and for some people it even had healing properties.

"All right, then, one won't kill you," Versavel yielded.

"Don't forget yourself," Van In shouted at his back.

The hoarseness had disappeared. He sank into the couch and followed the snowflakes whirling past the window. Such moments of intense happiness were few and far between. They made you scratch your forehead and left you tingling.

"Thanks, Guido."

The whiskey barely colored the bottom of the glass. Van In waltzed it and inhaled the aroma. He deferred the tasting.

Versavel put on a CD of Corelli music. The room was filled with the scent of crackling logs, and the harpsichord added an indefinable sense of tranquility and refined pleasure.

"What are you reading?" Van In asked after a moment.

Versavel held up the book. Van In read the title. "*Chaos,*" he reacted with surprise. "I don't remember reading it."

"Shame, Commissioner. It's fascinating."

"Take it home with you, Guido. I'll manage on my own. And I'll keep out of mischief."

It took the best part of fifteen minutes for Van In to convince Versavel that he felt fine.

"I'll be asleep in no time."

"Okay," said Versavel. "But you have to promise me two things."

Van In breathed a sigh of relief and snuggled under his blanket like a spoiled infant.

"Tomorrow you see a doctor."

Van In threw back the last drop of whiskey and nodded submissively.

"And if anything should happen during the night, you'll call me." Versavel rubbed his moustache a couple of times, a sign that he was worried.

"It's a deal, Guido. I'm here for the rest of the night."

Versavel seemed to believe him. He tossed another log on the fire.

"I'll lock up and slip the key under the door."

"You're a kind man, Guido. I'll see you at the station tomorrow."

Van In closed his eyes and waited for the sound of the key turning in the lock and being slipped under the door. It was like a factory siren at the end of a double shift. He bounced out of the sofa, went to the kitchen cupboard, and grabbed a reserve pack of cigarettes—of which Versavel was under the impression that he had taken the entire stock. Van In then lumbered down to the cellar in his bare feet and retrieved a dusty bottle of Rémy Martin.

A powerful northeast wind had picked up outside. Thousands of snowflakes died an inconspicuous death against the warm glass of the terrace doors.

Van In lit a cigarette, inhaled deeply, uncorked the cognac, and poured. He blew smoke into the glass, inhaled, and took a gulp of the amber fire.

Sure as he was that bank clerks everywhere spent their artless evenings in front of the box, he punched in the number of Philippe Depuydt. The phone rang three times.

"Hello. Pieter Van In here. Is Philippe there?"

"A moment." It was a woman's voice. "Philiiippe . . . telephoooone."

Van In could hear a child bawling and could almost smell the bland odor of talcum-powdered buttocks. It took a while before someone picked up the receiver.

"Philippe Depuydt? Pieter Van In here." There was an eerie silence at the other end of the line. "You remember me, don't you?" he said, as if they were best buddies. "We were in the same class at school. The Xavarian Brothers. You were always next to me in the study hall. We fought heroic sparring matches with our compasses."

"Yes. . . ." He sounded hesitant.

"I saw you Monday at the bank. I had an appointment with the manager and I saw you slink past his office."

"I'm afraid I can't help you, Pieter Van In." Depuydt smelled a rat. Nobody called an old school friend after twenty-five years just to say hello.

"Listen, good buddy. I know about your problem with the folks next door." Van In sought refuge in an authoritarian police voice. "There's nothing to be ashamed of. Noisy neighbors can be a real problem. I have similar issues myself," he lied.

"Perhaps, but. . . ." Depuydt sputtered.

"I can help you, Philippe. I know why the authorities haven't done anything about it."

Depuydt's heart started to pound in his chest. The dispute with Debaes, the manager at the Octopus, had been keeping him awake nights. He was begging for a solution.

"That's very kind of you, Pieter."

"I can end the whole thing once and for all, if you'll tell me why the bank is so determined to sell my house."

Silence. The background noise also disappeared, which meant that Depuydt had covered the mouthpiece with his hand. He was talking it over with his wife, Van In figured.

"Why should I believe you?" There was a hint of despair in Depuydt's voice. "Nothing's helped up to now, and if I violate bank secrecy I could lose my job."

"Bank secrecy," Van In laughed. "Let's not exaggerate. I'm just curious, that's all. My folks have lent me some money, so there's not going to be a sale."

Further consultation. This time Depuydt wasn't careful to cover the mouthpiece. Van In heard the voice of the female who had answered the phone. Van In's comment about paying off his debts had clinched it.

"Can you really stop the noise?"

"Within the week," said Van In without a flinch.

"Well," Depuydt hesitated, "there was never any intention of putting your house up for sale. A real estate agent has been combing the market for the last couple of years in search of mortgage risks. They've been putting the banks under pressure to divest themselves of people in financial difficulties."

"I'm listening, Philippe." Van In could hardly believe his ears. Banks were supposed to be aboveboard.

"That's all I know, honestly."

"Bullshit," Van In sneered. "I've always had my suspicions about Lonneville. He's as corrupt as. . . ."

"Leave Lonneville out of this," Depuydt pleaded.

"No problem, Philippe. I'm happy with the name of the real estate agent." He picked up his pen.

"Die Scone," Depuydt whispered. "But you didn't hear it from me."

"You get to sleep tonight, Philippe. That nuisance next door is history."

"I hope you're right. In any case, thanks for the trouble."

"I should be thanking you," said Van In. "And call me if anything goes wrong. Okay?"

Van In returned the receiver to its cradle and drew obstinate circles around "Die Scone" with his pen.

Van In headed upstairs after the late news and took a hot shower. He put on clean underwear and wriggled into his favorite jeans. He camouflaged the rolls of fat above his belt with a brightly colored sweater, a gift from Hannelore a few months earlier.

It was only a five-minute walk from Moer Street to Jan van Eyck Square. The snow was blowing a serious blizzard. Van In waded through the sludge, trying to keep a cigarette dry in the palm of his hand. He shuffled the length of Grauwwerker Street and slalomed deftly between the collapsed, half-snowed-under piles of dog shit.

A pair of disheveled couples were holding up the bar at the Villa Italiana, staring wearily at their drinks. Mario raised a listless hand and Jacques politely helped him with his jacket.

"Wendy van Wanten fans," the pallid waiter snorted. "They got the wrong night, of course. Should've been here yesterday."

Van In laughed. Jacques always used the same excuse if the place was empty.

"Is Véronique here?"

"She's upstairs glamming herself. Want me to tell her you're here?"

"No need. I know the way."

Van In made his way to the back, his heart pounding, opened the massive mirror door, and climbed the dark steep stairway. In contrast to downstairs, the upper floor looked more like a Warsaw slum. The paint flaked from the walls and colonies of black fungus festered on the ceiling like rotting seaweed. The air was stale, but nobody cared. The men who got this far usually had other things on their minds.

Véronique had the biggest room at the end of the corridor. Van In knocked and before she could say "come in," he pushed open the door.

Like most whores, Véronique had the taste of a twelve-year-old girl: bed linen in pastel colors, a pile of fluffy toys, and a vanity table in white craquelure with gold edging.

"Pierrot. I didn't think you would make it."

Véronique hopped from her stool like a brittle ballerina. Van In could see that she'd been using, but she made up for it with a waterfall of caresses.

"*Tu m'as manqué* . . . I missed you."

"I missed you too," he managed to squeeze in between a couple of kisses. Véronique had arrived in Belgium two years earlier without a valid visa, like so many other Eastern Bloc girls. When the police had finally picked her up, Van In took pity on her. She was twenty-two and smelled of the tundra. Her pronounced cheekbones, coral-red lips, and body that deserved the Nobel Peace Prize made his Russian seductress into an irresistible herb. He had grazed in her meadows and he was addicted to it.

"You called me," he said awkwardly.

She threw her arms around him once again and started to smother him with kisses.

"Let me make fix you a drink first. Campari?"

"If that's all you have," Van In sighed.

She rummaged behind a curtain, produced a bottle of Haig, and filled a couple of grimy glasses.

"Did you want to tell me something, *chou*?" he repeated in his best French.

Véronique gave him a glass and sat down on the edge of the bed.

"Is it about the German?" he asked.

"Fiedle?"

"No, the other one," he snapped.

"Pierrot, don't tell me you're in a hurry," she pouted. "A little more?"

Véronique filled his glass. Her carelessly fastened dressing gown fell open, but she didn't mind.

"That was no German," she said playfully.

Van In took a manly swig of whiskey and slipped off his jacket. The fake German wasn't going anywhere.

Enzo Scaglione was on a roll. He parked his slate-blue BMW in the shadow of Ghent's Saint Bavo Cathedral, popped some change into the parking meter, and headed toward the Wheat Market with a spring in his step. His expensive overcoat contained a bundle of crispy banknotes in its pocket: remuneration for blowing up Guido Gezelle.

His mother had always dreamed that her son would be a doctor or a lawyer. She had sent him to university against Scaglione senior's will. Enzo had studied in Namur, Leuven, and Ghent and kept it up for six long years until the day his mother was killed in a car accident. She'd been only forty-nine. A drunk driver had mowed her down at the front door of her house.

Three months later, Enzo had embraced the underworld. He was never going to get a university degree, but by this time he didn't give a damn. Today he had collected his fee, enough to turn even a hospital surgeon green with envy.

The Gravensteen gazed over the frozen castle moat like an alien monolith. The pristine snow on its battlements gave the aged giant an air of respectability. A tinkling tram traced parallel lines through the abandoned streets. The driving snow fuzzied the sharp yellow light of its headlamps. In contrast to Bruges, the authorities in Ghent let the snow lie, which was much safer for pedestrians. Enzo wasn't in a hurry. He savored the serene silence.

Robert Nicolai lived in a renovated apartment in the Patershol, one of Ghent's oldest neighborhoods not far from the university's cultural center, Het Pand. Enzo knew Het Pand like the back of his hand. He had regularly taken girls there for a screw when he was a student. But the dilapidated monastery had now been completely restored, and its former romantic charm had been bulldozed by the stiff respectability of the nineteen-nineties.

Nicolai was expecting him. The door swung open while his finger was still on the bell.

"Come in," he said with a welcoming smile.

Nicolai was youngish, good-looking, short of stature, but with the appeal of a trained bodybuilder. His long hair was tied back in a ponytail and his handshake was firm and dry.

"No problems?"

Enzo shrugged his shoulders and went inside. The apartment was sparsely furnished. The IKEA furniture was a perfect match for the whitewashed walls, and a couple of salmon-pink rugs graced the hardwood floor.

"Please take a seat, sir."

Nicolai didn't know his visitor's name, and Enzo wasn't planning to introduce himself. He chose a white beechwood rocking chair.

"Can I get you something to drink?"

Nicolai spoke Dutch with difficulty, but he did his best.

"Please," said Enzo.

"White wine?"

"Fine."

The awkward rhyme echoed the affected atmosphere.

"A very cozy apartment, Mr. Nicolai."

The broad-shouldered Walloon smiled shyly. He liked it when someone showed appreciation for his taste.

"I'll get a bottle from the refrigerator. Feel free to take a look around."

Enzo didn't need to look around. He had a sturdy file on the young man back at home.

Nicolai worked as a welder for a metalwork company. In spite of his modest income, he was addicted to luxury products.

He idolized Armani, collected antique toys, and was wild about fine foods. Having to conceal his excesses from the outside world didn't bother him. He lived a hermit's life and shared his secret passions with no one. He did the odd "job" now and then to finance his hobbies. He worked on assignment only, and for a fixed commission. He specialized in jewelry, but if he was getting low on cash he wasn't too picky.

"Can I take your coat, sir?" Nicolai suggested. "It's easier to talk that way."

He placed the bottle and the glasses on the mantel and helped Enzo out of his expensive coat.

"English?" he asked, without looking at the label. "Savile Row?"

Enzo nodded approvingly. He never got familiar with a "subcontractor," but there was something about this welder that he liked. The man shared his penchant for expensive, perfectly fitting clothes.

Nicolai uncorked the wine with a professional "pop" and filled the glasses. Pinot Noir also happened to be Enzo's favorite.

"I have the deposit with me," said Enzo after tasting the Pinot. "Four hundred thousand, the rest on completion. You'll find all the details in the envelope."

He fished the money and the instructions from the inside pocket of his jacket.

Nicolai nodded hesitatingly, as if he only now realized what was expected of him. The consequences could be far-reaching. Theft was one thing, but this. . . .

"I'm sure you're aware of the risks," said Enzo. He had detected the hesitation. Nicolai may have been an experienced burglar; but placing heavy explosives was the work of an expert, and that was definitely not something that could be said of him.

Nicolai tore open the envelope, evidently nervous.

"The green pages contain an outline of the security system," said Enzo in an obliging tone.

The Walloon appeared to misunderstand him, taking out the blue pages instead.

"Those are blueprints of the building," Enzo snapped.

"Sorry. I'll study everything later."

The wad of banknotes seemed to interest him more. He counted the ten-thousand-franc bills like an experienced cashier.

"The tower shouldn't be a problem," said Nicolai, full of himself now. "There are cracks and projections all over the place. I'll be at the top in less than half an hour."

Enzo shivered, in spite of the cozy warmth. He couldn't imagine anyone climbing the outside of a 250-foot tower without taking precautions. Looking out a third-floor window was already enough to make him dizzy.

"You can pick your own date," said Enzo, washing down his fear of heights with a healthy mouthful of wine.

"The sooner the better," said Nicolai enthusiastically.

"Before April first would be ideal."

"Don't be concerned. If it wasn't for the bloody snow, I'd be up there tomorrow."

Enzo had completely forgotten the snow. Nicolai obviously couldn't do the climb in such circumstances.

"But the snow never hangs around for long in Ghent," said the Walloon.

"No, but it can get bloody cold here."

"Not a problem. Last year I tackled a 1300-foot vertical climb in the French Alps in a noon temperature of fourteen degrees Fahrenheit," said Nicolai, oozing self-assurance.

"If you say so."

Enzo emptied his glass in a single gulp.

"This is the key to the baggage locker. I suggest you empty it as soon as possible. The police are in the habit of checking them, and they sometimes use sniffer dogs."

"In search of drugs, I suppose," said the Walloon with more than a hint of sarcasm.

Enzo blinked. The welder was getting cocky, and he didn't like it.

"There was a bomb alarm last year at St. Peter's Station. I don't think they used sniffer dogs then," Enzo snapped.

Nicolai laughed like a child at a fairground after winning a huge stuffed bear. Enzo took a deep breath and did his best to suppress his rage. He was half Sicilian and listed as a highly inflammable product. "I wouldn't take this so lightly if I were you," he snorted.

"Don't worry, sir. I rarely make mistakes."

"I hope so, for both our sakes, *amico.*"

Enzo got to his feet. The Walloon was on his toes. He fetched Enzo's coat from the stand and handed it to him.

"If problems arise, you can always reach me at this number," said Enzo, fishing a business card from his inside pocket and holding it up for the best part of ten seconds.

Nicolai barely glanced at it.

"Then I'll be on my way," Enzo continued dryly. He turned up the collar of his jacket and held out his hand. "The best of luck."

"Thank you. And tell your client everything will be just fine."

He sounded arrogant, and for a moment Enzo felt like an ordinary errand boy. The Walloon had balls, but his naïveté was a bad omen. Enzo turned to face him at the door.

"Repeat the telephone number," he barked.

Nicolai grinned and repeated the number without hesitation.

"If your climbing technique is as sharp as your memory, then no one has reason for concern. My client will be most appreciative," he added with unconcealed sarcasm.

11

"I THINK WE SHOULD BRING Versavel in on this. How can I work with the man when we're not singing from the same hymn sheet?" asked Van In in a formal tone.

Chief Commissioner Carton folded his mineworker's hands over his nose and audibly sucked in liters of air. "But you know the mayor's demanding secrecy."

"Which is evidence enough that Moens knows precious little about police business," Van In retorted. "Politicians are only interested in their image."

Carton loosened his tie. There wasn't a drop of moisture in the air. He walked to the radiator and checked to see if the humidifier had been filled.

"Nobody gives a fuck about these fucking things," he grouched.

"An investigation of this scale is too much for one man, Commissioner," Van In insisted. "I don't have enough time at my disposal, and I can't do everything by myself."

Carton turned and looked Van In in the eye. He was due to retire in three years. He had never wanted the chief commissioner's job.

"I heard you had another episode yesterday," said Carton in passing. "Are we on the mend?"

Van In nodded.

"No cause for concern, Commissioner. An empty stomach, a couple of cups of strong coffee, and a sleepless night. I guess I'm not eighteen anymore."

Carton appeared to be satisfied with this explanation. "So I take it Versavel already knows the score," he said, suddenly reverting to his formal voice.

Carton may not have had a college degree, but he was an excellent judge of character.

"How did you guess?" Van In sighed, pulling an innocent face.

Carton returned to his chair and parked his elbows on his desk. "Then the problem's solved," he said with a scowl. "*You're* in charge of the case. *You* bring Moens up to speed."

"Sorry, but I—"

"Spare me the excuses, Van In. Do me a favor. Go back to work and show me results. And remind Versavel to keep his mouth shut."

"I would trust the man with my life," said Van In. "Just like Mucius Scaevola."

"Moosius who?"

Carton was a fervent TV watcher. The name made him think of *The Godfather.*

"Scaevola was a Roman aristocrat who thrust his hand into an Etruscan fire to prove that—"

"Drop it, Van In. Your stories don't interest me in the slightest. *Capisce*?"

"Of course, Commissioner."

Carton didn't protest when Van In got to his feet and left the room, incensed. He had asserted his authority, and that was enough.

Versavel greeted Van In with a broad smile.

"Sleep well, Commissioner?"

"Like an angel, Guido. I heard you slide the key under the door, but only just."

In spite of the cutting east wind and the persistent blizzard, the sergeant was wearing a short-sleeved shirt. While the Bruges police didn't skimp on the heating, the main reason was his tan. He had recently returned from Lanzarote, and he was particularly proud of it.

"No more problems with the old ticker?" Versavel inquired.

Van In shrugged his shoulders. "Once a boss, always a boss," he said indifferently.

Leo Vanmaele stormed in at nine-thirty. The laughing leprechaun shook the snow from his shoulders like a wet dachshund after a walk in the rain.

"I owe you forty-eight Duvels," he crowed.

Versavel switched on his word processor and pretended to be busy.

Leo deposited a hefty dossier on Van In's desk.

"You don't have to read all this crap, of course," he quipped. "Lieutenant Grammens agrees with me one hundred percent: they used Semtex to blow up the statue. I'll spare you the technical details, but take it from me, the detonator system was professional stuff. We're not dealing with amateurs here."

"So we can rule out vandalism?"

"I'm afraid so, Pieter." Leo collapsed into a chair and unzipped his jacket. "Grammens even managed to trace the detonators to source," he said triumphantly. "In principle, they're for military use only."

"That's something, at least," said Van In. "If the detonators were stolen, there should be a record of it somewhere."

"Then we'll have to check at the European level," said Leo. "According to Grammens, electronic gadgets like that are only used in three countries."

"Germany, France, and Great Britain," said Van In casually.

"How did you know that?" asked Leo, surprised.

"The Krauts invent it, the French buy it, and the Brits get it for free from the Americans."

"Shall I contact Europol?" asked Versavel. They hadn't started quibbling, so he switched off his word processor.

"Europol? Don't make me laugh, Guido. By the time they connect up their computers, we'll be celebrating the second millennium."

"But we can't make light of the situation," said Leo. "Terrorists of this class aren't in it for the laughs."

"I had been hoping for a bunch of students," said Van In curtly. He opened the dossier and read the first paragraph.

"The analysis of the writing paper didn't reveal much either," said Leo.

Van In pushed Grammens's report to one side with a weary look on his face.

Leo went on. "Apart from three familiar sets of prints, the paper had been carefully wiped clean. The unidentified fingerprints on the envelope probably belong to the mail man, the sorter, the mayor's secretary, and all the others who pawed it at one time or another. If you go to the trouble to wipe the writing paper clean, you're not likely to forget to do the envelope."

"That sounds logical," Van In groused.

"But there's also good news," said Leo, upbeat. "I had a philologist take a look at the text."

"Jesus H. Christ," Van In groaned. "You promised me—"

"Don't panic, Pieter. I copied the letter and cut it up. The man has no idea what it's all about."

"Thank God."

Van In felt a stabbing pain in his chest but didn't let on.

"The letter contains sentence constructions that a Walloon or a Frenchman would never use. According to the philologist, it's pretty certain that we're dealing with a text translated from Dutch into French."

"The Dutchman," said Van In. "Guido, any news from the Dutch police?"

Versavel rubbed his moustache. "I had to cut things a bit short yesterday," he said diplomatically. "I didn't get the chance to. . . ."

"My fault," Van In grimaced. "We should contact them immediately."

Versavel got to his feet and nodded gratefully. "I'll fax them right away, Commissioner."

"Do that, Guido."

"There's been a complaint about a dud check," said Versavel with a sour look on his face.

Van In looked up, surprised. Leo had left fifteen minutes earlier, and he had been wondering what Versavel was up to.

The sergeant deposited the check on Van In's desk. "Recognize it?"

The color drained from Van In's face. "The bitch," he snorted.

"Under normal circumstances, some deputy public prosecutor would have found this tomorrow in his in-tray," Versavel grunted.

"And?" asked Van In, panicked.

"You can thank your lucky stars that Verbeke was on duty. Anyone else and you'd be fucked."

"You're an angel, Guido."

"I don't get it, Commissioner."

"Did Verbeke write up a report?"

Versavel fished a folded sheet of paper from his trouser pocket.

"Didn't he object?"

"Verbeke wouldn't bat an eyelid if a naked plumber appeared in his bedroom unannounced, looking for a leaky pipe," said Versavel with more than a hint of sarcasm. "I did it for Hannelore, Commissioner."

Van In was reminded yet again of Mucius Scaevola, who had held his hand over a fire until it was badly charred in an attempt to convince Porsenna that there was no point in continuing his siege of Rome. Versavel and the Roman noble were cut from the same cloth.

"You always jump to conclusions," said Van In in an effort to placate his assistant.

"Do you want me to believe you spent the whole time telling Véronique bedtime stories?"

"I needed information, Guido."

"That's James Bond's line," Versavel snapped.

"I mean it, Guido. Yesterday she told me—"

"So you *were* there?"

The prosecutor moved in for the kill.

Van In was ashamed and lowered his eyes.

"I'm done with her, starting now," he said. "I mean it, Guido."

"Spare me the promises, Commissioner. I'll pay the slut later tonight. Tear up the check and let's talk about something else."

Van In hadn't cried since the death of his mother, but at this moment he had an enormous lump in his throat and was on the verge of tears.

"Is there coffee, Guido?"

Versavel got the hint and turned around.

"Two sugars, Commissioner?"

Van In nodded when Versavel looked at him again and meekly accepted the mug of steaming coffee.

"The man who Fiedle spent the evening with wasn't a German," said Van In after a brief silence, reporting on what he had learned from Véronique. "It's getting more complicated by the minute."

"Was he gay?"

"Worse, Guido. Much worse."

"A politician?"

An explosion of laughter brought the necessary relief. Van In juddered in his chair, and for a brief moment his cares disappeared.

"It was Georges Vandekerckhove," he spluttered.

"The big boss at Travel Inc.?"

"The very one," Van In snorted.

"Are you going to question him?"

Van In grabbed a paper napkin and blew his nose. The tears trickled down his cheeks.

"If we don't do something," Van In finally responded, "Carton will have a stroke. And when a cop can't see the wood for the trees, he makes paper . . . lots of paper."

"Don't you need wood to make paper?" Versavel jested.

"Was that supposed to be funny, Guido?"

Van In felt the pain gnawing at his chest.

"Ecological harmony, Commissioner," Versavel explained. "Green is in."

"Maybe so, Guido," said Van In, "but let's be serious. Are you volunteering to inform Moens that we want to interrogate one of his captains of industry? And there's more cheerful news where that came from. Vandekerckhove owns the Villa. Did you know that?"

"Can't we pick him up for trafficking in women?" said Versavel eagerly.

Van In was aware that prosecuting Vandekerckhove would have personal consequences. He would be forced to appear in court and would have to face questioning. Versavel didn't need to be reminded of such complications.

"I think I'll pay an informal visit to Vandekerckhove tomorrow," he said. "If nothing else, I'm curious to hear why he didn't react to the death of his German buddy."

"Croos isn't going to like it," Versavel grimaced.

"Fuck Croos."

"And Creytens?"

Van In swirled the tepid coffee in his mug. Versavel was right, but. . . .

"If you ask me, an examining magistrate who's determined to bury a case can't be trusted. I bet you dinner in the Wittekop that he keeps his head down."

"Tenderloin flambé?" said Versavel, tongue in cheek.

"Not on the menu, Guido."

"Exactly, Commissioner. A simple steak. Who wants to get his fingers burned?"

"They should've made you Pope, Versavel. He gets to lecture people for a living."

"So I can expect to be punished for my impertinence?"

"Count on it," Van In teased. "You've got until tomorrow morning to find out all there is to know about a certain real estate agent here in the city."

"Planning a move?"

"Shut up and write, Sergeant."

Van In needed some fresh air, and Versavel didn't object when he rushed out of the office as if it was on fire. He rambled through the streets like a Don Quixote shadow and in less than an hour had crossed the city. He ended up on Burg Square, where an enthusiastic guide was herding his tourist charges like a flock of sheep into a nearby shopping gallery. In the shelter of the Steeghere—the monumental stairway leading up to the basilica—the guide eulogized Bruges, the "ever beautiful."

Van In was in the mood for something warm. The crackling log fire in a local tea room invited him in like the song of a charming siren. The temptation was great, but Van In reminded himself of Saint Anthony in the wilderness and resisted it. He headed for the Steeghere and wormed his way without flinching through the tightly packed tourists, who were listening indifferently to their "führer." When he emerged from the shortcut, he turned left and in no more than five minutes was standing beneath the impressive tower of the city's Church of Our Lady.

He stamped the snow from his shoes and hurried inside. It wasn't any warmer inside than out, but that didn't seem to bother the tourists. Some sat in the pews chatting about the gothic magnificence of the place as if they were watching the latest Spielberg.

Van In followed the left aisle to the altar, where Michelangelo's *Madonna* peered out over the heads of a group of twenty or so admirers. In spite of the signs scattered throughout the church inviting silence in five languages, an elderly church employee in an immaculate blazer was flouting the rules, informing the mixed assembly about the church's prized possession at the top of his voice. Van In joined them and listened with one ear to the man as he sang the praises of the Renaissance with great verve. His language was archaic and peppered with the kind of vocabulary you would expect of an art history dropout.

Van In grabbed a chair, sat down, and looked long and hard at the statue. The face of Bruges's *Madonna* bore a striking resemblance to the *Pietà* in Rome, as did the attire of the figures. Van In was no artist, but he couldn't escape the feeling that the expression on the Bruges *Madonna*'s face betrayed a hint of melancholy. The drapes and folds seemed stiffer than their Roman counterpart, and to him the Infant was a little out of proportion.

"Together with Leonardo da Vinci, my dear friends, Michelangelo was the most complete artist of the Italian Renaissance."

The church official held forth in French and English alternately.

"Don't forget that the fifteenth century marked the beginning of a new era. Michelangelo and Leonardo were the forerunners of a movement that opened up new horizons for Western European civilization. Michelangelo Buonarroti was a *uomo universale*. He was self-aware, arrogant, and quirky. He locked horns with popes and refused to submit to the ossified rules that limited artistic expression. Michelangelo's creations are refined works of art, and this statue is an excellent example."

Every head turned toward the *Madonna*. Van In looked on, amused. The guide was a pompous blowhard, but he had succeeded nevertheless in fascinating his audience.

"Permit me an anecdote," the man continued.

His audience was at once all ears, and that pleased him intensely.

"They say that when Michelangelo was commissioned to fashion the statue, he went in search of an appropriate model. He was intent on sculpting a young woman with the innocence of a virgin and the noble features of a lady. After a lengthy search, he found a girl who was prepared to pose for him, and because she had aristocratic blood in her veins he called her la contessina. While carving his statue, he fell in love with her, but his love remained unrequited. As was the custom in those days, *la contessina* was married off to a wealthy Florentine merchant. Michelangelo, who strongly opposed parochialism in all its forms, was so frustrated that he chiseled the initials MF in the statue's plinth."

The audience was spellbound. The guide's anecdote had made more of an impression than his complex explanation of the Italian Renaissance.

"Since we know," the man continued in a self-satisfied tone, "that Michelangelo never signed any of his other works, that makes our Bruges *Madonna* very special indeed. The statue is an ode to the love of a great artist for his Florentine sweetheart. 'MF,' ladies and gentlemen, stands for '*mia Fiorentina,*'" he concluded with a dramatic cadence. "My little Florentine girl."

The elderly church employee conjured a heavenly smile and accepted his tips with exaggerated gratitude.

Van In cast a final glance at the statue and ambled nonchalantly toward the exit. When he was outside, he realized that the icy church interior had offered protection after all from the cutting wind. He turned up his collar and tried to suppress his shivers by walking at a sturdy pace. An Irish coffee would do him the world of good.

12

"You don't sound very enthused," Versavel sniggered.

"Do you want to take my place?" Van In grunted. He lit a cigarette and started to pace nervously up and down.

"That's what you get, Commissioner. *Dura lex sed lex*—the law is hard, but it's still the law."

"And *durex sed* hard *sex*," Van In snapped. Versavel laughed out of politeness.

"Vandekerckhove isn't just any old bugger. Not to mention the fact that I don't have a leg to stand on," Van In sighed.

"What did he sound like?"

"God the Father. His lordship can see me at ten-thirty, but he has to be in Paris for a three-thirty."

"Then I'd get a move on," said Versavel. "Or shall I order one of our mounted colleagues to ride ahead of you and clear the way?"

Travel Inc.'s headquarters, a tasteless angular cube of mirrored glass and steel, dominated the skyline of Zeebrugge's harbor district. The multicolored signposts leading to the edifice were a waste of money: the monstrosity was impossible to miss.

Travel Inc. had started life thirty years earlier as a small family concern. Now it was one of the biggest tour operators in Benelux.

Georges Vandekerckhove had transformed his father's taxi business into a modern multinational. The company had an annual turnover of 14 billion Belgian francs and employed no fewer than three thousand people. Vandekerckhove and his youngest brother Ronald ran their business empire with a firm hand.

Van In was blessed with a more or less complete ignorance of macroeconomic models and the imperative laws that control the world of moneymaking. It didn't interest him in the least. He parked his Ford Sierra nonchalantly in the parking area in front of the building, next to the spaces reserved for the management. He stubbed out his cigarette in the unused ashtray and retrieved his jacket from the back seat.

The parking lot was kept free of snow. Travel Inc. didn't have an orange sun in its logo for nothing. If your business was promoting travel to warmer southern climes, you didn't want the parking lot in front of the company's motherhouse looking like a film set for *Amundsen Discovers the South Pole.*

Van In made his way to the central entrance hall and presented himself at the reception desk. The receptionist, a painted Barbie Doll lookalike and the product no doubt of some Flemish modeling academy, welcomed him with an American smile.

"Let me see if Mr. Georges is in his office," she said in cultivated West Flemish.

She worked the switchboard keys with the speed of a seasoned Internet surfer. As a phone discreetly buzzed elsewhere in the building, she glanced almost bashfully in Van In's direction. He instinctively pulled in his belly.

"Mr. Georges can see you in fifteen minutes," she said in a moment, pretending to be important. "If you wouldn't mind waiting?"

She pointed toward a sitting area surrounded by fake palm trees.

An enormous clock—a sun with huge blue hands—read nine-forty. Van In looked around for an ashtray but didn't find one. He lit a cigarette anyway. Miss Monroe coughed conspicuously but left him alone.

The telephone buzzed constantly, and just as Van In was crushing his third cigarette on the immaculate floor with the heel of his shoe, ex-Miss North Sea Cod gestured that he could go on up.

"Mr. Georges is on the sixth floor," she said, grinning from ear to ear.

Van In kicked thc cigarette butts under the fake palm trees and followed her pointing finger.

Travel Inc.'s headquarters were Georges Vandekerckhove's visiting card, and that was the way he wanted it. Lithographs by Dali and Modigliani graced the walls, and there was also a kitsch reproduction of Van Gogh's *Irises*. For Travel Inc., the destitute Dutchman's sun-drenched canvas signified cash.

The deep-pile wall-to-wall carpet in Travel Inc. orange and blue added an extra spring to his step. The obligatory couches were made of leather, their frames of tropical hardwood.

Hundreds of halogen lamps came relatively close to reproducing natural sunlight.

Van In announced his presence by pressing the buzzer next to the typical red and green panels: WAIT or ENTER. It took a good thirty seconds before the green ENTER panel lit up.

Georges Vandekerckhove was sitting behind his impressive desk with the telephone wedged between his cheek and his shoulder. His hair had been fashionably gelled and combed by an expensive hairdresser, but it still wasn't enough to disguise the fact that the boss of Travel Inc. was almost bald. In an ordinary suit, without the trendy shirt, extravagant silk tie, and liposome cream, he could have passed for an ordinary office clerk.

Vandekerckhove gestured nonchalantly that Van In should sit.

"Egypt's promising to be a fiasco this year," Van In heard him say on the phone. "Traffic fell by sixty percent over the last eighteen months. Hotel capacity is massive, of course. The five-stars are selling at less than cost. Even free flights don't seem to be making the difference."

Vandekerckhove laughed apologetically and pointed to a tray with a pair of chrome-plated thermos bottles. He pushed a porcelain cup in Van In's direction with his free hand.

"Turkey's down forty-five percent. Even Greece is suffering from this PKK business. Our people on Rhodes are at a complete loss after last year's bomb attack."

Van In grabbed a thermos and filled the cup. In contrast to the usual office sludge, he recognized the aroma of pure Colombian coffee, freshly ground and perfectly prepared. A rare treat.

"And Morocco isn't any better. As soon as people hear the word 'fundamentalist' on the TV, they cancel in droves."

"No, not Algeria," Vandekerckhove snapped in response to an apparent remark from the other end of the line.

"Our clients don't distinguish between Morocco and Algeria. For them, a burnoose is a burnoose and a camel is a camel."

The man at the other end of the conversation probably offered an apology, judging from the smile that appeared on Vandekerckhove's face and his cheerful tone as he continued.

"Ebola?" he roared suddenly.

There was silence for a moment. Van In presumed that Vandekerckhove was now being given a lecture about the deadly virus.

"Don't let it worry you. Central Africa is a limited market . . . a loss we can absorb without feeling it."

Van In looked out of the window for the sake of appearance. In the distance he could see a passenger ferry struggling valiantly against the North Sea tide.

"You're absolutely right. Before long we'll be left with Europe and nothing else, and let me tell you, my friend, the old continent is saturated. The Spanish have gone back to renting out goat sheds, and they even have trailers in the Provence with two floors."

Van In took a second cup, filled it with coffee, and slipped it across the desk. Vandekerckhove nodded jovially and sipped sparingly.

"No, that's news to me."

Vandekerckhove's voice changed pitch. In a fraction of a second, a look of concern filled his eyes.

"Listen, Jean. Call me back after ten tonight. I have an urgent meeting."

He wasn't ashamed to let Van In be a witness to his obvious lie.

"I'll take care of that this afternoon," said Vandekerckhove sullenly, and he ended the conversation.

"So what can I do for you, Commissioner?"

The sour expression on his face made way, as if by magic, for his infamous Travel Inc. Smile.

"Assistant Commissioner Van In. Pieter Van In."

He liked to introduce himself Bond-style: Van In. Pieter Van In.

"Precisely," Vandekerckhove laughed. "Sorry to keep you waiting. There's never a dull moment round here."

"The girl at reception was also pretty busy," said Van In amiably. "I imagine it's hard to find capable and presentable staff, both capable *and* presentable I mean." Vandekerckhove's smile suddenly disappeared. He pushed back his chair and folded his arms in expectation. Van In was uncharacteristically restrained. Vandekerckhove had consciously kept him waiting, so he felt no immediate need to come to the point.

"You have a magnificent company, Mr. Vandekerckhove. Business appears to be booming," he said, giving the impression that he hadn't been listening to the telephone conversation. "Not surprising, when you think of it. People want to travel, no matter what the economic situation is. Vacationing these days is big business. Correct me if I'm wrong, Mr. Vandekerckhove?"

"I wish you were right, Commissioner, from the bottom of my heart. But don't forget that the sector is under enormous pressure. The competition is cutthroat, and consumers punish us for the least mistake."

The cunning old fox didn't flinch.

"But aren't you insured against that kind of eventuality?" asked Van In with a twinkle in his eye.

Vandekerckhove ran his fingers through his thinning hair and took a symbolic sip of sugarless coffee.

"I presume you're not here to book a holiday." He clearly wanted to redirect the conversation.

"No, indeed, not for a holiday," said Van In obliquely.

Vandekerckhove's nerves shifted gear. His nostrils quivered and he started to rub his feet together.

"I wanted ask you a couple of questions in relation to the murder of Dietrich Fiedle."

Vandekerckhove remained emotionless. "Poor Dietrich. I read something about it in the papers."

He took off his glasses and rubbed the lenses with his silk tie. Then he shook his head. "Herr Fiedle was a valued business acquaintance. It's all such a pity. If this had happened in New York or Mexico City, we could write it off to occupational hazard; but in Bruges!"

Van In felt uneasy. All he had to go on was the word of a whore.

"May I ask when you last saw Dietrich Fiedle?"

Vandekerckhove threw back his head. Van In watched his every move. This was a crucial question.

"One moment, Commissioner."

He pressed the button on the intercom.

"Liliane, can you check and see when Mr. Fiedle was last here?"

"Certainly, sir," he heard Liliane answer.

Vandekerckhove smiled and replaced his glasses, clearly at his ease. Van In had never seen a fattened vulture with glasses before.

"And are you making progress with the case, Commissioner? I presume you at least have something to go on. Evidence, a tip?"

His bulging lips looked like a pair of bicycle inner tubes with a kink in the middle.

"We have a suspect," said Van In dryly. "But I can't reveal any details, as you can imagine."

Vandekerckhove was speechless for a moment, but Liliane saved the day.

"Mr. Fiedle was last here on February 15," the intercom announced.

"Thank you, Liliane."

His triple chin jiggled like Jell-O on the hood of a truck.

"So you didn't meet with him on March 11? Privately, I mean," Van In asked, pressing the point.

Vandekerckhove moistened his lips and pressed the tips of his fingers together.

"Mr. Van In." He stressed each syllable. "On March 11 and 12, I was in Nice at a conference."

The man's self-satisfaction was thick enough to slice, bordering on arrogance. Van In was at a loss. His entire theory was collapsing in front of him like a house of cards.

"And you have witnesses to confirm it?"

"Dozens, Mr. Van In," Vandekerckhove sneered. "Would you like me to name a few names?"

His chin jiggled once again, but this time the malignance in his narrow piggy eyes was undisguised. He pressed the button on the intercom with a resolute forefinger.

"Liliane, would you be good enough to bring in the reservations and tickets for my last flight to Nice?" Vandekerckhove leaned back in his expensive executive chair, evidently at his ease.

"There's no need, Mr. Vandekerckhove. I believe you, honestly," Van In said, making light of the situation. "We have to follow up every lead, you understand."

"But of course, Mr. Van In. Another coffee? Or can I tempt you to try something with a little more punch?"

"No, thank you, Mr. Vandekerckhove. We don't drink on duty," said Van In without batting an eyelid.

"Nonsense. It's almost eleven. An aperitif won't hurt."

"I'd rather not, sir. I want to be back in Bruges by twelve, and it's not going to be easy in this weather." For someone who had to be in Paris at three-thirty, Vandekerckhove seemed to be in no hurry.

Liliane was the prototype of the perfect secretary. She wore an elegant two-piece and trailed a cloud of Chanel n° 5.

"The reservation and the tickets, sir," she said discreetly. "And a copy for the Commissioner," she added unrequested.

"Thank you, Liliane."

She placed the plastic folder on his desk and disappeared without a sound.

"Mr. Fiedle wasn't having problems, was he?" Van In asked.

"Dietrich? No. But if Dietrich had enemies, then you'd have to look for them in Germany."

Vandekerckhove handed Van In the folder with the photocopied documents.

"Dietrich was a colorless man. He lived for his work. And I would be surprised if any of his friends and acquaintances were even aware that he held a top job at Kindermann. If you ask me, his murder was an accident."

People don't get murdered by accident, Van In wanted to say. "In any case, thank you for your cooperation, Mr. Vandekerckhove," he said instead.

"My pleasure, Mr. Van In. Feel free to call if you think I can be of further assistance."

Vandekerckhove got to his feet and accompanied Van In to the door. That was his way of rounding off a conversation.

Van In marched through the main hall. The conversation with Vandekerckhove had confused him. He couldn't understand why Véronique would have lied. Why had she called him in the first place? Vandekerckhove was her boss, more or less. By betraying him, she had put her future on the line. One word from mister big man at Travel Inc. would be enough to send her back to the tundra. Van In tore a piece of paper from his pocket schedule and wrote her name in block capitals followed by a wobbly question mark. Outside, the biting cold stole his breath and he sought the shelter of his car as fast as he could.

13

Examining Magistrate Joris Creytens went home earlier than usual. No one at the courthouse cared. The majority were happy he was gone.

After the seven-thirty news, he retired to his study as he did every night. He wife took care of the few dishes they had used at dinner and tidied the living room. She was planning to watch TV.

The examining magistrate had problems with acid indigestion. The pickled herring he had eaten at dinner hadn't agreed with him. But the frugal meal didn't explain his sullen mood. Suzanne was a nightmare in the kitchen and usually served crap. They had been married for thirty years and the only dish she was good at was instant soup. She once tried to prepare a joint of roast beef. Creytens remembered looking on with pain in his heart as she dumped the cremated lump of meat in the trash.

From that time on, Creytens had refused to invest good money in his wife's culinary escapades.

When he was still a young lawyer, the examining magistrate had already been quite stingy. His wife had thought "stingy" was an exaggeration, but had resigned herself to the reality of the situation after a couple of months. She came from a prominent, but not necessarily wealthy, middle-class family, and marriage to a lawyer was about the only security life had to offer her. She ate in the afternoon at a modest restaurant on Ezel Street and then picked up a frozen dinner from the store, which she later served to him. That way she avoided arguments with her indiscriminate husband who was happy with anything, and everything, as long as it was cheap.

Creytens was aware of what she did and, like his wife, he accepted the armed truce. He even took a little pleasure in the fact that she had no idea he knew she ate out every day.

In his study now, Creytens put on an old-fashioned threadbare jacket and checked the thermostat. Sixty-five degrees was more than enough. He didn't understand why his assistants looked like frozen rabbits half the time. The temperature in the courthouse was a tropical seventy degrees. It was little wonder that the judiciary had such a backlog. There was clear scientific evidence that cozy temperatures made people listless. Creytens blew warm air into his hands and sat down in his solid oak office chair. The thing creaked with a vengeance, its nasty springs protruding through its tattered leather upholstery.

Under the thin light of a sturdy floor lamp, he opened the file marked FIEDLE and leaned back. To help while away the long evening hours, he took a gilded box from one of the drawers in his old-fashioned rolltop desk.

A slender cigar from his deceased father's stock was the only luxury he was willing to permit himself. Some of the boxes dated back to shortly after the war, when his father, deputy public prosecutor Edgar Creytens, had had half a truckload of confiscated goods delivered to his house.

Creytens filled his lungs with the fusty smoke.

"Dietrich Fiedle," he sighed. "Isn't it a small world."

Joris Creytens had been only eight years old in 1944, but he still remembered Dietrich's father Franz as if it had been yesterday. The black uniform, the angular SS runes on the lapels, and the highly polished boots had always fascinated him. Between November 1943 and May 1944, Der Franz had been a regular visitor.

Creytens's father had idolized National Socialism, but had been intelligent enough never to side with the Nazis in public.

Der Franz always arrived a good hour after curfew. Creytens senior always made sure the door was slightly ajar. The SS officer usually stayed until late in the night, drinking superior French cognac and listening to Wagner. Their discreet friendship was never known to the public, and fortunately so: after the war, Franz had been condemned to death *in absentia* for crimes against humanity.

But Joris still had plenty of happy memories of the war years, including the chocolates filled with cherry liqueur and the fresh pineapple Der Franz frequently brought him as a treat.

The examining magistrate puffed sparingly at his sour cigar and relived the blissful memories.

He also remembered Ludwig Seiterich, a military adviser. In contrast to the more flamboyant SS officer, the reserved official wore a simple gray suit. When he visited, he and Creytens senior listened to Bach and argued about Hegel and Kant. He never brought chocolate bonbons. A simple handshake had to suffice. The only advantage of a visit from Seiterich was being allowed to stay up late. If he didn't make a racket, they even tolerated him as late as ten, but then it was bedtime, no excuses.

His father and Seiterich spoke French, so Joris was able to follow the conversation without difficulty. Like the children of many middle-class families, he had been brought up speaking French. His father was a widely read man, and listening to what he had to say was always interesting.

Creytens leafed through the file and paused to examine the photos of Michelangelo's *Madonna*. He remembered the conversation in question down to the last word.

It was early September 1944. The Allies had landed at Normandy three months earlier and were advancing toward the Low Countries. Seiterich had seemed nervous that sunny evening.

"I fear this will be our last meeting, my dear Edgar."

His father had had a bottle of champagne brought up from the cellar and offered a toast to peace and justice.

"They plan to remove the statue the day after tomorrow," said Seiterich after a couple of glasses.

"That's a pity, Ludwig. But what do you want me to do?"

"Mensch. What's the point? The war will be over in a couple of days. You're the warden at the Church of Our Lady. Do something. The *Madonna* is too precious."

"Let's not exaggerate, Ludwig. Do you honestly think they're worried about a statue at this stage of the game?"

"Nazis are capable of anything. They've looted half of Europe," Seiterich retorted.

"That's good, coming from you of all people," said Edgar stoically.

Seiterich shook his head and sipped the superb champagne. "You have influence, Edgar. I don't understand. How can you just sit there? Call the diocese. Have them hide the statue before it's too late."

"That wouldn't be wise, Ludwig."

"What do you mean?" Seiterich stared at his friend with suspicion.

"Because the order to remove the statue came from Berlin. Himmler doesn't want the American Jews to get their hands on it," said Edgar with a cynical smile.

The remark left Ludwig Seiterich pale.

"You're probably asking yourself where I get my information," said Edgar.

Seiterich nodded vacantly. The conversation was completely absurd. Who was the Nazi here?

"I presume you know Franz Fiedle," said Edgar cautiously.

"Yes, natürlich. But I have nothing to do with the SS."

"I know, Ludwig, I know. You are an intellectual, caught up like me in an insane war."

His words seemed to calm Seiterich, to a degree.

"Fiedle belongs to a special section of the SS. His presence in Bruges isn't coincidental. He was charged with the task of inventorying the city's important art treasures for potential 'repatriation.'"

"And you know all about this?" Seiterich sneered.

Edgar inhaled the acrid smoke of his cigar. He could see that the German was confused.

"The statue's relocation has been postponed time and again for logistical reasons. And as I said: a formal command arrived yesterday from Berlin. Himmler wants the Michelangelo, whatever the cost. And if we refuse to part with it, he's threatening to bomb the city with incendiaries."

"Nonsense, Edgar. You can't be serious. The war is lost. Himmler has other things to think about."

Creytens pictured himself now as he'd been then, between a couple of armchairs, guzzling cherry bonbons left by Der Franz on his last visit. Eleven o'clock had come and gone, and his father had had no idea he was still listening in.

"Franz Fiedle is a good friend, just like you. I don't think he's bluffing. He loves Bruges, and that is why he begged me to tell him where the *Madonna* is hidden."

"But the statue isn't hidden at all. It's where it has always been," said Seiterich, throwing his hands in the air in confusion.

"Precisely," said Edgar. "Then they won't have far to look."

"Mensch!"

Seiterich grabbed the bottle of champagne and unashamedly filled his glass. The military adviser was at his wits' end.

"There's one thing you need to understand, Ludwig. The *Kriegsmarine* has been ordered to point every gun, everything they've got in the direction of Bruges. Even the Resistance knows about it."

Seiterich furrowed his brow. The truth was slowly beginning to get through to him.

"Believe me, dear friend," Edgar drawled. "Michelangelo's *Madonna* will be safer in Germany, and after the war we're certain to get it back."

"If the facts of the matter become public, no one will believe your version, Edgar."

"Don't let that worry you. When all this is over, I'll be on the right side of the fence."

"I keep having to remind myself that we're the occupiers," Seiterich sighed. "I come to warn you that a unique work of art is about to be stolen, and you side with the enemy."

"I trust Franz Fiedle," Edgar insisted. He stubbed out his cigar and immediately lit another. "The city is worth more to me than a Michelangelo. History will be my judge."

Seiterich sat on the edge of his chair. From where Creytens was hiding, he'd looked like a gray leprechaun perched on a dried toadstool. "Why don't you believe me?" he protested. "I'm the military adviser here, and I assure you that the German Navy would never fire on Bruges. Never!"

"Can you really guarantee that, Ludwig?"

Seiterich blinked. Things had been fairly chaotic over the last few weeks.

"The glorious Wehrmacht is in tatters and on the run like a bunch of scared rabbits. Only the SS is offering any kind of resistance," said Edgar dryly. "I'm a pragmatic man, Ludwig. If you corner fanatics like that, they can do more damage in twenty-four hours than a regular army in four years. The SS has even been known to execute senior officials for ignoring a direct command from Berlin."

Seiterich snorted as if he was about to hyperventilate. "Then I hope history does indeed prove you right, Edgar. But I still have to follow my conscience. I hope you understand. If you refuse to cooperate, I'll have to do what I can without you to prevent the theft of the statue."

"Very commendable, Ludwig. But do you think they'll believe your version of events? You are the enemy, after all."

"So I can't change your mind."

"I'm afraid not, Ludwig."

Seiterich got to his feet, bowed stiffly, and shook Edgar's hand. "It's getting late," he said, "perhaps too late. I hope we meet again after the war . . . in better circumstances," he added with a hint of melodrama.

Edgar embraced him. *"Au revoir, mon ami,"* he said sincerely.

"Auf wiedersehen." Seiterich had arrived as a German and wanted to leave as a German.

Edgar accompanied the disappointed military adviser to the front door. Joris remained in his hiding place like a frightened rabbit. If his father discovered him now, there would be hell to pay. There were still a couple of bonbons on the tray. He would eat them first and then go up to bed as quiet as a mouse.

He cringed when he heard the door to the study creak open again almost immediately. His father never returned to the study as a rule, but now he was back. He picked up the phone and dialed nervously. A look of concern contorted his lips and he drummed the polished surface of his desk, fast and staccato.

"I know it's almost midnight, Father, but tell the bishop it's urgent."

It took five full minutes for the bishop to come to the phone. Creytens's impatient father puffed steel-blue clouds of smoke into the receiver. Suddenly he cleared his throat. The customary exchange of politenesses followed.

"Seiterich will definitely be contacting you, my lord. If we resist, they'll reduce the city to rubble."

There was a moment's silence, an opportunity his father used to rinse his throat with some lukewarm champagne.

"Of course the order has been given. If they don't find the statue, they'll turn their heavy artillery on the city," his father repeated, his patience now at its limits.

Another oppressive silence followed. Edgar stubbed out his cheap cigar and quickly lit a Camel. The bishop was probably consulting his vicar general.

"Thank you, Bishop," he heard his father say with a sudden sigh of relief. "Fiedle is a wise man. Take it from me."

Creytens clearly remembered the look of satisfaction on his father's face as he returned the receiver to its cradle.

He then made his way to the buffet and served himself a large cognac. Joris sat hunched between the chairs. His eyelids grew heavy and when his father didn't move to go upstairs, he finally fell asleep. The remaining cherry bonbons were left untouched.

Creytens stubbed out his sour cigar in an old-fashioned ashtray adorned with a skull and crossbones and the words *memento mori*.

Bruges had indeed survived the war intact, but neither Franz Fiedle nor his father had had anything to do with it. The city was only spared German artillery fire because a young Navy captain ignored orders from Berlin. Nevertheless, and on the bishop's explicit request, Michelangelo's *Madonna* was not taken to a place of safety. The Church of Our Lady was ransacked on the night of November 6–7, 1944 by a special unit. The *Madonna* was taken to the salt mines of Altaussee via the Netherlands and Mauthausen.

Both his father and the bishop had been under the illusion that they had saved the city from an inferno. The truth, however, was something else. Himmler had never planned to spare the city, with or without the *Madonna*. The naval captain who ignored his order only just escaped court-martial. His heroic actions remained a secret, and he died without recognition. The actual events surrounding the theft of the statue also never saw the light of day.

Creytens's father kept silent for the obvious reason that in those days fraternizing with a highly placed German official and an SS officer would have damaged his career, to say the least. The church at the time answered to no one.

Edgar Creytens was appointed public prosecutor in 1951 and was promoted four years later to prosecutor general at the Court of Appeals in Ghent.

Ten years later, Joris Creytens graduated from the University of Leuven. It took him seven years to get his law degree, and without his father's prestige he would never have reached the finish line. His short career as a criminal lawyer could be summed up in a single word: pathetic.

Edgar Creytens renewed his efforts, throwing all his weight into the balance. His youngest son was appointed Belgium's examining magistrate on his thirty-second birthday, an office he still held almost thirty years later.

When Edgar died, he left his incompetent heir an enormous fortune. Creytens knew where his father's money had come from, and that is why he was obliged to sweep the Fiedle affair under the carpet.

He closed the file and dialed Georges Vandekerckhove's private number.

"Hello, Joris." Vandekerckhove automatically grabbed the TV remote and pressed the MUTE button.

"It's about Fiedle. Complications, I fear."

"Nonsense, Joris. No one will try to connect us with Fiedle. I have a watertight alibi and you're unimpeachable."

"But I'm still concerned, Georges, and not just a little. That Van In has a nasty reputation."

"So what? We didn't kill Dietrich, did we?" Vandekerckhove laughed loud and hard. "And don't forget we have Leitner on our side. Dietrich was a risk factor. He drank too much, and that idiotic story about Michelangelo's *Madonna* might have had a damaging effect on the Polder Project in the medium range. He blabbed about it right and left the last couple of months. We're a respectable organization, Joris. Dietrich was a threat to the organization, a threat we couldn't tolerate. The sucker really believed that I had fallen from grace and that he had to lure me to Bruges. *He* was the one who had to die, not me."

"So it was a planned operation," said Creytens, carefully sounding his friend out.

"Of course, Joris. Don't let it worry you. Take care of the file and I'll do the rest."

"I can only hope it all works out, Georges," Creytens sighed. "We're already up to our necks in it."

"Apropos, now that I have you on the line. I was zapped last week by a traffic cop on the E40. My chauffeur was in a hurry. He was doing 120, I believe."

Creytens took a bone-dry cigar from the box on his desk. "I'll see what I can do, Georges."

"I appreciate it, Joris. See you next week at the club."

14

VERSAVEL ALMOST HAD A HEART attack when he opened the door to room 204 at eight-thirty that morning.

"Is Carton dead?" he asked, acting the fool.

Van In was staring at the word processor, playing its keyboard like an amputee concert pianist.

"Nothing of the kind, Guido. Life is a beautiful thing and I'm enjoying every minute."

Versavel hung his jacket neatly on the coat stand and stared at the commissioner with suspicion. "Did Vandekerckhove offer you a job?"

"You'll never guess," Van In laughed.

Versavel stroked his moustache. *He'll be depressed again in a minute and I'll have to pick up the pieces,* he thought. "Good news?"

"Excellent news, Guido. I've been to the doctor."

"*Now* I get it. When you didn't come back yesterday, I figured you and Vandekerckhove had gone on a spree."

Van In grinned like a satisfied baby. He saved his document with the F7 key and folded his arms.

"There's nothing wrong with me, Guido. My heart's okay and my lung capacity is six liters, no less."

"Smoke or air?" Versavel sneered.

Van In got to his feet and crossed to his desk. He had shaved and was wearing a clean shirt for once in his life.

"Shame I can't offer you a drink to celebrate this joyous moment," he said in an upbeat tone.

Versavel pulled a face when the commissioner hauled a bottle of rum from a secret drawer.

"So there's nothing wrong with you?" asked Versavel incredulously.

Van In opened a bottle of Coke and mixed himself a lukewarm cocktail.

"I have an ulcer, Guido. Can you believe it? A stomach ulcer! The doctor prescribed pills."

He pointed to a bottle of Logastric on his desk.

"If I stick to the pills, there's almost nothing I have to give up." Van In lit a cigarette and a took gulp of rum and Coke.

"Every drunk has his guardian angel," Versavel muttered under his breath.

"What was that?"

"That doctor of yours must be pretty special. Anyone who can diagnose a stomach ulcer without X-rays deserves a Nobel prize," said Versavel sarcastically.

"You're right, Guido," said Van In elatedly. "And if I win the lottery tomorrow, all my problems will be solved."

"So you don't mind if I start a pot of coffee?"

"According to the doctor, the only things I need to avoid are coffee and tea," said Van In, still upbeat. "But don't let me stop you. Your health, your risk!"

Versavel rolled up his shirtsleeves and switched off the word processor. The likelihood that the commissioner was going to need it any time soon was nonexistent.

"I still haven't heard from our German colleagues," Versavel said in passing. "I bet my little finger Croos has something to do with it."

Van In used the remains of the Coke to add a little color to a couple of ounces of rum. "Plus the fact that Jerries are unreliable by definition," he added with a scornful slur. This clearly wasn't his second drink.

"Anything on Die Scone?"

Versavel had checked them out at city hall the day before. "Nothing to write home about. According to the clerk, the firm has an excellent reputation, but he did confirm that they were keen on historical buildings."

"Who isn't?"

Van In propped his feet on his desk and yawned. He had celebrated his common or garden-variety stomach ulcer with fervor and had made his way directly to the station at seven-thirty that morning.

"And Frenkel?"

"Shit," said Versavel. "I completely forgot to tell you. Fifteen minutes after you left yesterday, we got a fax from Groningen. Commissioner Jasper Tjepkema is looking into the case. He promised to contact you sometime today. The military police have been charged with tracking him down."

"That's good," Van In mumbled.

He had hit a wall. The hastily consumed rum-and-Cokes and the agreeable temperature in the room were beginning to take their toll. He felt his chin bounce a couple of times against his chest.

"Wouldn't it be better if you went home, Commissioner?"

"Under no circumstances, Guido," he responded, each syllable delayed.

"I'll think of an excuse," said Versavel, refusing to take no for an answer. "Let me take you home. Have a good rest and we'll pick up again tomorrow where we left off."

"On one condition, Guido," Van In protested tamely. "Call Hannelore. Tell her the good news and tell her I want her in my bed tonight."

"At your command, Commissioner."

Sic transit gloria mundi, he thought.

Commissioner Croos of the Judicial Federal Police blew his nose with an already-soaked Kleenex. His head was pounding, and he had been sneezing like a dog with chili on its snout. The brand-new air conditioner pumped more dust into the room than it extracted, and the pile of moldy dossiers on his desk produced about as much pollen as an average forest.

Croos wadded up the dripping Kleenex and placed it beside him on his desk. Unlike so many of his colleagues, he refused point-blank to use toilet paper.

The sniveling commissioner took a swig of lukewarm coffee and popped a peppermint in his mouth to neutralize the bland taste of roasted malt.

He had received a second detailed report from the German federal police that morning. Was it because the Belgian prime minister and the German chancellor were such good buddies, or did those guys always work so fast?

Germans relate to creativity like pineapple trees to the North Pole, but you can never accuse them of sloppiness, he thought to himself with a sneer.

In less than a week, they had managed to reconstruct Dietrich Fiedle's life, get it down on paper, and have it translated into Dutch by an overpaid interpreter. They had even included a summary of his correspondence.

Croos sighed and submitted to yet another fit of sneezing. Fiedle's letters and personal notes contained explosive information, and while he had never been much interested in art history, the evidence was extremely convincing. Solving the German's murder paled into insignificance against this new background. If the press got ahold of it, Bruges would be shaken to its very foundations.

Croos wiped his nose with the back of his hand, pulled the telephone closer, and punched in Creytens's number.

"Good morning, sir. Commissioner Croos."

"Good morning, Commissioner." Creytens's voice was cold and thin, as always.

"I'm calling about the Dietrich Fiedle murder."

"Yes!" Creytens did his best to show at least some degree of interest. He had received a memo the day before from Commissioner Van In. That piece of shit was screwing around with one of the younger deputy magistrates. This interloper, *nota bene*, had informed him that he had traced a potential witness.

"New information has arrived from Germany," Croos said. "I'm afraid we have a serious problem."

"Is that so, Commissioner?" Creytens examined the photos lying in front of him on his desk. *Fucking Germans and their fucking efficiency*, he cursed under his breath. He could suppress the photos, but a hefty dossier and a memo from a smart-ass like Van In was a different matter altogether.

Croos sensed the investigating magistrate's almost physical disgust. Creytens was a dangerous man. He would have to tread carefully.

"Dietrich Fiedle states in writing that his father had Michelangelo's *Madonna* transported from Bruges to Germany immediately before the liberation."

The investigating magistrate fell deliberately silent. Croos hated imposed silences.

Creytens took an audible gulp of coffee. It was precisely to his taste. "Surely you don't see any relevance in such information, Commissioner," he said condescendingly. "I don't understand all the drama. Everyone knows that the Germans evacuated the statue to Altaussee on Himmler's command."

He used the word "evacuate" as if it was a humanitarian action.

"Of course, sir, but. . . ."

"But what, Commissioner?" Creytens bit his bloodless bottom lip. His angular mouth was twisted with rage. He searched feverishly for an answer that could muzzle Croos.

"According to Fiedle, his father had the statue copied by Jewish forced laborers," said Croos, pushing away his half-full mug of coffee and reaching for his soaked Kleenex. "According to Fiedle's notes, the Americans found a *copy* of the statue in the salt mines there in—"

"Altaussee," Creytens snapped, completing the sentence.

Creytens was both shocked and relieved at one and the same time. The *Madonna* had adorned the Church of Our Lady for no fewer than fifty years and no one had noticed the difference. And if he said nothing, it would stay that way. He didn't give a crap about the original.

"A *copy*, my dear Commissioner? Surely you don't believe such nonsense? The statue was examined by experts on its return, the best in the business. Michelangelo only made a couple of statues. Even a layperson wouldn't have been fooled by a copy."

As he did his best to overwhelm Croos with words, he grabbed one of the photos. It was the snapshot with the pokeweed in the background.

"Listen here, Commissioner. Every year, a handful of weirdoes claims to have seen the Loch Ness monster. There are at least five different heirs to the Romanov dynasty wandering the streets; and if you want, you can buy tickets next week in Brussels for the late Frank Sinatra's farewell concert. Give me a reason why the musings of some elderly German should be treated as authentic."

Anne Frank's diary is just the same, Creytens wanted to add, but he put the brakes on just in time. Croos may have been on the political right, but he was no revisionist.

"Fiedle's notes appear to be accurate all the same," Croos said. "He even mentions the name of the Jewish prisoner who made the copy of the *Madonna*. Such facts can easily be verified."

"Don't let it worry you, Commissioner," said Creytens in an unexpectedly honeyed tone. "You've done an excellent job thus far. I give you my personal word that no stone will be left unturned until we get to the bottom of the affair."

"The sculptor's name was Frenkel."

"I'll have it checked out, Commissioner."

"According to a police report, Adriaan Frenkel was one of the last people to see Fiedle alive," Croos courageously pressed his point.

"A remarkable coincidence," Creytens laughed nervously.

That fucking Van In must've passed on a copy of the memo to Croos. The bastard was going to pay. "Frenkel is a common enough name," he said dismissively. "But you're right, of course, Commissioner. It's our duty to follow every lead."

"No problem, sir. I'll do whatever is necessary."

"Croos," said Creytens, adopting the tone he liked to use with minor criminals. "I'll be taking care of things from here on. Is that clear?"

"Of course, sir." Croos had been in the business long enough to know that you didn't lock horns with a senior magistrate. Their "unimpeachable" status always gave them the last word.

"Shall I put the investigation on hold, or would you like me to shelve the file indefinitely?" Croos continued. He did his best to make the question sound subservient. It was a daring move, and he expected the magistrate to explode at any second.

Creytens felt the blood boil in his calcified veins. His first instinct was to cut the commissioner down a peg or two, but he spotted the trap just in time. Croos was no fool, and his question had been cunningly posed.

"Out of the question, Commissioner. I'll examine Fiedle's diary in person."

"At your command, sir."

"And I want to see all the documents, including copies."

"Copies, sir?"

Creytens perked up. The evident consternation in the commissioner's voice seemed genuine. "Excellent," he said, almost purring. Creytens considered treating the commissioner to a compliment. The rank and file liked that sort of thing. "You clearly have everything under control, Commissioner. It would save me a great deal of time if you would . . . I mean . . . if you would tell me what that 'explosive' diary of yours has to say," he fished in a friendly tone of voice.

Croos took a mouthful of lukewarm institutional coffee and was interrupted by a sudden knock at the door. Inspector Vermeire popped his head in.

"Commissioner, the deputy public prosecutor is—"

Croos signaled angrily that he should get lost, and Vermeire reluctantly did what he was told.

"Dietrich Fiedle was born on April 20, 1935 in Hallstatt," Croos began his diary-report to Creytens.

"Isn't Hallstatt in Austria?" Creytens interrupted.

Croos had put together a synopsis of the diary and counted his lucky stars that he had made the effort to check a number of details.

"Fiedle took German citizenship after the war," he answered with pride.

Creytens leaned back in his chair and lit a cigar.

"He was the son of Franz Fiedle and Ilse Weiss. Franz Fiedle was a professional soldier who experienced the hell of World War I in Poperinge in West Flanders. He was awarded the Iron Cross first class and made a career for himself in the *Sturmabteilung* in the early nineteen-thirties. He miraculously escaped the Night of the Long Knives and transferred to the SS in 1937. Two years later, he was promoted to the rank of major. As head of a special military unit, he scoured Europe during World War II in search of valuable works of art. On Himmler's command, he ransacked museums and private collections and had trainloads of art transported to Germany. Franz Fiedle performed his duties with considerable diligence. He was a cultivated man with the allure of a true-blue aristocrat. He was also extremely ambitious. When he got his way, he was the most civilized man in the world. But those who crossed him were treated with exceptional brutality. He had more than a hundred people executed in Russia because he narrowly missed confiscating a Fabergé egg."

"Is all this in the diary?" Creytens asked, his suspicions aroused.

"Yes and no," said Croos. "I'm also basing my words on the report provided by our German colleagues."

"Of course, Commissioner. Continue."

"There were rumors in Hallstatt that Fiedle senior had hung around with a certain corporal with artistic aspirations. You know the one. They had made each other's acquaintance at the front during the Great War. When the Führer-to-be was wounded in action and sent for treatment to a field hospital near Bruges, Fiedle visited his brother in arms several times. He used the opportunity to explore the city and immediately fell in love with it. The two comrades lost touch after the war, but in 1938 Hitler tracked him down and added him to his personal staff.

"Franz's son Dietrich grew up in a protected environment, spared in the idyllic setting of Hallstatt from the horrors of the war. Franz Fiedle abandoned his wife after the war and fled to South America, although he sent money on a regular basis to pay for his son's upbringing. Dietrich studied Classics at the University of Munich and turned out to be a typical representative of the German post-war 'economic miracle' or *Wirtschaftswunder.*

"When the tourist industry took off in the nineteen-sixties, Dietrich managed to bag a comfortable directorship at Kindermann's, and he watched the company grow into Europe's largest tour operator.

"Dietrich remained a bachelor. He was married to the firm. His ample salary allowed him to indulge in expensive call girls on a weekly basis."

"Thank God we don't live in Germany," said Creytens light-heartedly. "If what you say is to be believed, they must have the entire population under surveillance."

"But Dietrich Fiedle's existence was otherwise fairly nondescript," said Croos, almost apologizing for the man.

Creytens thought back to his childhood and to the tall and imposing SS officer. He found it almost inconceivable that the friendly Fiedle, who had treated him so often to a box of cherry bonbons, would have had innocent people shot for an egg.

"Extremely impressive, Commissioner."

"Thank you, sir, but in my opinion there is a genuine link between Fiedle's murder and the Michelangelo statue."

Creytens let the photos slip through his fingers. The story had confused him. Franz had always denied the atrocities, but Creytens the man was starting to have his doubts. Bonbons and murderers often go hand in hand, he thought, his anxiety beginning to peak. His father had assured him that Franz confined himself to "confiscating" artworks.

"I'm impressed, Commissioner. I suggest we send you to Hallstatt with a rogatory letter granting official authorization to collect more information." *A trip abroad on the Belgian state has been known to appease many a conscience*, he thought. "Give me a couple of days for the practical arrangements."

Creytens had returned to his holier-than-thou tone. Croos listened with his mouth wide open. Austria was a beautiful country. His wife wouldn't appreciate the idea of his going alone, but he could take care of that.

"We should also be aware of the economic implications, Commissioner. For that reason, I must insist that we keep the affair *intra muros*."

Croos grinned. Now he understood why Creytens wanted to sweep the dossier under the carpet. The investigating magistrate was alluding to the "principle of discretionary powers."

Bruges owed its very existence to mass tourism, and Michelangelo's *Madonna* was one of the city's top attractions. If you visit Paris you'll want to see the *Mona Lisa*, and if you go to Amsterdam the *Night Watch* is sure to be on your list. If the contents of the diary were to leak out, the damage to the tourist industry could be immense. Such circumstances gave magistrates the right to dismiss even serious cases if the consequences and the potential conviction of those responsible might be a danger to the public interest. Croos sidelined his personal animosity because he presumed that Creytens had this principle in mind.

"You can count on me, sir. This stays between us," he conceded conspiratorially. "We should carefully check all the information before we proceed."

"Very wise, Commissioner. We're probably dealing with a run-of-the-mill homicide. And why should we alarm the public with the contents of some obscure diary?"

"The public are only interested in headlines, sir. God only knows what kind of sensational front pages the press boys would come up with if they got ahold of this information."

"Precisely, Commissioner. I'm happy we're on the same wavelength. Have the material delivered to me, and I'll keep you informed of further developments. Agreed?"

"At your command, sir."

Croos returned the receiver to its cradle in slow motion.

Peering through the glass office door, Inspector Vermeire had no idea why the commissioner now had such an expression of bliss on his face. A couple of minutes earlier, he had appeared to be pretty upset.

The balding inspector knocked three times and opened the door just enough to stick in his tanned face.

"Deputy Martens wants a word with the commissioner," he said. "She's been swinging her ass up and down the corridor for a good fifteen minutes."

Vermeire, nicknamed the Rat, was fifty-six and known for his sexist remarks. He had a serious porn collection at home, put together in the nineteen-sixties when the vice guys turned porn confiscation into a sport.

"Let her in, for Christ's sake," Croos barked. Vermeire pulled back from the door opening like a startled Moray eel and winked at Hannelore Martens. She ignored the inspector's lecherous look and marched into the commissioner's office.

"Good morning, Deputy Martens."

Croos jumped to his feet and rushed to meet her. Vermeire followed the greeting ritual through the window. *Enough to confuse a blind eunuch*, he thought to himself, licking his lips. *Hot!*

"Your assistant informs me you're extremely busy, Commissioner. So I won't keep you."

Her sarcasm flew over his head. She was wearing a black jersey dress, tight-fitting, elastic, that adapted automatically to the shape of her body.

With a gallant gesture, Croos invited her to sit; then he returned to his desk. He spirited the soggy Kleenex into the wastebasket as inconspicuously as he could. Hannelore deliberately looked the other way and casually flicked her ponytail with the back of her hand. Her short hair bounced back into shape.

"I came to ask if we have new information on the Dietrich Fiedle murder."

She crossed her legs. Croos lowered his gaze and took a mouthful of cold coffee in the confusion. It burned like citric acid on an open wound.

"I sent you the autopsy report, ma'am, together with the official depositions and a list of the victim's personal possessions."

He hadn't told Creytens about this. If the investigating magistrate got wind of it, he would be in serious shit.

"Yes, Commissioner, they arrived safely. But I presume you also contacted the German federal police," she said with a hint of derision. "And I presume you had the lab take a look at the photos."

"The photos!" Croos covered his eyes with his hand. "I completely forgot about them. What an idiot. One moment, I'll contact Leo Vanmaele."

He grabbed the telephone. This was the opening move in a procedure known as "*le système parapluie,*" with an exclusively Belgian patent. The philosophy is simple: if you're in trouble, find a subordinate to take the blame.

"No need, Commissioner. I'm sure Mr. Vanmaele will let me know directly if there's anything unusual."

Croos bit his bottom lip. *Bitch*, he thought.

"Perhaps it's time to send someone to Germany with a rogatory letter," he said parenthetically.

Creytens would forgive him this indiscretion. A rogatory letter is, after all, an official document. She was bound to find out, sooner or later.

"Did the investigating magistrate talk to you about an official visit?" she said, fishing for more.

The wrinkles around his eyes tightened. "I can't say."

Hannelore didn't believe him. Police people often forget that they can be very clumsy liars.

"Then why raise the issue?" she snapped.

Croos tried to look her in the eye as he forced his lips into a relaxed smile. "Wouldn't a rogatory letter make sense, ma'am? For us, Fiedle is an unknown German businessman who happened to get himself murdered in Bruges for some shady reason or other. Extending our investigation to Germany might bring extra clarity."

Croos found his own argument convincing. He thought he had succeeded in distracting her, but from the frown on her forehead it didn't look as if she shared his opinion.

"And the witness?"

"Witness, ma'am?"

Hannelore leaned forward, and Croos did his best not to peer down her cleavage.

"Adriaan Frenkel. According to the police, he was the last to see the victim alive."

Croos suppressed a sigh. It was common knowledge that Van In and Martens were screwing each other, and there was little point in asking her where she got her information.

He stared at the deputy open-mouthed for a second or two, trying to work out why such a gorgeous specimen would want to hang out with a drunk like Van In.

"Didn't you receive the report?" she asked bluntly. "Surely someone has to contact Frenkel."

Of course someone should have contacted the Hollander, but Creytens had explained why it made sense not to. Croos knew well and good that young magistrates weren't much interested in the discretionary-powers principle.

"I should inform you, ma'am, that Investigating Magistrate Creytens has charge of the case," he answered evasively. "But I'm sure he would be happy to discuss the dossier with you personally."

Hannelore crossed her legs anew. The slit in her dress reached far above the knee. She now knew the score.

Tacent, satis laudant, she heard Professor Daems proclaim. Daems, like Timperman, was a monument. He taught criminology, and the auditorium was always full when he was lecturing.

Silence is answer enough. Daems resorted to Terence at the drop of a hat. A story did the rounds in her student days that a nervous freshman was rewarded with twelve out of twenty for blurting "Tacent, satis laudant" in response to a difficult exam question.

"Is there anything more I can do for you, ma'am?"

"No, Commissioner," she smirked.

The anecdote about the dumbstruck student stayed with her. Croos was convinced she was laughing at him. He turned his gaze away from her legs. When she stood, he remained seated like a paralyzed vulture.

"Have a good day, Commissioner."

"I genuinely hope so," he responded indifferently. The bitch left him cold. When she was gone, he summoned Vermeire and had him fetch a bottle of vodka from the store around the corner.

15

"Hi."

Hannelore scurried inside and gave him a shivering kiss. Van In had slept off his hangover and felt great. He was happy to see her.

"I'm making hot chocolate. Just for you. Take off your coat and grab a seat by the fire. I'll be there in a minute."

Under her beige gabardine raincoat she was wearing an amply low-cut dress in shiny silk. His T-shirts were longer.

"No wonder you're frozen to the bone."

There wasn't a lot of empathy in his words. He didn't have the energy, the concentration, needed for empathy: he couldn't keep his eyes off her when she was scantily dressed.

"I was just about to leave for De Korre when Versavel called. It's always sweltering in the stalls!" she said apologetically. "And I had to park the car in the Biekorf."

"What's a couple of hundred yards on foot for a date with Romeo?" Van In smirked.

"It's a little warmer in Verona at this time of year, Romeo."

She settled elegantly on the couch and massaged her own shoulders with her arms crossed. Van In retreated to the kitchen and poured a quart of milk into a saucepan.

"Versavel sounded worried on the phone," she shouted from the living room. "That's why I rushed over as fast as I could. So, what's the matter?"

Van In didn't hear her question through the clatter of cups and saucers. "When did Guido call?"

"Twenty minutes ago. He kept apologizing."

Van In stirred chunks of dark chocolate into the milk. He had to stir continuously to keep the mix from burning.

The powerful aroma of chocolate made her mouth water, even from that far away. A splash of cognac, and it was right up there with the nectar of the gods.

"Cognac?" he asked as if he could read her thoughts.

Van In knew what Hannelore liked, and the bottle was already uncorked.

"A splash," she shouted.

He managed a little more than a splash. In fact, if he had been cooking with gas, the whole thing would have gone up in flames.

"What's playing at De Korre?" asked Van In as he placed the cups of piping hot chocolate on the coffee table.

"*The Raphaels*, an absurd piece about deranged archangels." Theater wasn't his thing. And she didn't have to bother him with the details.

"Never heard of it. Modern, or what?"

"Postmodern," she chuckled. "That's why I didn't ask you to join me."

"Excellent, then I don't have to feel guilty that you're missing it," he said cheerfully.

Van In sat down beside her and wrapped his arm around her shoulder. He stared into the flames and didn't say a word. Versavel had contacted her. The commissioner's mood swings had been getting worse. Up and down like a bungee cord.

"Tell me what's wrong," said Hannelore after a minute. "Go on," she wheedled when he barely reacted. "Your servant is listening."

Van In wrapped his free hand around his cup, but had to let go right away.

"Muuuch too hot," he grumbled.

"Not yet," she laughed, "but we've got plenty of time for that later."

Van In's arm slipped from her shoulder, and he stared at the steaming cups of chocolate.

"Come on, out with it, Pieter Van In," she insisted. "There's something on your mind. I know it."

There was no sense in sulking and pouting. Van In cleared his throat. This was awkward. She loved him, and he had cheated on her.

"There's nothing to be ashamed about."

She took his arm and returned it to her shoulder.

"You been walking around like a peeved granddad the last couple of months. And don't try to put me off with any of that midlife-crisis crap."

The words "midlife crisis" melted his modesty, his lack of self-confidence, and made him defiant. Women had problems with menopause, okay, that was a fact. But the midlife crisis was the invention of a bunch of butch feminists.

"I'm waiting, Pieter Van In."

Her steadfast determination spiked his burgeoning defiance. He now understood why some successful business types were ready to part with a fortune now and again for the services of a leather-clad dominatrix.

"I've hit financial rock bottom," he finally admitted, reluctantly.

Hannelore listened attentively to his story. When he finished speaking, she checked the temperature of the hot chocolate, wrapping her hand around the cup. He had never seen her drink so greedily.

"You have a great place here, Pieter, don't get me wrong. But I can't figure why a real estate agent would be crazy enough to offer five million for it if he knows it would go for a lot less in a foreclosure auction."

"That's what I thought at first," said Van In. "But a quick call solved the mystery. Die Scone isn't a third-rate real estate agency, not by any stretch of the imagination. It's part of a much bigger concern. And guess who owns the controlling share."

"What difference does it make?" she asked.

"Does Travel Inc. ring any bells?"

Hannelore sat up and carefully put her cup on the coffee table.

"You can't be serious."

The warm blush on her cheeks and her wide-eyed surprise made him shudder.

"Travel Inc. is a massive company," he said. "If they're willing to offer such an inflated price, they must know there's a profit to be made."

"But the real estate sector is in crisis."

"And two years ago the pig breeders were up to their necks in swill," said Van In.

Hannelore looked at him and frowned. *He couldn't be drunk already*, she thought.

"Ease off, Hanne. Let me finish."

"Did I stop you?" She pulled him toward her for a cuddle. "Tell me. I'm listening."

"Well, a couple of years ago a television crew was interviewing a pig breeder. The reporter asked the hick farmer with more than a hint of condescension why he was buying up pigs left and right while the price of pork was nosediving."

"Sounds like a fairytale," Hannelore whispered. She rubbed his shoulder with the side of her head.

"Not far from it. And do you know what the farmer answered?"

"No," she said playfully.

"Now, when pork isn't profitable, nobody wants to breed. But that means a shortage in a couple of months, and then *my* pigs will be ripe for the slaughter."

"So you're saying that Travel Inc.'s expecting a rush on property in Bruges?"

"No idea. But Travel Inc. is the biggest tour operator in the country and Fiedle worked for Kindermann, which controls forty-five percent of the European travel market."

Hannelore shook her head, grabbed her cup, and took a mouthful of Van In's excellent hot chocolate.

"You're not trying to tell me that there's a connection between the Fiedle murder and the foreclosure of your house, are you?"

It was inadvertent, but her words were like a vicious slap in the face. Rage began to gurgle in his gut like seething lava. He had expected sympathy, but had hit a brick wall instead. An irrepressible hopelessness overwhelmed him. He fell stubbornly silent. His hand felt like dead weight on her shoulder.

Unlike Van In's ex-wife, Hannelore wasn't ready to throw in the towel. *If depression sets in,* she thought, *we can forget the rest of the evening.*

"But it's all hypothetical, Pieter. This house isn't for sale. I'll cash in some of my savings tomorrow and pay the arrears. More hot chocolate, please."

Her almost flippantly formulated suggestion stemmed the oncoming tide of melancholy. At least she understood him. It was time he got a grip.

He stood up and headed into the kitchen.

"We're not talking a couple of hundred francs, Hanne," he shouted. "And I've got no idea when I'd be able to start paying you back."

"I'll deduct fifty francs for every cup of hot chocolate you make for me." She pulled up her legs and snuggled into the couch. The warmth of the fire was making her sleepy. She thought of extra ways to spoil him later in the evening.

"But I can't accept your offer."

It didn't sound particularly sincere, but he still felt he had to protest, if only a little.

"Did I hurt your pride?"

"*What* pride?" he replied predictably.

"I know you, Pieter Van In. And I know this wasn't easy," she teased. "But you don't have to concoct a conspiracy."

What made her say such a thing? The irrational heavy-heartedness returned. He clenched his lips. His breathing accelerated and he was on the point of hyperventilating.

"You never let me fucking finish," he screamed.

Hannelore was shaken by his reaction. She'd thought that the tide had turned.

"Sorry, sweetheart. I wasn't trying to wind you up. It was a joke, nothing more."

She jumped to her feet and rushed to the kitchen. Van In was at the stove, stirring angrily. There were splashes of hot chocolate all over the place. He barely reacted when she pressed her body against his back. But he felt every bit of her, and the testosterone succeeded in pushing back the adrenaline, only just. The pressure in his chest subsided and his menacing jaw muscles loosened up.

"Make sure it doesn't burn, sugar, and tell me the rest when you're done."

Her body registered relaxation. The anger in his lips curled into the beginnings of a crooked smile. As he continued to stir, he felt his woes slip from his shoulders like snow from a roof.

"You're priceless," he said, positive and upbeat.

"You too," she laughed. "Literally, that is."

Van In was obliged to put the pan on the counter and take her in his arms. She smelled of warmed-up winter cold and charred birch logs.

"The insiders are saying that Travel Inc. and Kindermann's are about to merge," said Hannelore when she sensed the tension refocus on another part of his body.

"I read that too," he said, his voice thin and fragile. "But—"

"Don't forget the hot chocolate."

Hannelore preferred to take things slow. A quickie in the kitchen was okay for teenagers.

"Fine, but let me get on with it," he said with a hint of disappointment.

She gave him a peck on the forehead and returned to the living room like a prissy vestal virgin.

Van In told her about his meeting with Vandekerckhove over a second cup. When he was forced to reveal his source, she shifted the shoulder strap of her spotless bra. A routine gesture.

"Is she pretty, Véronique?"

"Not bad," said Van In impartially. "I did her a favor once and—"

"You don't need to apologize, Pieter. I believe you, honestly."

He gulped, but luckily she didn't notice.

"So you're still convinced there's a connection between the German and Vandekerckhove."

"Yes, I am."

Hannelore rubbed her nose pensively with the back of her forefinger. This was what she looked like when she was in court, listening to the defense.

"If you ask me, there's something not kosher about Vandekerckhove."

"Aha, at least they know that much at the public prosecutor's office," Van In exulted.

"They call him the Flemish 'Godfather,'" Hannelore admitted magnanimously.

"Just like his buddy Viaene, the trendy oil baron with the dodgy lead-free gas," he sneered. "The man screwed the state for three billion, and what did he get?"

"Three months suspended," she said, a little ashamed.

"But that never surprised me. It's a public secret that magistrates who filled up at his gas station got a discount."

"True," she said resolutely. "I filled up at Viane's. Does that make me corrupt?"

"Not corrupt . . . depraved, perhaps, and ever so slightly voluptuous."

"Cool it, big boy."

She leaned forward, and Van In's eyelids fluttered.

"Correction, slightly depraved and *very* voluptuous."

"If you keep this up, I'll be sleeping on the couch," she threatened. "And don't think the cognac's going to make me cooperate."

"It's the chocolate that does it," he drawled. "Beats oysters any day."

"Bluffer. Last time wasn't *that* great."

The memory of his wild encounter with Véronique helped his ego deal with the shock. Van In grinned like a cat watching the vet have a heart attack before he had the chance to castrate it.

"You're lying," he whined.

She pulled back indignantly into the corner of the couch.

"A pound of chocolate might—I say just *might*—make a difference," she giggled.

Van In leaped to his feet and made a beeline for the kitchen.

"That can be arranged, ma'am."

Hannelore fixed her dress and followed him. "Did it ever cross your mind that there's another common factor?"

Van In topped up the milk and crumbled an extra portion of chocolate into the pan, wielding his wooden spoon like a deadly weapon. Boiling hot chocolate spattered everywhere, some of it landing on Hannelore's cheek and left collarbone. Van In licked his lips like a caged chimpanzee. She let him indulge.

"Taste good?"

Van In growled in confirmation, but behaved himself nonetheless. Ever the gentleman, he knew she didn't like to go too fast.

"You mentioned something about another similarity," he said regaining control and reaching for the wooden spoon.

"The statues," she said, trying to sound unruffled. "They're almost each other's mirror image."

"Darling Hanne, you know how much I like it when you talk about images."

His words weakened her. She wouldn't have minded if he had pounced on her there and then.

Van In kept his composure and filled the cups. His self-control made her tingle from head to toe.

"Travel Inc., Creytens, and the statues. But you wouldn't take me seriously a moment ago."

"I've changed my mind, sweetheart."

Van In grabbed the Otard, held it up to the light, and tossed the remaining five ounces into the bubbling pan.

"There goes my beauty sleep," she pouted.

The way she purred made him think of letting go, like an animal, on the spot, no love, no foreplay. Twenty years ago he wouldn't have thought twice, but this was different, a courtship, the prelude to a sacred initiation, a precious stone, cut but still to be polished.

"There's power behind this, Hanne. People who don't like to be fucked around with."

Hannelore set the cups on a tray. The wind outside was kicking up a storm, and she craved the warmth of the log fire.

"I also don't understand why the Germans haven't responded to my faxes."

Hannelore lay on her side on the couch and he lay down beside her.

"Creytens?" she asked.

"Who else?"

"If you ask me, our buddy Croos is under the same pressure. He didn't say a word this afternoon. I presume Creytens doesn't know you're working on the Fiedle case."

"I sent him a memo yesterday," Van In grinned.

"You did *what*?"

"About Frenkel. How long is he planning to withhold information on the man?"

"But you could have contacted the Dutch police yourself," she said, surprised.

"I did, sweetheart, but Creytens doesn't know that."

She snuggled up to his shoulder. The hot chocolate was getting cold.

"Beware of Creytens," she warned.

"Creytens can go fuck himself. I'm more worried about the mayor."

He told her about the letter and his clandestine appointment as secret agent. "Terrorists don't write anonymous letters," he said. "They either claim responsibility for an attack or they say nothing."

"Don Quixote has been dead forever," she said softly. Van In slipped under the silky fabric of her dress, and his cool hand thrilled her.

"Why fall for a dumb idealist like me?" he asked, deadly serious.

"I've asked myself the same question, Pieter Van In. Maybe wayward knights are my type."

His hand crept higher and got stuck halfway up her back.

"I can't ignore it, Hanne. The world's a mess. Nobody gives a shit about the law, and everybody's locked up in his own little bubble of luxury. I've tried to fit in to this fucked-up society of ours, but—"

"Don't apologize. I'm the one who should be apologizing. I should never have doubted your good intentions."

The wind and the crackling log fire heralded the bliss that was to come.

"Thank you, Hanne."

She heard him sob and caressed his head. The tears soaked her dress. Only now did she realize how much he loved her.

"I've something to confess, sweetheart."

"Shush," he said. "You don't have to confess anything."

She pressed against him, freeing his hand to explore further.

"Will you marry me?" he asked.

Hannelore was on the verge of tears herself.

"I mean it," he said with a lump in his throat.

"If you insist," she sniffled.

Van In raised his head and looked her deep in the eye. She could see the corners of his mouth tremble.

"What did you expect me to say?" she asked.

Van In couldn't contain himself any longer. "'If you insist. . . .' Jesus H. Christ!"

Van In was the first to let go, and moments later they were rolling on the couch, screaming with laughter.

16

ROBERT NICOLAI TOOK THE NUMBER 4 bus in front of the Bruges train station heading into the center of town. According to the euphoric statistics published every other day by the bus company, the number of passengers had increased by forty percent since the introduction of the new traffic-circulation plan. They must have based their figures on random spot-checks. Nicolai was all alone.

The somber statue of King Albert I on horseback seemed to come to life for a moment in the fierce light of a sun harp that pierced the blanket of cloud. The bus crunched its way through the grit and melted snow. The layer of snow on the parks and rooftops was fortunately still intact, its decorative white making Bruges appear more romantic than it already was. This was weather for poets and painters, not for a bomber on a scouting mission.

Nicolai didn't have to wait in line at the ticket office on the first floor of Bruges's Belfort. Of the few tourists visiting the place, only a handful were up to paying the hundred-franc fee to climb the 366 steps of the medieval bell tower. He was standing behind an elderly gentleman who had paid for his ticket with eager enthusiasm. A huddle of noisy French schoolkids provided a running commentary. They seemed to be taking bets on whether the old man would reach the top or die of a heart attack halfway.

Nicolai passed through the turnstile, which kept an automatic visitor count. For security reasons, no more than seventy-five people were allowed to climb the tower at one time. There wasn't much danger of them reaching seventy-five today.

"Excuse me," he said to the old man as he squeezed past.

Nicolai wanted to climb the tower at his own pace. He took note of the security cameras, positioned at strategic locations. The number of cameras was more than sufficient and every door was fitted with a contact magnet. Security at Bruges's Belfort was as he had expected: excellent.

When Nicolai reached the top floor, he checked the roof structure and the window recesses for infrared detectors. He found none. There was a camera above the entrance that covered roughly half of the space. While he was still alone, he quickly explored the west side of the tower, the side that remained out of range of the camera.

He hoisted himself onto a broad windowsill, lay flat on his belly, and stuck out his head as far as he could. The sheer verticality of the wall made no impression on him. For a climber, two hundred feet was like the first step on a ladder.

Nicolai wasn't interested in the magnificent view. He concentrated on the wall. He ran his fingers over the stones in search of splits and loose pointing. When his finger snagged in a groove, he tensed his muscles. The stones were less fragile than he had expected. No erosion, no crumbling.

The sound of thudding footsteps on the stairs heralded the arrival of the others. He recognized the piercing voices of the French schoolkids.

Nicolai slipped to the floor and did what tourists do: placed his elbows on the icy windowsill and peered out over the silent, snow-covered city.

The sinewy Walloon hoped it would soon thaw. His client had been unequivocal. He wasn't to leave a single trace.

As the shivering French schoolteacher chanted the praises of Bruges and the schoolkids boisterously drowned her out, Nicolai turned his attention to the interior of the tower.

The Belfort is an octagonal structure. In each corner, a solid vertical beam supports a system of trusses that seem to hold the tower together.

The trusses, eight beams radiating toward the central point, are further reinforced by slanting crossbeams, making each buttress look like an oversized gallows. The central point consists of a square frame supporting the bourdon, the largest bell in the carillon.

To blow up the tower's roof, he would have to place four pounds of explosives in the "armpit" of each gallows. After detonation, the concrete floor would hold up a little longer than the masonry and the concentrated energy of the blast would blow out the walls like the sides of a magician's box. That's what he had been told by an expert. According to his client's wishes, only the upper part of the tower, the so-called "lantern," was to be blown apart. The rest was to remain intact.

A couple of Dutch girls snapped each other's photos endlessly. They were both wearing miniskirts and thin sweaters. Nicolai didn't understand how they could bear the cutting wind. The French schoolkids stayed until the carillon rattled its half-hourly ditty. They sucked up the decibels, and when the mechanism fell silent they shouted for more. But their teacher was frozen to the bone and paid no attention.

Jan Brouwers struggled to the top at four forty-five. He was wearing a greasy kepi and a shiny navy blue uniform. A poorly knotted regulation tie peered over the neck of his sweater.

"Ladies and gentlemen," he thundered. "De toren gaat dicht, on ferme, we are closing, cerrado."

About a dozen curious visitors were still in the tower, among them the elderly man, who had taken half an hour to climb the stairs, the two Dutch girls, and an English couple.

The towerkeeper repeated his announcement and gestured that everyone should take the stairs ahead of him. The English couple, who had reached the top only ten minutes earlier, responded spontaneously and obediently commenced the downward climb. The others pretended they hadn't heard the man, but the shivering city employee knew that one. He gently herded his hard-of-hearing flock toward the stairs and paid little attention to their protests. Nicolai made sure he was the last, slipping between the row of complaining tourists and the towerkeeper.

"You must get a lot of visitors," he said, half looking back.

Jan Brouwers was happy to hear someone who spoke Flemish. Nicolai's accent didn't bother him. He scratched under the rim of his kepi, and his stern expression made way for a relaxed smile.

"More than a hundred thousand a year," he sighed, with an undertone of restrained pride. "And we deliberately limit the number of visitors. Otherwise the tower would start to lean like the Tower of Pisa."

Brouwers had switched instinctively to his Bruges dialect. He figured Nicolai was from Ghent or thereabouts and that he would understand.

"You know the one, in Italy," he explained with an affable air of omniscience.

"And you have to keep an eye on it all."

"Not anymore. Everything's electronic these days. See that camera there?"

He pointed upwards. Nicolai knew there was a camera above them, but did his best to appear surprised.

"And then there's them infrared detectors," he added, his pride no longer concealed.

Nicolai nodded, curiosity written all over his face.

"They built them into the cameras three weeks ago." Nicolai now understood why he hadn't seen any; all the more reason why a person should never trust outside information, even if it's supposed to be airtight.

"If a bird flies through here at night, the cops are at the door in five minutes. We used to have to do the rounds ourselves, but now it's a lot easier. Once the system's switched on, we can take it easy."

The towerkeeper visibly enjoyed the opportunity to hold forth.

"Do you live on the premises?" Nicolai asked casually.

"Jesus, no. I just take care of the tower. The janitor's downstairs. What a dope . . . and he doesn't give a toss about anything. You should see him. They pay those bastards a fortune and we end up doing all the work."

Brouwers may have been a mere tower-watcher, but he considered himself miles above the janitor. Janitors and their like were on the bottom rung of the civilization ladder.

"And did you ever lock anyone in by accident?"

"Me? Not in a month of Sundays," said Brouwers indignantly.

"Hasn't anyone ever tried to get locked in on purpose?"

"They'd have to be crazy. The temperature up here at night is enough to freeze your balls off, if you'll excuse my French. Certainly in the winter."

"I can imagine," Nicolai laughed.

By five o'clock, everyone was standing outside on the square in front of the Belfort. The old man was holding on to the railings at the bottom of the stairs, out of breath.

"By the way, do you happen to know if there's a specialist food store in the neighborhood?" Nicolai asked the towerkeeper when the man was about to go inside.

"What was that?"

"One of those fine food stores," said Nicolai.

Brouwers needed time to think and stared threateningly at the sky as if he'd see the answer in the clouds.

"Somewhere I can buy caviar," Nicolai explained.

"Caviar," Brouwers echoed. "You mean those black fish-egg things they always serve on toast?"

"The very ones."

"Delhaize, perhaps. It's not that far."

Brouwers felt honor-bound to provide a detailed set of directions.

"They might even sell it in the Carrefour, and that's just around the corner," he said enthusiastically.

Nicolai didn't press the point. He thanked the man, crossed the square, and headed in the direction of Oude Burg Street. Brouwers stuck up his hand and Nicolai waved back in return.

He should have said nothing about the caviar. It wasn't unimaginable that the towerkeeper would remember the conversation later, and that might be problematic. His client had insisted he do nothing to draw anyone's attention.

So what? A man obsessed with infrared detectors wasn't likely to remember anything useful. He also found it hard to imagine that a simple soul like the towerkeeper would make a link between a tourist asking for a fine food store and a bomb attack. *Fuck the client,* he thought.

Was it his sixth sense that made him turn left on Oude Burg Street instead of right, or had he only half understood the towerkeeper's directions? Whatever the case, he had found what he was looking for. *Deldycke—Purveyors of Fine Foods* was right in front of him.

"I'm sorry, sir, but we don't stock Beluga," said the slender countergirl with a suspicious smile.

Nicolai was wearing a beat-up pair of jeans and a tatty woolen jacket. He didn't exactly look the type to be asking for the most expensive caviar on the market.

"What about Royal Black?" Nicolai asked, with a hint of arrogance. He fished a ten-thousand-franc note from his jeans pocket and smoothed it out on the counter.

She smiled again, this time apologetically.

Nicolai looked the salesgirl in the eye. She was an extremely attractive specimen. Even the metal-rimmed glasses and the tight, brushed-back hair didn't spoil the impression. When she leaned over to open a compact refrigerator, he was treated to the outline of a muscular upper torso and an angular derriere.

"One ounce or two?" she asked, taking a couple of flat round tins from the refrigerator.

"Make it four ounces. I'm hungry."

She turned, her dark brown eyes glistening like sequins on a cocktail dress. Her smile was now halfway between disbelief and admiration.

"No need to wrap it up," said Nicolai when she reached for a polystyrene box. "But if you can organize a plastic spoon, I would be more than obliged."

The bubbly salesgirl was so impressed, she scurried into the kitchen, leaving the other tins behind on the counter. Nicolai was taken by the charming creature's legs. They were in perfect harmony with the rest. No sign of the balloon calves that often plague women who wear high heels.

When she returned with the spoon, he slipped the ten-thousand-franc bill across the counter.

"Make it a round five thousand," he said amiably, leaving the remaining hundred and eighty francs on the counter. "For the spoon," he insisted when she refused to accept the tip.

Nicolai stuffed the five thousand-franc bills into his jeans pocket as if they were small change and strutted toward the door. He could feel her gaze burning a hole in his back.

Wool Street wasn't busy. As soon as the museums closed their doors, Bruges changed into a ghost town. A car or two whizzed past with its headlamps dimmed. Nicolai sauntered in the direction of Market Square and sought shelter in the Vier Winden, a café with a heated terrace. He waited for nightfall, when the Belfort was bathed in beams of light.

The waiter smiled shyly when Nicolai left the change on his table and headed off.

"Have a good evening, sir," he said, almost subserviently. Nicolai paraded like a windblown tourist along Halle Street and turned left at the end. He passed the Delhaize, which turned out to bc an ordinary supermarket. *Salmon or cod roe, perhaps,* he thought to himself, *certainly not caviar.* But he couldn't really blame the towerkeeper for confusing such rubbish with the real thing. He crossed a couple of streets in search of the best view of the west side of the Belfort. In Stone Street he fished a pocket telescope from his jacket and took his time studying the tower's smooth exterior walls. The first stage would be a piece of cake. He had spotted a downspout on Halle Street that would get him up to the roof of the halls beneath the Belfort in no time at all. The remaining two hundred feet were going to put his climbing talents to the test, unless he opted for the east side. The last challenge, getting from the corner turret to the sound louvers, was his biggest problem. He was going to stick out like a fly on a whitewashed wall. A moonless night would be ideal.

Nicolai lowered his telescope. He figured he could be at the top in twenty minutes if all went well. He was determined to get the job done in less than an hour and a half, which made three in the morning the best moment to start the climb. According to statistics, even the hardiest of cops would be ready for a nap at that time of the night.

Inspector Vollekindt of the Special Detective Division kept a careful eye on the tourist with the telescope. Under normal circumstances he probably wouldn't even have noticed him. Thousands of people a year use telescopes to peer at the Belfort, but Vollekindt had been given orders to take note of anything or anyone suspicious.

He pulled a compact Nikon from under his trench coat and snapped a few shots of the fishy tourist. The camera was loaded with super-sensitive 2000 ASA film. The light of a burning match was enough to ensure perfect photos.

Vollekindt followed the man and stopped by the window of De Reyghere's bookstore. The location allowed him to keep a perfect eye on the "suspect."

Nicolai sought shelter in one of the niches at the bottom of the Belfort and installed himself on a broad windowsill like a tramp settling in for the night. He barely noticed the man in front of the bookstore.

He nestled into a corner and prized open the can of caviar with the bottom of the spoon. This was the height of decadence. He scooped a generous spoonful from the tightly packed tin. The gray crispy globules exploded between his tongue and the roof of his mouth. The saline nutty flavor of the Royal Black served as foreplay to a refined oral orgasm.

17

COMMISSIONER JASPER TJEPKEMA OF THE Groningen police called Van In's private number. He knew it was Saturday, but he considered his reasons important enough to not have to wait until Monday.

"Is this Assistant Commissioner Van In?" The Dutchman's voice was clear and extremely agitated. "It's about Adriaan Frenkel."

"Who? What?" Van In mumbled.

Carton had just given him a serious dressing-down. The previous day's escapades had evidently gone down the wrong way.

"Can you repeat that?" the Dutchman asked politely.

Van In tapped the mouthpiece with his finger, pretending it was faulty.

"Just a second, I'll pick up on another phone." He waited ten seconds and cleared his throat.

"Good morning, Commissioner Tjepkema. Pieter Van In speaking."

"That's much clearer," said Tjepkema. "I'm calling about Adriaan Frenkel."

"Have you been able to track him down?"

"Well, yes, in a manner of speaking," said Tjepkema. "Sorry to have kept you in the dark for so long, but we had been watching his apartment in Groningen and there had been no sign of him for days. Then one of the detectives discovered that he was spending time at his holiday home on Schiermonnikoog Island."

"Excellent," said Van In. "Have you been able to question him?"

"That's the problem. Frenkel is dead. His holiday home was burned to the ground last night."

"Jesus H. Christ."

"What was that?"

"Jesus H. Christ," Van In repeated.

Tjepkema raised his eyebrows, but didn't take his Belgian colleague's odd exclamation any further.

"The fire department found his charred remains in the living room. We don't know the cause of death yet. The autopsy should tell us more."

"A pity," Van In sighed. "Have you searched his apartment in Groningen?"

"I have a team on it as we speak. I'll let you know right away if we find anything new."

"That's very good of you, Commissioner Tjepkema. I'm afraid our friend Frenkel was caught up in a hornet's nest. This fire seems a little too convenient for my liking."

"So you think Frenkel had information that wasn't for public consumption," Tjepkema concluded.

"To say the least," said Van In. "I'm giving priority to the investigation at this end. It's high time we rounded things up. As soon as I know more, I'll contact you."

"We have a deal, Commissioner Van In."

"Call me Pieter."

"Okay, Pieter. Jasper's fine by me too. I'll fax the autopsy report as soon as I have it."

"And I'll keep you posted on evolutions here in Bruges."

"Excellent," said Jasper Tjepkema.

Versavel had followed the conversation, more or less. But the sergeant wasn't exactly in the best mood either. He too had been put on the carpet by Carton, and the old bastard hadn't pulled any punches. He had even threatened sanctions if the same excesses repeated themselves.

"Frenkel's dead," said Van In almost enthusiastically.

Versavel didn't react. He switched on his word processor and started to type up a report.

"Is something the matter?" asked Van In, surprised.

Versavel stopped typing and looked sternly at Van In.

"I think we should focus on the bomb attack," he barked. "We've been on the case for five days and haven't made an inch of progress. If we keep it up, we'll have the public prosecutor's office on our ass."

"Come on, Versavel. We stood up to De Kee for eight years. Don't tell me you're buckling under for Carton."

Versavel returned to his word processor and said nothing.

"Guido! After everything we've been through together. Don't do this!"

"There's a fundamental difference between Carton and De Kee," Versavel replied dryly. "De Kee *thought* he knew it all, but Carton is right, Pieter. It's getting out of hand."

"What's that supposed to mean?" Van In laughed sheepishly.

"You know exactly what I'm talking about, Pieter. You drink too much. You used to know your limits, but the last couple of months. . . ."

"Can't a man celebrate being declared fit as a fiddle?" Van In snorted.

"A stomach ulcer isn't what I call fit as a fiddle," Versavel retorted.

"Okay," said Van In. "According to you, I neglect my work. The old bastard's treading water; and because he enjoys a drink now and then, the moral crusaders have decided he's suffering from premature dementia. And that from a . . . from a . . . "

"Fucking faggot!" Versavel completed his sentence and shook his head. "I feel sorry for you, Pieter."

"Yeah, right. And spare me the Hannelore speech."

Versavel said nothing and returned to his work. He had finally said what he had to say. Anything further would only make things worse.

"If it's okay with the boss," Van In said angrily, "then I plan to concentrate from now on on a still-unsolved bomb attack. And because the investigation isn't likely to make much headway if overdue paperwork nails us both to our desks, I've decided to hit the street. Or does the boss think we can solve the case by staring at a goddamn word processor?"

The entire floor shook when Van In slammed the door behind him. He was so angry, he almost knocked over a young cop.

A motley bunch of visitors was poring eagerly over a selection of hefty reference works in the sweltering reading room, a representative cross-section of intellectual Flanders: a couple of awkward students, a balding writer specializing in legends and folklore, a pair of encyclopedia hags, and an elderly lady who had signed up for an ikebana course and wanted to read all about it in advance.

A civilized young gentleman complete with neatly trimmed stubble and tortoiseshell frames was manning the counter.

"I'd like to consult the *Bruges Trade Journal* for 1967, if I may," said Van In before the young clerk had a chance to say "good day."

Van In was rarely mistaken when it came to sizing up civil servants, but this time he was wide of the mark: the young man was on his toes and exceptionally friendly.

"Certainly, sir. Shall I fill out a form for you?"

"Thank you," said Van In, overwhelmed. He didn't like surprises. Bureaucrats were supposed to be rude and impolite.

"Take a seat at one of the tables in the meantime. I'll bring you the documents as soon as they're available."

If the friendly smile that followed was anything to go by, the young clerk meant every word.

Less than five minutes later, a dust-covered bundle of frayed newspapers appeared on Van In's table wrapped in a musty marbled cardboard binder that had clearly seen better days.

"Would you like the entire year?" the clerk asked.

Van In looked at him, not sure what his question meant.

"This is the first semester," the young man explained.

"Thank you, but this will be enough to get me started."

Newspaper articles from the time were all he had to go on. By some coincidence or other, the public prosecutor's officc had managed to misplace the file on the '67 bomb attacks. At least that's what Croos had told him. Van In turned ten pages at a time until he came to the edition dated February 17. The headline said it all: BRUGES ROUSED FROM ITS SLEEP BY VIOLENT EXPLOSION.

He read the article, which covered an entire page, and allowed the old-fashioned language to irritate him.

"In the early hours of Monday February 13 around 3 A.M. a powerful bomb exploded on Burg Square. The device had been equipped with a timer and had been placed at the entrance to the courthouse. Alarmed residents rushed to the scene in their night attire and observed the resulting havoc with great consternation."

The journalist described the force of the explosion and the reaction of the locals who had been torn from their sleep in well-turned, melodramatic sentences.

"Unimaginable damage was done to the centuries-old stained-glass windows of the Basilica of the Holy Blood. . . . A great loss for the city of Jan Breydel. . . . No trouble or expense should be spared to restore the magnificence . . . residents shocked at such a barbaric act of terror. . . . Governor sizes up the disaster in person. . . ." Van In read the article line by line. He was still none the wiser. Coverage of the event was sprawled all over the two following editions of the weekly paper. The judicial inquiry struggled to get started. The public prosecutor's office interrogated a number of random suspects, and the entire affair was shelved with alarming speed. The perpetrators were never found. Bruges's public prosecutor's office chugged along in those days like a Soviet Trabant declared unfit to drive: it produced a lot of smoke and made a lot of noise. In less than half an hour, Van In had read all the articles dealing with the bomb attack.

Not of a mind to return to the station with his tail between his legs, Van In thumbed back through the pages. It made him feel nostalgic. An article near the front caught his eye.

The police had arrested five troublemakers after a scrap at a nightclub on the coast. The gang's leader, Luigi Scaglione, and his cronies were being held in Bruges's prison, waiting for their case to be called to court. The journalist had clearly sunk his teeth into the affair and had managed to spread it out over six reports. Van In read each installment with increasing astonishment.

"Excuse me, sir. The reading room closes at twelve-thirty." Van In glanced at the enormous clock in front of him in disbelief. It read twelve-forty. He looked around. The room was empty.

"We open again at two," said the young clerk. He had already put on his coat and gloves.

Van In could have pulled out his police ID and flatly insisted that the young man show some patience. American cops did that all the time on TV.

"Sorry," he said with a smile. "I lost track of time. I'll come back this afternoon."

He closed the musty pile of newspapers and followed the clerk to the door.

"Shall I reserve the entire year for you?" he asked as if he was talking about a best-seller.

"Yes, do that. Thanks a lot."

Van In had to get used to the biting cold outside. He thought about treating himself to a couple of Duvels on Market Square, but changed his mind. Versavel's sermon had haunted his thoughts while he was reading. They had worked together for more than eight years now, and he had never seen the calm and collected sergeant so worked up. It made more sense to go home now and return at one-thirty with some apologies.

The sun suddenly broke through the clouds. A patch of clear blue sky peered through the monotonous gray. According to the weather guys, things weren't likely to improve any time soon. The forecast was still snow, for at least three more days.

Van In made his way to the Vette Vispoort bathed in sunshine. The sun followed him to the front door of his house.

He found a can of mackerel in tomato sauce and a banana in the refrigerator. He emptied the mackerel onto a plate, sliced the banana, and started a pot of coffee brewing. As the coffee machine perked and spluttered, he tidied up the living room. He found a book under the coffee table and was about to return it to the bookcase. . . .

"That's odd," he mumbled. "*Chaos.*"

Van In vaguely remembered that Versavel had been browsing through it that Wednesday when the sergeant had tucked him in.

He opened the book and started to read. He poured himself a cup of coffee with the book in hand and sat down at the kitchen table. Completely captivated by the intriguing read, he squashed the slices of banana into the tomato sauce and wolfed it down together with a chunk of mackerel. The unusual combination was delicious.

It was already dark when Versavel rang the bell. No one answered, and he headed away, fearing for the worst. The commissioner was capable of anything when he was depressed. For once in his life, he genuinely hoped that Van In was in a pub somewhere.

"Hey, Guido," he heard Van In shout.

He turned back and saw the commissioner in the doorway, waving.

"Thank God," Versavel sighed, retracing his steps. "I thought you were out. I've been ringing the bell for the last five minutes."

"Come inside, Guido."

Van In had propped the book under his armpit.

"Sorry for leaving you out in the cold. And I mean that both literally and figuratively."

Versavel took off his coat, and Van In hung it neatly on the coat stand.

"Will you accept my apologies for this morning?"

The sergeant stroked his moustache and grinned. The Versavel Van In knew and loved.

"Of course, Commissioner. I wasn't exactly easy on you either, and when you didn't show up. . . ."

"You were right, Guido. It was time someone told me the truth. But you have to promise me one thing."

"Anything, Commissioner."

Van In ushered him into the living room and switched on the light.

"Promise me that you'll call me Pieter from now on. I've been sick of that Commissioner crap for years."

"At your command, Pieter," Versavel laughed.

Van In tossed a couple of firelighters into the fire, lit them, and arranged four logs of beech on the grate.

"Sorry I abandoned you this afternoon, but you're partly to blame . . . indirectly."

He showed him the book.

"I finished it in one go, and I think we should let chaos theory loose on our mystery to see where it gets us."

Versavel took a seat and stared at the book. He was certain Van In hadn't been drinking, but. . . .

"But I'll come back to that later. First let me tell you what happened at the city library."

Versavel nodded submissively. He wanted to give the commissioner every credit.

"Do you remember the Scaglione gang?"

Versavel placed the book at his side and furrowed his brow.

Van In rattled off energetically: "1967, a brawl in Knokke. Five people arrested, including Luigi Scaglione, a notorious gangster stationed in Marseille."

"Weren't they settling some score or something?" asked Versavel after a moment.

The wood began to crackle and fill the room with a pleasant smell of smoke.

"Exactly. Scaglione claimed that the nightclub owner owed him a million, and when the man refused to pay, his cohorts laid into him."

"It's coming back to me," Versavel mused. "A bit of a looker, that Scaglione."

"I hadn't thought about it that way," Van In sighed. "And don't try to tell me that's all you know about the case."

He poked the fire and maneuvered the logs into the best position.

"There were problems with the court case," Versavel said. "Scaglione insisted on appearing in front of a French-speaking tribunal, and I believe he finally got his way. The case was transferred to the district court in Tournai a couple of months later. If I'm not mistaken, he got a six-month suspended sentence."

"There's nothing wrong with your memory, Guido. According to the papers, the judge decided on February 7 that Scaglione was not to be tried in Bruges, and on February 13 a bomb exploded in front of the courthouse."

"But Scaglione certainly couldn't have had anything to do with that. Why would he use a bomb to press home his demands if they had already been granted a week earlier?"

"Indeed," Van In mumbled. "That's what was bothering me too."

"It's not a bad argument, I'll give you that; but even if your theory tallies, I still don't get what a bomb attack from 1967 has to do with the attack on Guido Gezelle almost thirty years later."

Van In didn't seem the least discouraged. "Do you know who the public prosecutor was in 1967?"

Versavel nervously stroked his moustache. Van In was in dangerous waters.

"Edgar Creytens, the renowned father of our infamous investigating magistrate."

"I hope you aren't starting to see ghosts, Commi . . . Pieter, I mean."

"There's a lot more where that came from," Van In continued with enthusiasm. "According to the papers, Scaglione was an experienced deep-sea diver, and a loose-lipped gang member declared to a journalist that they had just returned from Lake Toplitz in the Austrian Alps."

"With all due respect, Pieter, I'm having a hard time following this."

"Patience, Guido, patience. I once saw a documentary about Lake Toplitz. Insiders claim it's where the treasure of the Nibelungs is hidden."

"The *what*?"

"SS gold, Guido."

"You don't say."

Van In stuck to his guns. "The German press paid it a ton of attention in the nineteen-fifties. *Stern* magazine even organized an enormous expedition in search of the lost gold."

"And did they find anything?" asked Versavel curtly.

"Chests full of British pounds and U.S. dollars," Van In reluctantly admitted. "But where there's smoke—eh?"

At that moment, an angry gust of wind forced smoke down the chimney, making Versavel cough.

"That'll teach you," said Van In in his stride. "And if you had paid more attention during geography class, you would have known that Lake Toplitz is a stone's throw from Altaussee."

"And what would that tell me?" Versavel had decided not to wind Van In up.

"That the Allies found a large number of art treasures in the salt mines of Altaussee in 1945. All of them stolen by the Nazis."

"Michelangelo's *Madonna*," said Versavel, feigning surprise.

"Finally," Van In snorted.

Versavel confined himself to a modest nod. The story sounded completely implausible, and the link between the 1967 bomb attack and the death of Fiedle was about as believable as the existence of a relationship between Princess Diana and the tramp who slept on the bench in front of Kensington Palace every night.

"Isn't Hallstatt also nearby?" asked Versavel incidentally.

"Jesus H. Christ. Where did that come from?"

"You shouldn't have been so quick to accuse me of not paying attention in geography," Versavel smirked.

"Any more surprises up your sleeve?"

Versavel grabbed the book and carefully examined its cover.

"If I tell you that Bostoen led the investigation in '67, you'll probably lose it completely," he said dryly.

"State Security Bostoen?" Van In screamed.

"I have to admit, he did shoot right up through the ranks after that," Versavel humbly conceded.

18

VAN IN WAS AWAKENED ON Sunday morning by a pelting downpour. The weather man was wrong again. He had forecast snow, but in Van In's bedroom it was a tropical seventy degrees. Hannelore was lying on top of the duvet, sleeping like a newborn Venus.

Van In switched on the bedside lamp and carefully got out of bed. Hannelore turned on her side and grabbed his pillow without interrupting her dream.

He stood by the window and gazed at the dark waters of the Reie canal. Huge drops of rain trickled down the glass, and dozens of gurgling drainpipes joined forces with the clatter of the pouring rain. The water washed the thick layer of snow from the rooftops, its fluorescent white melting like fat in a fire. Darkness once again took possession of the row of houses on the other side of the canal. Van In glanced at his watch. It was five past six. He had only had four hours of sleep. Before turning the light back off, he took time to survey the pale-skinned beauty breathing silently on his bed, still fragrant from their moment of intimacy.

Downstairs, he started the coffee and lit a cigarette. He cherished such moments of intangible tranquility, listening to the rain, his eyes half-closed.

When the coffee was ready, he made his way to the lounge, lit the fire, put on his headphones, and slipped a CD of the orthodox monks of Chevetogne into the player. He sweetened his coffee with two lumps of sugar and added a dash of cream.

With his feet on the coffee table, he submitted to the embrace of the melodious Slavic tones and tried to empty his mind. The tranquility and the music had the same effect on his mood as the pure air he had inhaled deep in his lungs ten years earlier on a visit to the North Pole. His eyelids grew heavy, and the flicker of burning logs worked on his mind like a hypnotist's watch. Just as he was about to doze off, he had a moment of oneness with the cosmos, with an all-penetrating presence. For the first time in his life, Van In realized just how insignificant he was.

"Hello."

He was vaguely aware of someone removing the headphones. Hannelore was curled up beside him.

"Wakey, wakey."

She smelled of shower gel. A wet lock of hair clung to his cheek when she kissed him on the lips.

"Jesus H. Christ. Did I oversleep?"

"It's seven forty-five," she teased. "You're going to be late for work."

Van In jumped to his feet and stared at her in confusion. She was wearing a pair of his buttonless pajamas.

"I've taken care of breakfast," she laughed.

"That's sweet of you, but I don't have time for breakfast. Shut the door after yourself, I'll see you tonight."

Hannelore couldn't control herself any longer, exploding with laughter.

"It's Sunday, Commissioner!" she giggled, jumping to her feet and pinching his cheek. "Sunday, no work, lazy day, making dinner for the little lady. That's what you promised yesterday."

"Sunday!" Van In roared.

He grabbed Hannelore and pulled her onto the couch.

"Jesus H. Christ, you almost gave me a heart attack."

"You, a heart patient?" she jeered. "I didn't see any signs of it last night."

"Careful," Van In threatened. The pajama jacket hung loose over her shoulders. "You're asking for it."

"First, breakfast."

She made herself decent and took him by the hand.

Van In never ate breakfast when he was alone, but the sight of her tucking in gave him an appetite.

"Jesus H. Christ, that tastes good," he said between mouthfuls.

Hannelore buttered a slice of toast and dipped it in her coffee. "How long have we known each other?"

Van In put down his cup and licked the jam from his upper lip.

"Eight months and ten days," he said with certainty.

"You're like an ex-smoker keeping track of his smoke-free existence."

"I wish," he sighed. "Cigarette?"

"Later."

She took a slice of toast and piled it high with honey.

"There's one thing I've always wanted to ask you."

"Do I look like someone who never betrays his secrets?"

"Well," she hesitated. "It might be a stupid question, but what in God's name is the 'Jesus H. Christ' thing all about?"

Van In was taken aback. He had expected a completely different question.

"Do you really want to know?" he said, relieved.

"Mm-hmm," she nodded.

Van In poured himself a cup of coffee and offered her a cigarette.

"I don't like to admit it, but my grandmother had an affair with a German during the First World War. His name was Helmut Kohl."

"Small world," Hannelore giggled.

"Don't laugh," said Van In. "Just because my grandma hung around with a German doesn't mean I—"

"Get on with it," she interrupted him, losing her patience.

Van In took a spoon and stirred his coffee slowly and deliberately.

"The affair didn't last, of course, but Helmut reappeared after the war. My grandmother was married by then, but he continued to be a friend of the family."

"Pieter," she pleaded. "Will you please get to the point?"

"My grandfather was a very tolerant man," he continued unruffled.

"Pieter Van In, I mean it."

"Helmut always joined us for Christmas, and when dinner was over and my grandmother asked if he had enjoyed the meal, he would always say: *ich bin schon im Himmel*—I'm in heaven."

"I don't get it," said Hannelore disappointed.

"If I can believe my mother, he said it all the time. And as a child, I mimicked him and used to say 'Benson im Himmel.' When he died, my mother said 'Now he's really in heaven, with Jesus.' As I got older, 'Benson im Himmel' made way for 'Jesus H. Christ.' 'H.' is for Helmut. But to be honest, it's time I dropped it."

"Why?"

Van In took a deep drag on his cigarette and exhaled the smoke through his nose.

"Simple," he said with a twinkle in his eyes. "Forget Helmut: I'm in heaven myself."

Robert Nicolai started his day with the usual routine. He worked out for a good half hour on a complicated fitness machine and then washed off the sweat under a cold shower. Experienced masochists know that ice-cold water can take the body to unparalleled heights of ecstasy. Nicolai savored the pain that preceded the ecstasy. When he was climbing an impossibly steep mountain face, he longed for the moment the pain in his fingers became unbearable.

He scrubbed his body with a coarse brush. His blood reached the boiling point, and he only turned off the shower when the water started to feel warm to the touch. He then dried himself carefully, put on clean underwear, and concluded his exercises with a hundred knee bends in front of the mirror.

A typical breakfast was fruit juice, hard-boiled eggs, muesli, and cod liver. Outside, the first tram of the day cut its way through the mushy gray melting snow. He didn't have to open the curtains to know that the thaw had set in.

Nicolai enjoyed his breakfast and thought about Wednesday night—or, really, early Thursday morning. He had prepared the operation down to the last detail; if this morning's forecast was to be believed, Northern Europe was looking forward to an area of high pressure, and that meant good weather. He lit a cigarette to celebrate. He always lit a cigarette before an important job.

He spent the rest of the morning organizing his climbing gear. A genuine climber always pays a lot of attention to his material, making sure everything is as it should be.

Nicolai was known as a perfectionist. He started by laying each item out in front of him. He rolled out the nylon cable and tested its supporting power on a rafter in the attic. He examined every inch of the rope without hurrying himself. He then checked his harness, his figure-eight descender, the carabiners, and the pitons.

Nicolai considered taking a chalk bag. Magnesium powder could be traced, but it was a risk he was willing to take. He only got dressed after everything had been thoroughly checked. He planned to call the client that night. The wee small hours of Thursday morning seemed to be the ideal moment to risk the climb.

Herr Leitner studied the faces of the men gathered around the table. Ernst Vögel, a thickset fifty-year-old with ruddy marbled cheeks, nibbled at a croissant and brushed the crumbs from the table after every bite. Vögel had succeeded Fiedle as the company's Benelux manager.

Klagersfeld, the society's general secretary, stirred his coffee with the grace of a recently resuscitated mummy. Heinz Witze sat opposite Leitner. He was in charge of finances. Fiedle's death was a boon to his strategy. The fusty accountant had never concealed his conviction that the Bruges venture was a bad medium-range investment. Scaglione had done a perfect job and the ambitious Vandekerckhove was convinced that he had acted on Leitner's orders.

An elderly man sat in a wheelchair by the window.

"Operation Canal Grande has reached a decisive phase."

Otto Leitner placed his hands flat on the table as if he was about to stand up. Vögel looked at him pityingly. From the way the imperator was leaning forward, it was clear to see that his piles were acting up.

"In two weeks' time, Bruges's administrative council will examine the Polder Project, and it looks as if the present coalition is going to agree to our plans."

Witze shook his head and scribbled a couple of observations. Manfred Klagersfeld tried to decipher them, but refused to put on his glasses.

"The next phase is set to cost us at least five million," said Witze in a toneless voice. In contrast to the others, he had good color and seemed in the best of health. He had just returned from a fortnight in the French Antilles.

"Ach, Heinz. You always say that," Vögel responded, evidently irked. "What does five million mean? The Bruges region is worth a hundred times more. And don't forget we get the port of Zeebrugge as a bonus, and you know how important Zeebrugge is."

"Then there's the added value of the properties we've purchased, Heinz," said Leitner with a painful smile.

He continued to hold himself up with his hands as he searched in vain for a comfortable position.

"Two hundred restored residences with a surplus value of twenty-five thousand apiece. That alone covers the extra outlay," said Klagersfeld. "Doesn't that compensate for the 'reconstruction' of a stupid tower?"

Witze combed back his thinning hair with his fingers.

"No one can guarantee that the attack on the Belfort will bring the people of Bruges to their knees," he protested. "We can hardly blow up every monument in the city."

"Why not?" said Klagersfeld, raising a bony finger.

"I don't understand why you have to look for problems all the time, Heinz. Don't forget the three thousand new housing units. With the profit they bring in, we can reconstruct half of

Bruges if we want. Look at Warsaw. Not a single tourist will notice the difference."

"Gentlemen, gentlemen, we need to maintain our unanimity."

Konrad von Metternich didn't need to raise his voice. The assembly fell silent in an instant. The elderly man turned his wheelchair and rolled gently toward the conference table.

"Our company is growing," he cautioned. "Profit is our first priority. We need the Low Countries, and what better prey than Flanders?"

They all nodded in agreement. Von Metternich was a living legend. His great-uncle had been one of the co-founders of the society, and while he had no official function, no one dared contradict him.

"Anyway, if I'm not mistaken Travel Inc. will be covering the cost of restoring the tower."

"With our money," Witze carped.

"Our respected colleague von Metternich is right. A mere five million should not prevent us from pushing through our plans."

"And if the entire tower collapses?" asked Witze, unable to conceal his skepticism.

"Then the Flemish themselves will pay the tab," said Klagersfeld. "Fiedle foresaw such an eventuality. The man consigned to plant the bomb is a Walloon. One hour after the explosion, the police will be tipped off and the poor fellow will be arrested. According to Fiedle, the Belgian legal authorities will link the bomber with the MWR, a Walloon extremist movement."

"And you believe you can turn the Flemish against the Walloons," said Witze, still skeptical.

"It doesn't have to be civil war, but the process will cause commotion enough," said Leitner, smiling.

"Fiedle was a genius. Even if his first plan backfires, we can profit from his second."

"But it'll never come to that," said Klagersfeld in a conciliatory tone.

"The Polder Project can't fail. Our research has made that clear. In the next few years, Bruges's inadequate tourist policy will lead to a massive loss of tax revenue. The city already has a debt of four hundred million DM, and privatization is in fashion."

"I fear you underestimate the people of Bruges. I can't imagine them leaving their city in droves to resettle in the polders," Witze grunted.

"But they will if we set the rental value of the new houses low at first," said Leitner. "Most people are having a hard time dealing with city rents."

Konrad von Metternich stirred his glass and took a sip of his freshly squeezed pineapple juice. The elderly man was fed up with the discussion. He tapped the side of his glass with a silver spoon.

"Dietrich Fiedle prepared this operation with precision," he said, sure of his words. "The previous city council had agreed to cooperate, but no one could have foreseen that the elections would throw such a monkey wrench in the works. The new mayor rejected our plans, but he isn't able to turn back the clock on everything. The traffic-circulation plan imposed on the city by Herr De Kee and Herr Decorte is beginning to bear fruit. The new system of traffic loops is forcing traditional businesses out of the city. Rents are set to fall, placing us in a position to acquire extra property. These are the facts. Research has also shown that the majority of Bruges natives are getting a little tired of the tourist torrent. The inconvenience is a serious burden and no one feels at home in the city anymore. These are also facts.

"The creation of a bedroom community with modern housing is the obvious solution. The procedure was applied in Venice with success. The city became an open-air museum without inhabitants, and that is precisely what we want in Bruges. The difference with Venice is that we have no influence. Bruges is another matter. The city is bankrupt, and the demand for historical open-air museums has never been greater. A couple of bombs can shift the balance in our favor. No one will tolerate the resulting empty properties, gentlemen. If the people leave the city, our patrimony will be worth its weight in gold. I know plenty of wealthy Europeans who would hand over a fortune for a house in Bruges. And that's also a fact."

"Herr von Metternich is completely right," said Leitner. "I couldn't have sketched the situation any better."

Klagersfeld and Vögel nodded approvingly.

"With all due respect, Herr von Metternich, I think we're overlooking one important element." Witze took off his glasses and looked around at the out-of-focus assembly. "The success of the operation depends primarily on Vandekerckhove. Fiedle made all the arrangements with him, and no one knows the precise details of the final phase of the plan."

"Promote him to head of department," said Klagersfeld, "and he'll be eating out of our hands."

"Excellent idea, Manfred."

Leitner scribbled a note.

"Are we agreed, then?"

Even Witze had nothing more to say. He had lost the battle. The death of Fiedle had solved nothing. Von Metternich had set his mind on Bruges, and it would be foolish to openly attempt to thwart the old man's plans.

19

"Good morning, Commissioner Van In."

Mayor Moens scribbled his signature at the bottom of a routine letter.

Van In formulated a polite greeting and sat down in the chair at which the mayor had pointed.

"Good news?" asked the evidently relaxed mayor, rolling back his chair and crossing his legs.

"Let's just call it 'news,' sir."

Moens fiddled with the tip of his nose and encouraged Van In to continue.

"We received a file on Friday from State Security, but I'm afraid it's not going to be very useful."

Moens let go of his nose as if he had suddenly realized he was not alone in his office.

"Of all the groups considered a danger to the state, only one matches our profile. They call themselves the Mouvement Wallon Révolutionnaire, MWR for short. In the winter of 1976, a State Security 'spy' happened to overhear a conversation that took place in a club room at the back of a café in Liège. Four students were carping about wealthy Flanders, which was threatening to bulldoze impoverished Wallonia out of its economic existence. The discussion was occasioned by the sale of a luxury hotel in Spa to a buyer from Oostende. The new owner had sacked the Walloon staff on the spot and imported Flemish replacements, complaining that the Walloons didn't speak enough Dutch and that they were too lazy to work."

"The man may have had a point," Moens grinned. He had his own little pied-à-terre in the Ardennes, and as a dyed-in-the-wool supporter of the Flemish Movement he was convinced that the Walloons could use a taste of their own medicine. They had exploited and terrorized Flemish laborers for more than a century.

"The situation bothered them," Van In calmly continued. "They feared the effects of the forthcoming federalization and were convinced that an autonomous Flanders would tighten the purse strings and reduce the flow of money into Wallonia. After a couple of Westmalles, ironically enough one of Flanders's best beers, they decided to wage war against what they called Flemish colonialism. They planned to imitate the Cellules Communistes Combattante, or Communist Combatant Cells, and organize a campaign of terror to draw attention to the situation. The State Security informant took note of the conversation and passed it on to his case officer."

"And you don't call that good news?" Moens scowled.

"The problem is that the MWR only managed to distribute a few pamphlets and organize a couple of meetings, which no one attended. They were suspected of a number of arson attacks on Flemish-owned property in the Liège region between 1976 and 1979, but the judicial police were never able to substantiate their claims."

"Of course not," Moens snorted. "In Wallonia they know how to keep the lid on things."

Van In wasn't of a mind to pay attention to the mayor's remark. "Just to be sure, we checked out the current alibis of the founding members of the MWR," he said wearily. "Claude Dufour is an engineer and works for a major construction company near Brussels. He's currently on assignment in Kuwait. Jacques Hendrix teaches communication studies at the University of Louvain-la-Neuve. The man is suffering from AIDS and requires constant nursing."

"Typical. Those communication studies people are all the same," Moens interjected sarcastically.

Van In resisted reacting yet again. He had long known that politicians were rarely the people they pretended to be.

"Grégoire Bilay has a senior position at the Ministry of Health, and Alain Parmentier entered the Dominican order last year."

"And the others?"

"There were only those four founders, sir. After 1979, nothing more was heard of the MWR. But for the sake of completeness, I should mention that Bostoen at State Security suspects that someone has revived the movement. In his opinion, the July 11 incident has something to do with the MWR revival. It may have been trivial, but it was enough of a spark to rekindle their fire. Inflammatory pamphlets have been spotted in a variety of places in Wallonia in the past months."

Moens radiated like an applicant who had finally been given a job after his thirty-sixth psychological screening. July 11 was carved in his memory like hieroglyphics: as the Flemish community celebrated its national day, the king had visited Bruges and had been broadcast on all the TV stations singing the Flemish national anthem.

"Why so modest, Commissioner Van In?" said the mayor, shaking his head. "Surely this represents a breakthrough in the investigation."

"I'm not convinced, sir," said Van In, digging in his heels. "Terrorists always claim an attack."

"Nonsense. Look at what happened in America and Japan, Commissioner."

"That was the work of religious fanatics or fundamentalists." He forgot to add "sir." "If you ask me, these guys have different motives."

Moens planted his elbows on his desk and treated Van In to a stony stare.

"It's my job to ensure a subjective sense of security among the citizens," he said. "National television is going to be breathing down my neck this afternoon, Commissioner. I'm obliged to tell them we're making progress. Do you know how many people have already cancelled their Easter vacations?"

"No idea," said Van In listlessly.

"Thirty percent. If we don't succeed in reassuring the public, I fear for the worst."

"The potential revival of the MWR won't make much of a difference to the percentages," said Van In sternly. "And don't forget, the Walloons are also potential visitors."

It was as if someone had opened all the windows in midwinter. The temperature in the mayor's cozy office dropped forty degrees on the spot. The mayor may have been right, Van In thought. The man was begging for a breakthrough and was desperately trying to protect the city from an even bigger disaster.

Moens took a deep breath and was just about to read the insubordinate commissioner the riot act when Van In's pager started to beep.

Saved by the bell, thought Van In, taking back everything he had ever said about the irritating gadget.

"Excuse me, sir. Do you mind if I make a call?"

Moens pointed at the phone on his desk, stood up, and made way for his subordinate. A flock of gulls fought over a dried-up slice of ham in the garden.

Van In rejoiced at the sound of Versavel's voice.

"I'll be there as fast as I can, Guido. No . . . no need to send a car. I'll walk."

Moens registered the click and turned.

"New developments," said Van In, deadpan. "Our Dutch colleagues claim they have valuable information at their disposal."

"So what are you waiting for, Commissioner?" said Moens grumpily.

They shook hands by way of formality, and Van In took to his heels. He passed Decorte in the corridor. The councillor for Tourism didn't even deign to look at him.

"Perfect timing, Guido," said Van In, puffing and panting. He had covered the distance between city hall and the police station in less than ten minutes.

"Tjepkema said it was personal," said Versavel, wondering what Van In had meant about timing. "He said he was sending a fax in ten minutes from then."

Van In was gasping for a drink, but he left the bottle in his secret drawer undisturbed. To compensate, he lit a cigarette. After three puffs, the fax machine started to churn out paper. Tjepkema was punctual.

When Van In read the first lines, he understood why his Dutch colleague had called his office first and only then sent the fax. This was explosive stuff.

The handwriting was shaky, but its regular tiny letters and almost perfectly straight lines betrayed its author as an educated man.

Steiner stood in the doorway grinning while fifteen prisoners rolled the massive block inside over a carpet of birch trunks. I stood in front of the stone in amazement. As a sculptor, I had always dreamed of Carrera marble. But the SS had never asked for statues before. They were always after paintings, and I had reproduced them en masse together with Zalman Rosenthal and Oler, a French Jew. The three of us were mesmerized as we watched the emaciated detainees win the almost hopeless battle against the sturdy limestone, inch by inch. When they had delivered the marble block to the designated spot, Steiner screamed 'raus, Dreckjuden, *as he always did.*

The shadows disappeared like mist in a balmy summer breeze. Then the Unterscharführer approached me. I looked down and waited anxiously for what would happen next. I inhaled his breath through my nose. The German stank of rotten food and cheap tobacco.

"I have a job for you, Dreckjuden,*" he bellowed. "The commandant wants you scum to carve a statue for him." I stood stock-still. Oler and Zalman were standing behind me, and must have felt a whole lot safer.*

"He wants a copy of this statue, Schwein," he raved.

It was only when Steiner hit me with his lash that I realized he wanted me to look up. Blood poured over my right eye from the cut he had just put in my eyebrow. Steiner was holding a postcard, and I immediately recognized the statue. I realized in an instant that this job was a death sentence. No one could copy a Michelangelo on the basis of a photo.

"Do you understand, filthy Jew?" Steiner raved further.

"Ja, Herr Unterscharführer," I whispered.

The SS officer forced the butt of his lash under my chin and pushed back my head. He looked me straight in the eye, and all I could do was outstare his wild gaze.

"The commandant wants the statue in three months," he said with cynical satisfaction. He then roared with laughter, slapping his thighs like a little child.

We stood still until the drone of his marching boots ebbed away. Oler was the first to move. He approached the block of marble with respect and ran his bony fingers over its unhewn surface.

"If they don't have the original, maybe we can dupe them," he said optimistically.

Twenty-two months of Nazi terror had broken his spirit. The diminutive painter looked at me as if he knew the commission intrigued me.

"This is the opportunity of a lifetime, Meir. Have you any idea how much such a block of Carrera costs? Before the war, you would have gone crazy," he said almost jeeringly.

Zalman rarely said anything, but this time he nodded enthusiastically.

"Rumors are doing the rounds that the Allies are nearing Brussels. Three months is quite a long time. Let's see what we can do."

Three days later, they arrived with the real statue. I couldn't believe my eyes. The presence of the Michelangelo had a discouraging effect. I was lucky to have Zalman and Oler to keep my spirits up. They never let it show that we were working on an impossible commission. Zalman helped me with the sculpting, and Oler polished the marble when I had completed a segment. Steiner paid us daily visits and gave us dog's abuse. We were happy that our monumental task was showing signs of progress.

"Schneller, schneller!" *the SS man raved, but fortunately that was all he did.*

After seven weeks working eighteen hours a day, the copy was starting to look more and more like the original Madonna. *At least that's what Zalman and Oler thought. We worked with passion, and I couldn't deny that the statue was beginning to radiate a melancholic beauty. News that the Americans were getting close to the Rhine gave us courage.*

Just as we were planning to slow down a little, all hell broke loose. Steiner barged in one morning, ranting like a man possessed. Oler took the brunt of his anger. It was a miracle that he survived the beating.

"Fucking Jews! The statue needs to be ready in two weeks. And what do you call this? A monstrosity! Don't you love the blessed virgin?"

Steiner was foaming at the mouth. He had given us three months. This would barely be two. Perhaps the Allies had reached the Rhine!

"This is the mother of Christ, the God you hooknose bastards nailed to the cross!"

He turned on Zalman Rosenthal and kept hitting him until the fragile artist sank to the floor covered in blood.

When the SS man's rage was spent, it was my turn. He bore down on me, snorting, his expression wild, his eyes distraught with fear. I prayed to HaShem. A real God doesn't concern himself with earthly trivialities, *I thought to myself. But that was something the German would never understand. God isn't a magician, ready to solve trifling problems by pointing his finger. God is love. God shows us the way. I felt no bitterness when the Aryan laid into me mercilessly with his lash.*

"Beginning tomorrow, I shoot five filthy Jews," he snorted, "and the same every day until the statue is finished."

Oler did what he could, but he was forced to throw in the towel. He was urinating blood, and he died just before we were transported to Auschwitz. Zalman and I were now working twenty hours a day. The executions continued unabated. The copy was ready on the night of 24/25 December. We had hurried to complete it before dawn and so spare five lives.

When Steiner arrived that morning, we proudly stood to attention.

"Dirty ass-lickers," he jabbered. "You did that on purpose! Well, since it's Christmas, you can say goodbye to twenty."

"Fucking Kraut," said Van In, shaking his head. "This is enough to make anyone boycott Volkswagen."

"It explains the pokeweed," said Versavel. "Fiedle had the statue copied and shipped to South America."

Van In set the fax aside.

"Meir Frenkel," he said under his breath. "Meir Frenkel. MF. 'Mia Fiorentina' or 'Meir Frenkel.'"

"What was that, Commissioner?"

"Chaos, Guido, chaos."

"You were trying to tell me something about that yesterday."

"You read the book too, didn't you?"

"If you hadn't kept interrupting me, I might have managed to read it, yes," the sergeant crustily observed.

Van In lit a fresh cigarette and clasped his hands behind his neck. "Do you want the expert version, or should I wait until you've finished the book?"

"I already got the gist of it," Versavel responded defiantly.

"Okay, tell me."

The sergeant nervously rubbed his moustache. He wasn't a fan of this sort of intellectual verbal diarrhea.

"If you ask me, chaos theory has its roots in popular wisdom," he said self-consciously. "Small leaks sink big ships. It's all about situations that start simple and then become so incredibly complicated that the results are no longer predictable."

"Bravo, Guido. How many pages did you read?"

"Thirty," said Versavel.

"Then let me summarize the remaining 250. Chaos works with fractals, making it relatively easy to measure complicated forms such as the volume of a cloud or the craggy surface of a Norwegian fjord. The weather is a typical example. According to classical models, forecasters try to chart systems of cyclones and depressions on the basis of countless measurements and thousands of different parameters. The results are rarely satisfactory. The weather isn't ready to submit to a handful of mathematical formulas. Chaotica offers an alternative. According to the author, a Peruvian farting in the Andes can disrupt the weather system to such a degree that—in defiance of classical calculations—a tropical storm develops off the coast of Bangladesh."

"Jeez," Versavel laughed. "That's a fart I'd like to hear."

"There's no such thing as a stable system," Van In continued, unperturbed. "Minute discrepancies find their way into every process, and classical mathematics can't account for them. Such anomalies can only be dealt with by chaotica. And don't forget that the same minute defects manifest themselves in all sorts of different domains. Let me give you an example."

"Finally," Versavel sighed. "I don't understand any of this."

"Me neither, but I'm doing my best."

Versavel grinned. He hadn't heard the commissioner preach this kind of pseudo-intellectual twaddle for years.

"Scientists discovered by accident that running faucets will start to whistle if there's turbulence in the pipes. The tone increases an octave if the water pressure is increased by 21.7 percent. A trivial phenomenon in itself, perhaps, but it gets interesting when other scholars come to the conclusion that you need to increase the oscillations in an electrical circuit by 21.7 percent if you want to double the frequency."

Versavel yawned in Van In's face. He was beginning to suspect the DTs.

"Which is proof that chaotica functions in different domains," said Van In, proud as a peacock. "So why don't we use it to solve crime?"

"Shall I make some coffee?" asked Versavel with a worried expression on his face.

"No objections, Guido. Stop me when you get bored."

"No way, Pieter. Your modus operandi fascinates me."

"Modus operandi is for criminals with no imagination, Guido. This is what the Americans call brainstorming."

"And you can only ward off a storm with chaotica," Versavel teased.

"The Dutchman bugs me," said Van In as Versavel spooned coffee into the filter.

"The Peruvian fart?"

"So you do understand after all," said Van In with a hint of admiration.

"Small leaks sink ships. Chaotica is as old as the hills," Versavel repeated.

Van In stretched his legs. The sun was shining outside, and its oblique rays accentuated the presence of dust on the filing cabinets.

"If the Dutchman is an accidental factor, we have to be extremely careful. Without strong evidence Vandekerckhove will grind us to pulp," said Versavel, switching on the coffee machine and returning to his desk.

"Tell me something I *don't* know," Van In sighed. "But without Frenkel, we would never have found out that Vandekerckhove had something to do with the murder."

20

Jasper Tjepkema was expecting a call from Belgium. The words of Adriaan Frenkel's recently deceased uncle Meir had also made a deep impression on him.

"Hello, Jasper. Pieter Van In here, Bruges Police."

"Hi, Pieter. I take it you've read the fax."

Tjepkema was due for retirement in six months. He had lived through the war, and the excesses of the Nazis still chilled him to the bone.

"Unbelievable, don't you think?"

Van In gestured to Versavel that he should listen in. "The serpent has closed the circle," he said cryptically.

Tjepkema didn't react. Belgians often used strange expressions he didn't understand, and he didn't want to appear stupid by asking for an explanation.

"If you ask me, Frenkel was murdered, Jasper. The killer set the house on fire to get rid of the evidence."

"But he didn't succeed," said Tjepkema. "Meir's notes were in Frenkel's flat in Groningen, not on Schiermonnikoog Island. He stopped at the flat on his way from Bruges to his holiday house. A neighbor on Schiermonnikoog confirmed that he arrived on Monday evening."

"That's something the killer could never have known," said Van In.

"Unless he asked around," said Tjepkema. "I'll send a team to question his neighbors in Groningen."

"Excellent, Jasper. Is there news from the autopsy?"

"I'm expecting the report tomorrow, Pieter. Do you think he murdered Fiedle?"

"We have to wait for some DNA results: there was a tiny piece of tissue under one of Fiedle's nails. If the blood group matches, we'll know we're moving in the right direction."

"You must be running out of time," said Tjepkema with a hint of pity.

A DNA test took two weeks and offered close to 100% certainty. A test to determine a blood group only took minutes, but was virtually useless in terms of evidence.

Van In wasn't planning to take his colleague into his confidence. The connection between the bomb attack and Fiedle's murder was nothing more than a hypothesis, and he was beginning to have serious doubts about it.

"Fiedle was a big shot," he answered evasively. "The quicker we get this behind us, the better."

"Beware of political pressure," Tjepkema laughed. "Those bastards don't have a clue about police work."

"Good advice, Jasper. It sounds as if you guys have the same trouble up north."

"It's all over the place, my friend. We deal with it differently this side of the border, but people are people wherever they are."

"That's what I call a word of encouragement," said Van In in good spirits. "When the case is closed, you and your wife are welcome for a day out in Bruges, my treat. I'm anxious to meet you both."

"It's a deal," said Tjepkema. "Janet will love that." Van In gave him his phone number, and they agreed to keep in touch on a regular basis.

"What do you think, Guido?"

Versavel took off the headphones and scratched his moustache.

"If Frenkel's the fart that turned the system upside down, why was he killed? Because of something he heard, or witnessed?"

It took a few seconds for the meaning of his words to penetrate.

"The *Madonna* or Vandekerckhove," said Van In.

"Have you got a better idea?"

"So you're beginning to believe me," Van In nodded approvingly.

"I never said your chaos theory was worthless," Versavel defended himself. "But it certainly doesn't make things any simpler."

Versavel sat down at his word processor and opened the Fiedle file. "Let's see what we have so far."

Van In joined him, peering at the screen over his shoulder.

"Fiedle is spotted in the Villa Italiana in the company of Vandekerckhove, director of Travel Inc.," said Versavel. "Adriaan Frenkel happens to be sitting within earshot and listens in on their conversation. Later that night, Fiedle takes a beating and Frenkel leaves the city post-haste. Vandekerckhove denies he was in Bruges that evening, and a few days later Dutch detectives find Frenkel's charred remains in Friesland. The judicial police are doing their best to sweep the case under the carpet on the insistence of Investigating Magistrate Creytens."

"Well, I'll be," said Van In in admiration. "I thought you just typed words into that thing, but this is an exceptionally clear analysis of the situation."

Versavel blushed. A compliment from the commissioner always made his day. "And there's more," he beamed. "A photo of Michelangelo's *Madonna* is found in Fiedle's wallet. Leo Vanmaele identifies the vegetation in the background as pokeweed, a plant that doesn't grow in the Northern Hemisphere. The statue was copied at the end of the Second World War by a certain Meir Frenkel. The original is most probably in South America. Meir Frenkel dies on March 8 this year. The elderly artist's diary occasions his nephew's hasty visit to Bruges. Two days after that visit, terrorists blow up the statue of Guido Gezelle. According to State Security, the attack was the work of an extinct Walloon splinter group."

"Keep going, Guido," said Van In enthusiastically. "I don't understand why you don't publish these stories. You have talent, man."

Versavel finally got into his stride.

"There appears to be a connection between Fiedle, the *Madonna*, and the 1967 bomb attack. The *Madonna* was recovered after the war in Altaussee. Dietrich Fiedle lived in neighboring Hallstatt. In 1967, a criminal gang under the leadership of a certain Scaglione avoids prosecution in Bruges and is given a symbolic prison sentence in Tournay. Six days after the decision to transfer the case is made in chambers, a powerful bomb explodes on Burg Square. Those responsible are never found. Spicy detail: Scaglione and his cronies had just returned from a diving expedition in Austria. An indiscreet gang member tells a local journalist that they had found 'the treasure of the SS,' a fortune in gold hidden by the Nazis at the bottom of Lake Toplitz. Altaussee, Lake Toplitz, and Hallstatt are only a couple of miles apart. At the time Scaglione and his gang were avoiding trial, the father of our current investigating magistrate, Creytens, was prosecutor general. He was probably the one who gave orders for the case to be transferred to Tournay. Inspector Bostoen was in charge of the investigation, and now he's one of the top boys in State Security. Bostoen also suggested the possibility that the MWR had risen from its ashes like a phoenix and had chosen Bruges as the target of its terrorist activities after the July 11 incident."

Versavel was happy as a kid at Christmas. "If we ask the right questions," he said with pride, "the solution is at our feet."

Van In was impressed. Versavel was up there with Hercules and his twelve labors. He had just cleaned the stables of Augias.

"Let's check the name of Scaglione's 1967 defense lawyer," said Van In.

Versavel was taken aback. The commissioner often had a surprise up his sleeve, but now he was having trouble following his line of argument.

Van In explained: "If Scaglione was responsible for the bomb attack in '67, *something* must have gone wrong between the moment Edgar Creytens transferred the trial to Tournay and the Monday on which the bomb exploded. Scaglione's lawyer has to know what." Van In was deep in thought, his brow furrowed. "And why was Vandekerckhove so determined to prove he was in Nice the night of the murder here?"

Versavel took note of the question.

"The next point is the most delicate," said Van In in a dull tone. "If I'm not mistaken, the threat of further bomb attacks is intended for Moens, to put him under pressure. The question is. . . ." Van In hesitated. He was skating on exceptionally thin ice. ". . . does the city council have to make a certain decision soon in which the mayor holds the decisive vote? And if so, *which* decision?"

"I'll do my best, Pieter," said Versavel. "Let me start with the lawyer."

"Good," said Van In.

In the old days, you could get information on "friends" of the police with a simple phone call to the local Records Office. But the new law on privacy has made that impossible. All the files are now held by the National Records Office and are only accessible to the federal and local police. At least that's what they say.

Van In identified himself on the phone as police commissioner and within five minutes a list had been faxed to his office of all the Scagliones registered in Belgium. He then called Missing Persons and asked for Enzo Scaglione's dossier. An obliging inspector referred him to the public prosecutor's office in Neufchâteau.

"I've got Scaglione's lawyer on the line." Versavel winked at Van In with the receiver in his hand. "His name's Dewulf, and I'm afraid he's deaf as a post."

Van In took over and tried to speak as loud as he could. Dewulf might have been hard of hearing, but his memory was unimpaired. He remembered the Scaglione case as if it had been yesterday.

"It was decided in chambers to refer the case to Tournay on February 6," said the elderly lawyer without hesitation. "I only heard about it eight days later. The reason it took me that long to find out was that I had just had an operation, and my wife didn't want my substitute to visit me in the hospital."

"So Scaglione was only informed of the decision on February 14?"

Van In wanted to shout hooray.

"The fifteenth, actually," Dewulf corrected him like a know-it-all schoolteacher. "I remember how much it excited him. He still owes me money, by the way."

Van In thanked the man profusely and lit a cigarette. It was only his third that day, and he was proud of it.

Scaglione thus had had, or had *thought* he had, a motive to organize a bomb attack on the courthouse in Bruges. But just as a mountain climber discovers new challenges every time he conquers a difficult peak, new questions inevitably arose in an inquiry. How, for example, did a gangster from Marseille manage to put pressure on Edgar Creytens, and why hadn't Fiedle's killer finished him off on the spot? Were they dealing with an amateur, or was Frenkel simply an accidental witness to the murder?

He left chaotica for what it was and tried to concoct a simple solution. There were two possibilities where Creytens was concerned: money, or blackmail.

Gold seemed the most attractive motive. The treasure of the SS was estimated at several billion. Van In grabbed a pen and frantically scribbled some notes.

Hannelore rang the doorbell on the stroke of eight forty-five P.M. Van In removed a pot of sauerkraut from the burner and hurried to the front door.

"I've made your favorite," he said in the best of form.

"Good for you," she said listlessly.

"Is something wrong?"

She took off her coat and tossed it nonchalantly on a chair. She was wearing jeans and a turtleneck sweater.

"Don't be silly," she barked. "Of course there's nothing wrong. I'm just beat. It's a free country!"

Van In ran his fingers through her wet hair.

"Did you get a carpeting from the prosecutor?" he asked, sensing that something wasn't right.

She shook her head and made her way to the kitchen as if she wanted to evade him.

"Sauerkraut," she mumbled. "You should always keep a hundred jars in the house."

Van In shivered at the thought. *Women and pickles, what else could it mean?*

"No problem," he said. "I'll go to the store tomorrow."

She grabbed a wooden spoon, returned the pot to the heat and stirred mechanically.

"I forgot to take the pill on Tuesday," she said after a few seconds. "Didn't even cross my mind."

"So what?" Van In laughed. "Once is no big deal. I'm forty-three, Hanne. I drink like a fish and smoke like a chimney. According to statistics, my sperm is about as fertile as an orange pit in the Siberian permafrost."

"Don't underestimate mother nature, Pieter Van In. I fell victim to ovulation on Tuesday."

Only a deputy prosecutor could make ovulation sound like a crime. Van In wasn't sure if he should laugh or throw a comforting arm around her shoulder.

"The sauerkraut smells good," he said.

She turned and smothered him with kisses.

"I'm watering at the mouth," she snorted. Van In took the wooden spoon.

"Are you still up to setting the table?"

"Would it be so terrible if I was pregnant?"

He stopped stirring and grabbed her firmly.

"I would be over the moon with joy, Hanne."

The sound of sizzling sauerkraut put an end to the embrace.

"These are the last two jars," he said apologetically.

Hannelore took a couple of plates and danced toward the kitchen table.

"There's still a bottle of white in the cellar."

Van In had been dry for forty-eight hours, but Hanne's hints had inspired him to give in to temptation.

"A copy of an airline ticket doesn't prove Vandekerckhove was in Nice for four days," she said a minute later, between bites.

Van In offered her what was left in the pot, and she shoveled it greedily onto her plate.

"The south of France is only an hour from Brussels by plane," she continued. "There are some, let's call them the stinking rich, who wouldn't think twice of flying back for half a day, leaving time for a visit by limo to Bruges and Ghent."

"Versavel checked all the flights."

He helped himself unnoticed to a second glass of wine.

"The private jets too?"

Hannelore ate like a starved construction worker.

"I'll take that as a no," she grinned when Van In didn't respond.

By nine fifty-five, they had cozied up in the living room. Two glasses of wine had never tasted so good.

Van In let her lean on his shoulder, and he turned on the TV.

Moens appeared on the screen after a piece about the war in Bosnia.

"According to a recent police report, the bomb attack was the work of an extremist Walloon faction. . . ."

"Jesus," Van In groaned.

Hannelore woke with a start when he turned up the volume from six to ten.

"According to State Security, the Mouvement Wallon Révolutionnaire has been active for almost twenty years," said the journalist taking the interview.

"That's correct," said the mayor.

Moens was wearing his best suit, but was struggling to disguise his thick West Flemish accent.

"In the nineteen-seventies and eighties, the MWR was responsible for a wave of arson attacks in Wallonia, in most instances on Flemish-owned property. Just like today, they never claimed responsibility for their terrorist activities."

Moens used long complicated sentences, and it was close to a miracle that they made any sense at all.

"Are you expecting further attacks, Mayor Moens?"

Moens turned to the camera like a tormented Churchill. "The security services are on red alert, and the minister of the interior has just granted permission for two special-intervention platoons to be positioned at strategic points in the city throughout the night."

"So the citizens of Bruges can sleep secure?"

Moens conjured a smile that would have made many a U.S. presidential candidate jealous. "Bruges at this moment is unconquerable," he declared with pride. "We're determined to nip any potential acts of terror in the bud."

Van In zapped angrily to a commercial station. Anything was better than Moens's bullshit.

"In a hundred years' time, they'll be able to use his statement for high school TV," he growled. "The fall of Western democracy in ten installments."

Hannelore let him blow off steam.

"Anything else worth eating in the house, Pieter?"

Van In looked deeply into her eyes.

"There's a jar of pickled herring in the refrigerator," he said, not quite sure what she was on about. "Don't tell me you're really—"

"Go get it. I'm starving."

"Are you serious? I thought you were joking. How can you be so sure, for Christ's sake?"

"We'll see who's laughing in nine months," she said playfully.

Van In wasn't in the mood for a discussion on women's intuition. He got to his feet and headed for the kitchen.

"There are still three of them swimming in the jar."

"I'll take all three, and pour the juice in a glass."

Van In didn't protest. As a father-to-be, he just did what he was told.

21

Precisely a week had passed since person or persons unknown had blown up the statue of Guido Gezelle. The day after the mayor's melodramatic TV interview, Flanders's right wing was up in arms and the newspaper headlines were as plain as the nose on your face. No more shilly-shallying: the annual transfer of billions of francs from Flanders to Wallonia had to stop. The Flemish authorities held emergency consultations, and a variety of organizations threatened concrete action. Flanders was a powder keg, and one stupid statement had lit the fuse.

"Moens just farted," Versavel observed with undisguised sarcasm. "The system's gone haywire."

Van In put down his newspaper and lit a cigarette. "The Flemish are a hardy bunch," he said resignedly. "They'll swallow almost anything. But if you touch their historical patrimony, they lose it big-time."

"And why now?" said Versavel. "The bomb attack was last week, and it hardly made the news. Now they're rolling out the heavy artillery."

"Odds on, the news editor is from Bruges."

"What do you mean?"

Van In tore a sheet of paper from a notepad and scribbled in jagged letters: "Vandekerckhove / Zeebrugge / billionaire–Bostoen / Bruges–State Security–Creytens / Bruges / investigating magistrate–X / Bruges? / press."

Versavel studied the names. "What connects them?" He grabbed the telephone directory for Brussels from his desk and looked up the TV station's number.

Van In stubbed out his half-smoked cigarette and lit another.

"Mr. Lanssens isn't in his office? Can I reach him at home?" Versavel fiddled with his moustache, his pen at the ready. "It's extremely urgent," said Versavel. "It's about yesterday's broadcast. We're following a new line of inquiry, and I'm certain Mr. Lanssens—"

Versavel nervously tapped the edge of the receiver with his fingers.

"No, I need to talk to him personally." It took a full minute, but then Versavel gave the thumbs-up and started to scribble Lanssens's details on the back of a piece of scrap paper.

"I have the number of his car phone," Versavel beamed.

In less than five minutes, the National Records Office computer coughed up an answer to the sergeant's question.

"Lanssens is Bruges-born and -bred. He moved to Brussels in 1968. Before that, he was a journalist with the *Bruges Trade Journal*."

"The man who wrote the series of articles on our man Scaglione. I should have guessed," said Van In enthusiastically. "Long live the chaotica."

Versavel nodded pensively. The commissioner's loopy theory was sounding more plausible by the minute.

The telephone interrupted his musings.

"Hello, Sergeant Versavel speaking."

Van In lit a cigarette and smiled when Guido tried to respond in French.

"C'est très gentil," he heard him say. *"Oui."*

A silence followed and Versavel plucked nervously at his moustache. *"Bien sûr. Je vous donne le commissaire Van In."* Versavel handed him the receiver with a scornful smile. "They found a file on Scaglione," he grinned.

Hannelore had never been to police headquarters before, but no one asked for her ID. A young officer accompanied her to room 204.

"Au revoir," she heard Van In say as she walked inside.

"That was Neufchâteau, sweetheart," he said, upbeat. "The Scagliones have a bit of a reputation. Our friend Luigi retired to Sicily in the seventies; his son Enzo still lives not far from here. There's no such thing as coincidence."

"I've got news too," she said. "On Saturday, March 11, Fiedle rented a Learjet from Abelag Private Jet Leasing. According to the flight plan, it took off at four-thirty P.M., destination Nice."

"The bouillabaisse," Van In roared.

Both Hannelore and Versavel were dumbfounded.

"Bouillabaisse?" they echoed.

Van In grinned like an adulterous woman who had just witnessed a judge hit her husband with a massive alimony schedule.

"Tub gurnard and zander, the fish they typically use in Mediterranean fish soup. Fiedle had bouillabaisse in his stomach."

"But you can eat bouillabaisse anywhere in Europe," Versavel observed dryly.

"Of course you can," Van In said. "But don't try to tell me this isn't right up our alley."

Hannelore took off her coat and sat gracefully on the edge of Van In's desk.

"The jet was on standby until four-thirty A.M., and then it returned to Belgium with a single passenger."

"Vandekerckhove?"

"The pilot described the man as elderly and heavyset. I faxed him a photo of Vandekerckhove."

"And?"

"Nothing. The passenger was wearing a scarf over his face and didn't say a word to the crew."

"Now we know at least that Vandekerckhove lied," said Versavel. "The nocturnal trip makes him very suspect."

"I presume it's enough to have him arrested," Van In mused. "A DNA test would certainly simplify matters."

Hannelore nodded. If Creytens refused to cooperate, she would go directly to the public prosecutor.

"So you think Vandekerckhove killed Fiedle," she said bluntly.

Van In was aware that he couldn't give a flippant answer to her question. If the test was negative, Hannelore would look like a fool, and young magistrates were very vulnerable beings, especially at the public prosecutor's office.

"Actually, I don't," he said unexpectedly. "I can't imagine Vandekerckhove busying himself with the dirty work, and certainly not right in the middle of Bruges."

"What are you planning to do?" she asked in despair. "Surely you don't think he's going to volunteer a DNA sample."

Van In tried to order his thoughts. There were so many elements he had to account for.

"Give me a minute. I think it's time for another little chat with Tjepkema."

The Groningen commissioner had been just about to call Van In when his phone rang.

"Hello, Jasper. Pieter here."

"Talk about telepathy," Tjepkema grinned. "The results of the autopsy arrived just fifteen minutes ago."

"And?"

"Frenkel died from a blow to the skull. The fire was to get rid of the evidence, as you thought."

"The blood group?" said Van In impatiently.

"A-positive. Is that any help?"

"No, Jasper. The skin under Fiedle's nail was O-negative."

"Shame, Pieter. It looks like you're going to have to wait for the results of the DNA test."

"Thanks anyway, Jasper."

"Perhaps this might help," said Tjepkema, trying to be optimistic. "According to a couple of locals, someone came asking about Frenkel on Thursday evening. One of them referred him to the holiday house."

"Do you have a description?"

"We certainly do," Tjepkema beamed. "Male, thin build, five-ten or thereabouts, thirty to thirty-five years old, straight black hair, trendy dresser with a southern European look."

"Scaglione," Van In whispered.

"What was that, Pieter?"

"You're a star, Jasper."

"My pleasure, Pieter. I'll call if I have more news. 'Bye."

Hannelore was fidgeting with her blouse, and Versavel stared at Van In with bated breath.

"Vandekerckhove's off the hook," said Van In, "unless he's O-negative."

"Maybe they used a hired killer," said Hannelore matter-of-factly.

"Who's 'they'?" Versavel appropriately wondered.

"No idea," Van In sighed. "I think I need to take time out for a couple of hours."

"Then I'm going with you," Hannelore chirped.

The fire was still smoldering when they arrived back at the house. Van In adjusted the thermostat to 72 and tossed a symbolic log on the grate.

"Carton's going to be looking for you later," she teased.

"Then the luck's on your side," he retorted sarcastically. "Magistrates don't need an excuse when they take a couple of hours off."

"The courts aren't soft on men who molest their pregnant wives," she snapped.

"I almost believed you, Hanne," said Van In wearily. "But I checked a couple of books this morning. It's impossible to tell if you're pregnant after a week."

She walked to the refrigerator.

"Any pickles?"

"No, sweetheart. If you want gherkins, you'll just have to buy them yourself."

"Oh, how I wish I was Mrs. Van In," she pouted.

"Please, Hanne. I came home to think."

"Would Holmes like a jab of morphine, or shall I make a pot of coffee to stimulate the old gray matter?"

"There's some cake in the cupboard," he said resignedly.

When Van In stormed back in at six-thirty with two jars of pickled gherkins, Hannelore was sitting in the living room with an exceptionally pale young man.

"May I introduce Xavier Vandekerckhove?" she said with a gracious gesture of the hand.

Van In looked like a child who had just received a visit from ET. He recognized Véronique's frail, slightly balding bag carrier immediately. This was Armageddon, he thought with a sigh. Hannelore seemed highly amused.

"Xavier can spare you a bunch of mental acrobatics; true, Xavier?"

The timid young man nodded. Van In put the gherkins in the refrigerator and poured himself a cup of coffee. A Duvel would have tasted a lot better.

"Good evening, Commissioner Van In. I suppose I'm the last person you expected to see."

You can say that again, Van In thought, obliged to agree. He broke into a cold sweat.

"I've been in two minds whether to contact you, but circumstances compel me. . . ."

Xavier spoke like someone who had just visited a speech therapist. He articulated every syllable.

"That's very courageous of you, Xavier."

Van In cast a desperate glance in Hannelore's direction, but she was playing the Queen of Sheba.

The young man didn't beat around the bush.

"I wanted to talk to you about my father and about Thule."

Van In sat down and took in a mouthful of lukewarm coffee.

"Very few people know that my father has two sons. Ronald was always Daddy's favorite. I'm the problem son. No one's heard of me."

Xavier was clearly having a hard time. His pointed adam's apple bounced up and down in a frenzy.

"Father thinks I'm mentally unbalanced and refuses to let me be part of the business. But that doesn't mean I'm retarded, you understand."

"I'm already convinced," said Van In in an optimistic tone.

"That's why I asked Véronique to tell you about my father. He really was in Villa Italiana on March 11."

Van In froze. "True, yes, that's what she told me," he said nonchalantly.

If Xavier coughed up any more details, Bruges would soon be one more unmarried mother the richer.

"Véronique's a sweet girl. She goes with anyone and everyone, but that doesn't bother me. No one knows that I'm in love with her."

Xavier knew how to build up the tension.

"I thought you'd be able to solve the case on the basis of my hint, Commissioner. But I had no way of knowing that my father would come up with a watertight alibi."

"Not as watertight as he thought," said Van In. "We've already discovered some holes in it."

"Thank God," Xavier sighed. Beads of sweat formed on his forehead. The glow of the dancing flames gave his ashen complexion a yellowy sheen.

"But tell me something about Thule, the name you mentioned a moment ago," said Van In.

He hoped that Hannelore wouldn't notice how desperate he was to change the direction of the conversation.

Xavier nodded submissively. "Electronics is my hobby," he said with a hint of pride.

Hannelore looked at Van In. He avoided her stare. They were both thinking the same thing: Xavier seemed far from balanced.

"Please be patient, Commissioner. I'll get to the point in due course," said the delicate young man, anticipating their surprise. "My father gave me free rein, and money was never an obstacle. But what started as a pastime turned into a nightmare."

Van In lit a cigarette. Hannelore pulled up her legs and huddled into a corner of the couch. The young man's story intrigued her immensely.

"In my free time, I installed listening devices in every corner of the house. You should know that I was never allowed to be part of anything. If we had visitors, I was always banished to my room. The listening devices gave me the feeling that I was joining in somehow. That's how I discovered Thule," he said with a weary smile.

"Does the name Thule have anything to do with Fiedle?" asked Hannelore.

"It certainly does, ma'am. You should know that the Thule Society is almost a hundred years old. It started off as a pan-German order of knights with branches in the business world and politics. Dietrich Eckhart, one of the order's founders, is said to have confided in one of his friends in 1919: 'We need a man who can bear the sound of a machine gun. Those bastards'—he meant the Jews and the communists—'need the fear of God put into them. We don't need a gentleman officer, we need working class with a loud mouth. He has to be vain and unmarried; then we'll get the support of the women.'"

"Well, I'll be damned," Van In grumbled. "It sounds as if Mr. Eckhart and his cronies got what they wanted."

Vandekerckhove's son concurred with an alert glance.

"According to reports, Eckhart was an adviser to Hitler for a time. He inspired him to write *Mein Kampf* and helped organize the Wannsee Conference when the Nazis adopted the Endlösing—the 'Final Solution.'"

"A jolly little club," Van In snorted.

Fascist stories like this gave him goose bumps.

"I found the information in an encyclopedia," said Xavier. "According to the source, the Thule Society was disbanded in 1944."

"Which is probably not true," said Van In with an undertone of disbelief.

"I'm afraid you're right, Commissioner. Thule has never been more active. But their tactics have changed. Now their goal is economic dominance."

"A fascinating theory, Xavier," said Hannelore. "But what does it have to do with Bruges?"

"Good question, ma'am."

Van In got to his feet and shuffled to the kitchen.

"Beers all around?" he asked.

"A Coke for Xavier," Hannelore shouted at his back.

Outside, the sun's last rays disappeared behind a gold-rimmed cloud.

"Thule evolved over the years into an exclusive club of businessmen. Their only goal was to make money, and the end always justified the means. They have connections with the mafia and are trying to worm their way into the European Parliament."

"Jeez," Van In exclaimed. "And your father thinks you're backward."

Xavier sipped carefully at his Coke. The compliment clearly pleased him.

"Let me spell it out," he said. "Thule wants to pocket Bruges and turn it into a sort of medieval Disneyland. Their strategy is very simple. They've been buying up property in the city for quite some time via my father's real estate company, exclusive residences that they plan to sell later to a privileged few."

"Jesus," Van In grunted. "That's why Invest Bank was after my house."

"My father is on the Invest Bank board of directors," Xavier confirmed.

"The bastard," Van In snorted.

Hannelore smiled. She was happy that she had been able to solve the house issue.

"But there's a whole lot more. To achieve their goal, they need to eliminate Bruges's shopkeepers and business owners and evacuate its inconvenient population. Locals just get in the tourists' way. The traffic-circulation plan was a first step in undermining the confidence of the business people. By making the city inaccessible, they ruin hotel tourism and force the people living in the periphery to shop in the suburbs. The major shops and chains simply relocate and the smaller businesses go bankrupt. Their place is taken by the multi-national wage slaves who concentrate on selling 'Belgian' chocolates, lace, and sandwiches to day-trippers.

"The second phase is the creation of a bedroom community outside Bruges. The same idea was introduced in Venice decades ago. The city itself is an open-air museum and amusement park, and its employees live in Mestre, an artificial appendage to the city of the Doges."

"The polders. Do you remember those photos of Fiedle's?" said Van In, slapping his forehead with the palm of his hand.

Xavier took more than a little pleasure in being able to surprise the commissioner.

"My father wants to reconnect Bruges with the sea. Agricultural labor law is squeezing out the farmers, and more and more of them are selling out. They plan to use part of the polders as a nature reserve to pacify the Greens. The rest is earmarked for residential estates. There's a European consortium that has plans to build three thousand new houses along the Bruges-Zeebrugge axis."

"That's why they need Moens," said Van In.

"According to Fiedle, the mayor constituted a serious obstacle and wasn't to be underestimated," Xavier concurred. "The city's previous administration had already signed off on the project. 'The Pride of the Polders' would already have been a fact if the elections hadn't tossed a monkey wrench in the works."

"So the death threats and bombings were designed to force Moens to give his support," said Hannelore, shaking her head.

"In part, ma'am. The attacks were intended to create anxiety. While the city's businesspeople are reeling from the effects of the economic crisis and the traffic-circulation plan, an additional crisis, brought about by a wave of terrorism, was guaranteed to bring them to their knees. No one can afford another bad season."

"Unbelievable," Hannelore shivered.

Van In lit a cigarette. Too much information. His head was spinning.

"Is Creytens a member of Thule?" he asked.

Xavier produced a notebook. "Creytens, Lanssens, Bostoen, you name it. They're all part of one massive plot."

"And the MWR?"

"Afraid not, Commissioner. The revival of the MWR was concocted by Bostoen. If they can prove the Walloons were responsible for the bomb attacks, then the hunt is on. And a witch hunt is precisely what Thule is after."

"Creative stuff."

Van In poked the fire and stared at the pallid young man. Xavier and chaos theory were a perfect match. His testimony allowed Van In to create order in what was otherwise a series of apparently unconnected people and events. He now knew that Creytens had passed on information about Adriaan Frenkel via Thule to the man who had killed him.

22

NICOLAI ARRIVED IN BRUGES SHORTLY before noon. The young Walloon was inconspicuously dressed in a black track suit and a short woolen jacket. His nylon rucksack contained two hundred feet of thin-gauge climbing rope, a pair of pliable shoes, a harness with a figure-eight descender, a dozen or so pitons, and a sack of magnesium chalk. He was carrying a sports bag without a logo in his right hand.

He had called his client the evening before. The message was short: I climb tomorrow.

"Okay," was the response from the other end of the line.

It was a couple of degrees warmer in Bruges than in Ghent. According to the official forecast, temperatures that night weren't expected to drop below 45°, slightly overcast with a moderate southerly. This was the ideal moment, the moment he had been waiting for.

Nicolai took the bus to the center of town, passing the statue of King Albert on horseback for the second time. His muscles quivered, and an accelerated pulse pumped adrenaline-rich blood to every part of his body. Nicolai was always nervous before a climb. He knew from experience that he would only calm down when he had confronted the enemy face to face.

He got off the bus on Market Square, under the indifferent gaze of Jan Breydel and Pieter Deconinck. The diminutive Walloon looked up with a degree of admiration at the men who had once fought for Bruges's freedom.

In 1302 they had defeated the cream of France's cavalry in the Fields of Groeninge in Courtrai. They had fought for their freedom and confronted the tyranny of an arrogant feudal liege. Cities such as Bruges, Ghent, and Ypres had struggled hard to cast off their vassal state and had aspired to greater independence by extorting various privileges. Priceless documentary evidence of their successes was preserved in the Belfort. The tower functioned as a shrine to the rights these "free citizens" had toiled to acquire. The halls beneath symbolized freedom of trade.

Nicolai had prepared his task to the last detail. He had spent the last few days reading whatever he could find on Bruges. The Walloon considered it important to know his adversary through and through.

Nicolai had enormous respect for the thirteenth-century tower and the chunk of history the proud Belfort harbored within its walls. But he had come, nevertheless, to mutilate Bruges's fortress in exchange for a handful of silver.

Van In had tossed and turned the entire night. Hannelore had sought refuge on the couch downstairs. In moments of crisis, she preferred to leave him to his own devices. Truth be told, Xavier Vandekerckhove's story had also taken her unawares.

The world was a rational place these days, she thought, or pretended to be. Solutions that appeared out of the blue could be hard to digest.

She brought him a cup of coffee in bed and found him snoring loudly. When a kiss didn't work, she shook him by the shoulder.

"Eight o'clock, honey, time to get up!"

Van In opened his eyes in a daze, blinked in the brightness of the light, and pulled the blankets over his head in a temper.

"It's Sunday," he growled.

Hannelore shrugged her shoulders, left the tray on the dresser, and took off her clothes. She snuggled up against his back, and within thirty seconds he was wide awake.

"It's Wednesday," she said.

When they were done, Van In lit a cigarette and looked at his alarm clock.

"Twenty past eight," he grumbled.

"You're not twenty anymore," she teased.

Van In stubbed out his cigarette and made his way to the bathroom, mature perhaps but still an Apollo.

"Are you free tonight?" he shouted before turning on the tap.

Hannelore followed him, pulled back the curtain, and joined him in the shower.

"I can't hear you."

They stood under the hot shower for ten full minutes. When they were getting dressed, Hannelore couldn't resist ruffling his dripping wet hair with her fingers.

Van In was waiting for her at the courthouse around seven-thirty that night. He had hurried to be on time. He and Versavel had spent a busy day organizing all the paperwork. Now his heart was pounding. With a little luck, this sordid business would be over by the morning.

They didn't have much trouble finding Enzo Scaglione's farm. The farmhouse was clearly visible from the old Roman road connecting Torhout with Diksmuide. A narrow winding gravel track led up to the property.

One side of the farmyard served as an asphalt parking lot with room enough for three cars. Scaglione had commissioned a landscape gardener with a painful lack of imagination to design the remainder. What was supposed to be a garden consisted of a patch of uniformly mown grass with a trio of birch trees in the middle, and an elongated rose bed running parallel with the front of the house.

An obligatory privet hedge shielded the green wilderness from prying eyes.

The farmhouse had been completely renovated. The old narrow windows had been replaced by expensive and more substantial frames, and a rickety but picturesque two-part stable door had been restored and preserved. Scaglione had left the white exterior plasterwork untouched, together with the tarred black strip along the bottom of the wall. A niche above the door still housed a polychrome plaster statue of the Blessed Virgin.

Van In parked the VW Golf on the asphalt in front of a massive barn door.

"Do you think he's at home?" asked Hannelore as she stepped out of the car. She shivered as a gust of icy wind cut through her jacket.

"We'll soon find out," said Van In optimistically.

Enzo Scaglione had seen the police vehicle drive up the gravel track. He had prepared for this moment a thousand times. His heartbeat slowed, though, when he realized there was only one car. If they had come for the reasons he was expecting, there should have been more of them. As the VW Golf approached at an exasperatingly slow pace, he tried to work out what he had done wrong. Frenkel was dead, and he was the only one who could have queered the pitch. The Dutchman had followed Fiedle for some reason or other, and he hadn't been able to finish him off as he had planned. Good thing the German had died from his injuries. He couldn't understand how the cops had made the connection. Herr Witze had assured him that Frenkel hadn't reported a crime, and the investigating magistrate who was handling the case was a prominent member of Thule.

Enzo carefully concealed his Magnum in a specially carved hollow in one of the beams supporting the ceiling. He had carved out the secret compartment himself and attached a door that could be opened and closed with the flick of a finger.

"There's light inside," said Van In, pointing to the chink in the heavy curtains.

"Be careful, Pieter. Are you armed?"

He shook his head.

Hannelore was afraid, but she too refused to back off.

Van In inspected the front door. There was no bell. He clenched his fist and knocked.

Enzo took a deep breath, ran his fingers through his hair, and headed for the door. He waited to open it until the policeman had knocked a second time.

"Good evening," he said stiffly.

"Good evening, Mr. Scaglione. Van In, Bruges Police."

He deliberately didn't introduce Hannelore.

"May we come inside?"

An ordinary cop, he thought with suspicion.

"Of course."

Enzo let them pass and pointed to a comfortable lounge suite. "How can I help you, Mr. Van In?"

He grabbed a chair and positioned it beneath the beam with the secret compartment.

"This is an informal visit, Mr. Scaglione, more or less," Van In smiled affably. "Do you mind if I smoke?"

"Feel free. There's an ashtray on the side table."

As Van In lit his cigarette, Scaglione suddenly had an exceptionally unpleasant thought. On Sicily, hired killers sometimes pretended to be policemen. The woman was only a distraction.

Scaglione got to his feet and rested his hand on the side of the wooden beam.

"I don't have the police at the door every day," he said apologetically. "But isn't it usual for you to identify yourself first?"

"No problem."

Van In reached into his inside pocket. Enzo propped the tip of a finger in the groove above the compartment door.

Van In produced his police ID, and Enzo dropped his hand.

"The farm here is a little remote," he laughed nervously. "You can never be careful enough."

Neither Van In nor Hannelore reacted to his transparent cliché.

"May I ask the reason for your unexpected visit, Mr. Van In?" He straightened his tie and sat down again.

"I presumed you would know the reason, Mr. Scaglione. Don't you read the papers?"

Hannelore braced herself. She planned to hit the floor if Scaglione made a false move.

Enzo shrugged his shoulders. "How could I possibly know, Mr. Van In?"

"Last week, someone blew up the statue of Guido Gezelle," said Van In coolly.

The atmosphere in the tiny living room was extremely tense. Hannelore watched Scaglione. The man was pretending to be nervous, and that worried her.

"You probably think I followed in my father's footsteps," Enzo drawled.

His eyes glistened like polished silver. Van In said nothing and blew a cloud of smoke toward the ceiling.

"I'm afraid I'm going to have to disappoint you, Mr. Van In. My father is dead. He abandoned my mother when I was a student. I earn an honest wage. Look around you. The BMW in the garage is my most precious possession."

Van In nodded superficially. The living room furniture was basic, the television prehistoric, and the paintings on the walls were garage-sale and worse.

"If I had come to arrest you, I wouldn't have come alone," said Van In, easing the tension. "To be honest, the past doesn't interest me."

Enzo made a vague gesture with his hand.

Van In continued: "I know in the meantime that the Mouvement Wallon Révolutionnaire is no big deal. Thule has been trying to pull the wool over our eyes, and the society almost succeeded."

Scaglione didn't visibly react to the word "Thule."

"Whose idea was it? Fiedle's? Vandekerckhove's? Bostoen's? Or yours, Mr. Scaglione? I'm curious to know what's next on the program."

"Mr. Van In," Scaglione protested. "Forgive me, but I really don't have a clue what you're talking about."

The Sicilian pretended to be upset. Hannelore registered his reaction down to the last detail.

"Then let me come to the point, my dear Enzo."

Van In had confused him. The unexpected use of Scaglione's first name was consciously timed.

"If I'm not mistaken, your mother was killed by a drunk driver eight years ago."

Scaglione jumped to his feet. *An excellent opening move*, Van In exulted.

"Sit down, Enzo, and listen carefully."

Scaglione collapsed onto his chair like a sack of flour. Van In knew he had won the argument. The man's emotional reaction to the death of his mother was still intense, in spite of the intervening years.

"The killer"—he used the word on purpose—"did a runner and the case was never solved. But what you don't know, Enzo, is that the police were bribed."

Scaglione looked up. He gritted his teeth, and his upper lip trembled, a not-uncommon reaction for a southern type, for whom the boundary between unbridled sadness and vindictive rage was often extremely narrow.

"And you said nothing," he roared, flying from his chair and pacing up and down.

"Take a seat, Enzo. I only discovered the truth yesterday."

Van In had succeeded in completely disorienting Scaglione. He had confronted him with a feeling of guilt he had been carrying around for years. Enzo had come home late that night. He had promised his mother he would go shopping with her to the market, and when he didn't show up she had decided to go alone. At least that's what it said in the official police report Van In had received by fax from Neufchâteau.

"So you know who killed my mother, Mr. Van In?"

"And I can prove it, Enzo."

Scaglione took a deep breath and turned around. His sadness had dissipated and his penetrating gaze gave Hannelore the shivers.

"I guess the information isn't free of charge," he said impassively.

"That's what I was trying to explain, Enzo. I want the bombings to stop."

Scaglione started to pace up and down again. A Sicilian's oath of secrecy was a sacred thing, but he was also half Belgian.

"I'm informed that the bomb attack has to do with 'The Pride of the Polders.'"

Scaglione glanced skittishly in Van In's direction. This cop knew more than was good for him.

"The bomb was intended to pressure the mayor into approving the project. Blowing up Gezelle was a warning. Am I right?"

Scaglione nodded, searching feverishly for a solution to the dilemma that was tearing him apart.

"Okay, Enzo. We're off to a good start. Take a seat, then we can discuss things calmly."

Scaglione obeyed like a fractious jailbird. "Good, but first I want to know who killed my mother," he said.

Van In lit a cigarette and offered the packet to both Hannelore and Scaglione.

"Do I look like someone who doesn't keep his word?" he asked, feigning a huff.

"No," said Scaglione.

He suddenly got to his feet and crossed to an old-fashioned dresser next to the oil stove. Hannelore tensed her muscles. Neither she nor Van In were at their ease. *What if I've overplayed my hand*, Van In thought. The clatter of glasses broke the tension. Enzo turned to reveal three gold-rimmed shot glasses in one hand and a bottle of amaretto in the other. He set everything down on the coffee table, pulled up his chair, and poured unasked.

"The Belfort is the next target," he said as if he was announcing a sports event.

"When?" Van In barked.

"Next week."

"When exactly?"

"Wednesday," said Scaglione without emotion.

"How?"

"I don't know, Mr. Van In."

"Who?"

Scaglione shrugged his shoulders.

"I only spoke to the man by telephone. *He* called *me*. I have no idea where he lives."

Van In emptied his glass of sweet amaretto in a single gulp. Hannelore followed his example. She was happy all the commotion was over.

Scaglione refilled the glasses. He looked relieved.

"Are there other bombings on the cards?" Van In asked.

"I don't think so. After the Belfort, Travel Inc. will make the city of Bruges an offer. Vandekerckhove will cover the restoration costs in exchange for approval for his polder project. He'll be more subtle, of course, but that's the gist of it."

"I can picture him now," Van In concurred.

"And now the name of the killer, please."

Van In wiped his lips with the back of his hand.

"I'm a man of my word, Enzo."

He produced two sheets of paper from his inside pocket and gave them to Scaglione.

"This is a copy of the official police report. When you lodged a complaint with the local police in Neufchâteau, they tracked down a witness. The man described the car and was able to remember the first two letters of the license plate. A list was generated of every Mercedes with license plates beginning with AV. The local police in Bruges located a dark brown Mercedes with license plate AV 886. They put together an official report that was delivered to the public prosecutor's office two days later. In spite of the serious dent in the radiator, they didn't pursue the case, on the advice of Investigating Magistrate Creytens. The man in the car was Georges Vandekerckhove, Enzo, the man whose dirty work you've been taking care of."

"Creytens?"

"You know him, apparently," said Van In nonchalantly.

Scaglione realized he had let something slip.

Hannelore found it strange that his reaction to the name of the killer was minimal.

"My father was a friend of the Creytens family for years."

"Creytens senior, I presume."

"Who else?" Enzo snapped.

"Aha, yes, the Nibelung treasure," Van In jested. "How could I forget that little episode? So your father found the treasure after all."

Scaglione said nothing and gulped angrily at his amaretto.

"Come on, Enzo. That inquiry was shelved a century ago. Everyone knows that Creytens senior referred your father to the courts in Tournay. But our Luigi was an impatient man. Instead of waiting until the prosecutor general had convinced the local judge that a court case in Bruges would be ill-advised, he gave orders from prison for his comrades to place a bomb in front of the courthouse. He was unlucky. His lawyer was sick and hadn't been able to inform him in time that the judge in Bruges had already agreed to his request to have the case heard in a French-speaking court."

Scaglione grabbed the Amaretto. Van In noticed that his hands were trembling. The circle was almost complete, he thought, his mood upbeat.

"The question is: how did a gangster like Luigi manage to put the screws on a high-ranking magistrate?"

"Gold," Scaglione screamed. "Gold makes people crazy."

"I asked what Prosecutor General Creytens had to do with the case," Van In stubbornly insisted.

"Creytens managed to smuggle a senior SS officer out of the country after the war. The man took him into his confidence and told him about the treasure at the bottom of Lake Toplitz. He contacted Creytens again in 1966 and promised him and Vandekerckhove two million dollars if they successfully smuggled the gold to Paraguay."

"Why 1966?" asked Hannelore, joining the conversation for the first time. Scaglione paid little attention to her.

"Thule was disbanded in 1944 and restarted in 1966 by a number of greedy industrialists. The new generation came to the conclusion that war had been too blunt an instrument. They concocted an alternative strategy. Saber-rattling was out of fashion. They planned to dominate Europe in a different way, and they needed money. Young Vandekerckhove grabbed the opportunity, and that's how he came into contact with Creytens."

"So the neo-Fascists called in their little nest-egg," said Van In cynically.

History had revealed how the SS had managed to acquire their gold reserves.

"That's one way of putting it," Scaglione concurred. "But transporting sixteen tons of gold turned out to be easier said than done. Vandekerckhove arranged to meet the manager of L'Etoile."

"The unfortunate nightclub boss," Van In confirmed.

"Correct. He dumped the gold on the black market."

"And got a little too greedy," Van In guessed.

"Precisely. My father didn't like cheats and decided to teach him a lesson." Enzo threw up his hands and heaved a deep sigh.

"But you were only a child in 1966," Hannelore observed, unable to conceal her skepticism.

"That's correct, ma'am. My father never spoke about his professional activities, but in our world every good story gets passed on from generation to generation."

"I think you're crazy, Pieter Van In," said Hannelore as she got into the car. "The man is clearly guilty, and you pretend there's nothing wrong."

Van In lit a cigarette and blew the smoke against the steamed-up windshield.

"In court, they never stop whining about evidence," he said dryly. "Should I arrest Scaglione and watch him get released in twenty-four hours?"

Hannelore swallowed the rest of her critique. Van In was right.

"Scaglione will never betray the operation. Never," said Van In as he started the car.

"But surely he just did."

"All he did was identify the next target, the Belfort. But I'm convinced he knows more . . . the exact time, the identity of the bomber."

"He said Wednesday."

"True, that's what he said."

When they reached the main road, Van In shifted from third to fourth and hit the gas.

"Scaglione wanted the name of the man who killed his mother. He knows well and good that we're powerless."

"But he didn't really react when you named Vandekerckhove," she said, still unconvinced.

"He didn't need to. As far as he's concerned, Vandekerckhove is already a dead man."

"Are you serious?" she asked, finding him hard to believe.

"He's Sicilian! Lay a finger on their mother, sisters, wife, and you're history."

"I don't like it when you keep that kind of thing from me, Pieter."

Van In didn't react. Half a mile along the road, he slowed and turned onto a narrow dirt track. Hannelore stifled her disappointment. She felt like a schoolgirl, ditched after a passionate three-week relationship.

"Do we have to wait here much longer?" she asked after ten minutes.

"Are you cold?" He started the car and turned up the heater.

"Don't be such an idiot, Pieter."

He tried to put his arm around her shoulder, but she pushed him back.

"You are a self-centered bastard," she said angrily.

Van In tried to snuggle up to her.

"Leave me alone."

He obeyed submissively and pulled back.

"Don't forget our marriage plans," he soothed.

"Think again."

The heater was on full blast, but it wasn't enough to melt the ice that separated them.

"You're making me think I'm the enemy," he said after a moment's silence.

"That's your own choice, Pieter Van In."

"I love you, Hanne."

"Don't think you can buy yourself out of this with that kind of talk," she spluttered. "I want to know what's going on."

"I'll tell you later," said Van In obstinately.

"Why not now?"

"I don't want to get you into trouble. If I confide in you now, I'll be exposing my sweetest magistrate to serious professional error."

"As if that hasn't happened already," she snapped.

"Not according to the law, my darling deputy."

He caressed her and she slipped a couple of inches closer.

"Why are we waiting here?"

"Because," Van In whispered in her ear, "following a suspect is allowed by the rulebook."

She dropped her defenses, and their first argument as a couple was defused.

"So you think Scaglione has somewhere to go."

"It wouldn't surprise me," said Van In conspiratorially. "Did you notice the shoes he was wearing?"

"Black loafers," she answered, proud of her attentiveness.

"Correct. And did you check the floor?"

"Polished," she said with a frown.

"And the oil burner was at its lowest setting, in spite of the comfortable temperature."

"Please, Pieter, get to the point. This is killing me."

Van In pulled a face that would have made a professional clown jealous.

"We were lucky. Scaglione was getting ready to leave the house. He had taken off his slippers and turned down the burner. Our visit messed up his plans."

She looked at him, unable to follow.

"Next to the chimney . . . a pair of house slippers."

"So?"

"Well, Enzo Scaglione was raised by his mother. She taught him to change into his slippers if he was in for the night."

"Pieter Van In," Hannelore cautioned, "I don't know where to begin with you. If you notice that kind of detail, then. . . ."

"Then you're going to feel uneasy."

"Count on it," she said. "A policeman who presumes someone's planning to commit a crime because he's still wearing his outside shoes at eleven-thirty is a bit of a. . . ."

"Genius?" Van In grinned.

"Stop it."

Just as he was about to slip his hand under her blouse, the radio crackled. Versavel's timing was beginning to get on his nerves.

"Hello, Pieter."

"Hi, Guido."

"Am I interrupting?"

"Is he interrupting, Hanne?"

"Sorry, Pieter, but this is something you need to hear."

"Okay, speak."

"Croos faxed a photo earlier this evening of a certain Nicolai. The man was observed and photographed by routine surveillance not far from the Belfort. Turns out our Nicolai is a notorious sneak thief."

"And Croos waits until now to let us know," Van In sighed.

"The boys in Ghent broke into his apartment and found a floor plan of the Belfort."

"Jesus H. Christ."

Van In tried to keep his cool. If he sounded the alarm now and nothing happened, he would be making a complete idiot of himself. He first had to know what Scaglione was up to.

"Nicolai's off the radar. According to a neighbor, he trains three times a week at an indoor climbing wall in Courtrai."

"And they haven't seen him?"

"Negative, Pieter. I thought it was important to bring you up to speed."

"That's good of you, Guido. If I have more information, I'll contact the duty officer. Thanks, Guido."

"Sleep well, and say hello to Hannelore."

She grabbed the microphone. "'Bye, Guido."

At one-fifteen A.M., Enzo Scaglione drove out of the gravel track that led to his farmhouse and onto the main road. He was wearing a heavy gold chain around his neck, a gift from his mother for his twenty-first. There was a transmitter on the passenger seat, the kind you use to control model airplanes, the kind you can buy in shops. He had changed its frequency. The transmitter had a range of half a mile, and its frequency was now tuned to the detonators Nicolai would install in a couple of hours.

23

THE NIGHT WAS DARK AND mild, as he had predicted. Nicolai had kept a constant eye on the tower from midnight onward. A two-man police patrol did its rounds every twenty minutes, following the same regular trajectory: Market Square–Burg Square–Blinde Ezel Street–Dyver Canal, and back via New Street and Old Burg Street. Increased surveillance was annoying, but it wasn't much of a threat. The police were checking windows and doors. Neither of them was interested in the Belfort.

Nicolai timed their routine to the point of weariness and then positioned himself behind one of the pillars of the Pro Patria Gate on Kartuizerinne Street. He had swapped his sneakers for climbing shoes. The rope was under his track suit, coiled over his shoulder and across his chest.

When the patrol turned out of sight into Halle Street, he started his stopwatch and attached the explosives to the outside of his rucksack. He crossed the street with the invisibility of a cat and sought shelter in the shadow of the massive walls at the base of the tower. He stopped halfway at a downspout. A quick glance was enough. The street was empty and there were no lights to be seen in the surrounding windows.

The old market halls at the base of the tower form a closed square around an interior courtyard. The tower rises from the roof of the main building on the Market Square side, with Wool Street to the east, Old Burg Street to the west, and Halle Street to the south.

Nicolai had opted for the Halle Street side because it was more or less uninhabited and its narrowness almost completely restricted any view of the tower.

It took him less than a minute to climb the downspout onto the roof of the halls. He lay flat on his belly for a second, listening intently, and then scurried across the pitched and slated roof. Once over the crest, he was invisible from the street. His climbing shoes didn't make the slightest sound. He reached the foot of the tower in no time at all. *Now for the real climb*, he thought to himself. He rubbed magnesium powder into his hands and pulled himself up with the help of an anchor plate. The wall between him and the corner turret was relatively rough-hewn. He covered the distance to the first parapet in less than five minutes, hid behind the balustrade, and took stock. A quick glance at Market Square was enough. It was traffic-free, a vision the city's puritan traffic experts could only dream of. The silence was overwhelming, and every window was as blind as the eye of Polyphemus. In eleven minutes precisely, the police patrol would turn into Halle Street.

Nicolai crept with caution behind the balustrade to the east side of the tower where he could make use of the down pipe that led directly to the bottom of one of the second-level turrets. The chances of being seen were slightly greater, but it was worth it for the time it saved.

It took him three minutes. The balustrade, with its rounded arches that connected the four turrets, provided sufficient cover. As he waited for the police patrol to pass, he wandered like a wayward tourist to the west side of the tower. He waited a full ten minutes to be sure, and then commenced his climb of the northwest turret. Its enormous pinnacle provided plenty of handholds and footholds, and he was able to save a few costly feet by crossing the stone buttress to the tower wall.

The final part of the climb to the belfry windows was smooth and vertical. Nicolai explored the wall. The tiniest irregularity was enough for an experienced climber. He was almost two hundred feet above the ground, and the cold cut into his fingers. He stopped searching for a moment and rubbed some warmth into them. He took a deep breath and tried again. He finally found an opening in the pointing, wormed a finger into the gap, and pulled himself up. His curved feet sought support against the wall. An enticing wall anchor was only six feet away. His head was now at the same level as his contorted finger. He knew he could only hold this position for a minute more at most. One more handhold and the anchor would be within reach.

He carefully explored the surface of the wall. In spite of the cold, he started to sweat. His left foot searched every square inch. The seconds ticked past. The proud tower was putting up a fight, he thought, still determined to defeat it. Cramps in his arms finally forced him to let go. He lowered himself back to the top of the buttress. Two minutes later, he was back on the level of the balustrade.

It was three-thirty and he was now behind schedule. His only option was to try the southwest side. To avoid running the slightest risk, he waited until three-forty. According to his calculations, the police patrol would be in Wool Street at that moment.

Centuries of exposure to fierce rain had left the southwest wall in a much rougher state. Nicolai cursed himself for not thinking of it earlier. With the help of a protruding stone, he easily reached the first wall anchor, and from there it was a piece of cake. The anchors formed a sort of dotted black line all the way up to the belfry windows. It was three-fifty when he pulled himself onto the window ledge. It would only take him half an hour to place the explosives. Detonation was scheduled for five-thirty A.M., and by that time he would be safely ensconced on the first train to Ghent.

Nicolai unrolled the cable and placed the explosives as designated. He then attached the wires to the detonators. He was done in less than his half hour.

The descent was effortless. He abseiled to the street in three stages, using a double rope.

Scaglione parked his BMW in High Street—ironically enough, right in front of the former police headquarters. Van In saw him brake, and turned into Ridder Street.

"Keep an eye on him. I'll call for backup."

Hannelore stationed herself on the corner of Ridder Street and High Street. The flash of a cigarette lighter confirmed Scaglione's position.

"Van In here."

He ignored the obligatory call ID.

"Marc Vandevelde, I'm listening," the officer responded with a drowsy voice.

Van In jumped at the crackle of the radio and carefully closed the car door.

"I want the center of Bruges evacuated . . . immediately."

"What was that, Commissioner?" Vandevelde was suddenly wide awake.

"Evacuate all the residents of Market Square and the surrounding streets, on the double," he whispered angrily.

Van In understood Vandevelde's sluggish reaction. He had almost given up himself before Scaglione had finally driven from his home to a local disco, where he downed cappuccinos till four A.M.

"And contact the special intervention squad at the local police barracks. Tell them there's a bomb attack in progress."

"Commissioner?"

"Vandevelde," Van In barked. "I want you to sound the alarm, code red."

Silence. Vandevelde had eighteen months of service in front of him, and it wouldn't be the first time Van In had caused a commotion for nothing.

"Can you confirm, Commissioner?" he asked, still not quite sure how to respond.

"Vandevelde," Van In growled. "There's a rumor going around that you just bought a boat and that you're looking forward to causing trouble along the Belgian coastline, but let me make this one thing clear: if you don't do what you're told on the double, I'll make sure you never meet the payments on that fucking boat of yours. Understood, Vandevelde?"

The wailing sirens made Scaglione jump. Van In heard the engine of the BMW start and dragged Hannelore back to the Golf.

"The bastard's doing a runner. Why in Christ's name do they have to make so much fucking noise?"

Scaglione drove his car with one hand on the wheel. It was five-fifteen. He hoped the Walloon had finished on time. He ripped along Philippestock Street, his tires screeching, and turned into Vlaming Street. When he passed the city theater, he grabbed the transmitter and activated the signal. No explosion. He tried again. Nothing. *Fuck*, he said and hit the gas.

Market Square was hermetically sealed and police vehicles with whirling blue lights were parked everywhere. Major Adam, commandant of the anti-terrorist special intervention squad quartered in Bruges, was standing between the two fast-food stands in front of the Belfort.

The Belfort's concierge, a thin man in an old-fashioned dressing gown, nervously opened the enormous doors. Twelve members of the elite squad covered Adam's back. They were wearing military helmets and bullet-proof vests. Twelve Uzi barrels pointed ominously in the direction of the helpless concierge.

For more than an hour, fifty police officers searched the halls. There was no sign of explosives. The security guard manning the switchboard in the Coach House insisted that there had been no break-in and no alarm.

The neighborhood had been evacuated in the meantime. The governor had activated the requisite contingency plan, and the people living within a given distance of the Belfort had been transported to Boudewijn Park and given shelter in the main hall. A local TV camera crew had arrived just in time to shoot some film of the chaos.

Van In requested assistance twice as he tried to keep up with Scaglione's BMW, but the governor's contingency plan had used up all the available manpower. He gave up the chase just outside Beernem and headed back to Bruges.

"Why didn't you call in the local guys?" Hannelore asked. "You didn't even release his license plate number."

"We foiled the attack, didn't we?" said Van In, in a buoyant mood. "Don't worry yourself, Hanne. It all went better than I expected."

"Pieter Van In," she barked. "I demand an explanation, and I want it now."

"Scaglione is more useful if we let him do his thing for a while," Van In laughed.

"What?"

"Sorry, honey. But at this stage of the game, I don't want to compromise you."

"Where have I heard that excuse before?" she sneered. "And what if the bomb explodes without Scaglione?"

"Then our luck ran out. Did you hear anything?"

The experts from bomb disposal took over the search at six-thirty. A team of three, dressed in protective clothing, searched the tower from bottom to top. The elite squad from special interventions stood lookout and the officers of the Bruges Police sought cover in the surrounding streets. Van In and Hannelore had stationed themselves at the beginning of Vlaming Street.

At seven fifty-five, the bomb-disposal guys found the explosives. Van In followed their conversation on his walkie-talkie.

"There's enough here to blow up half the fucking tower."

"And the detonators?"

There was silence for a while, followed by a hoarse laugh.

"The idiot attached them backwards. You can announce the all-clear. Our terrorist is either an amateur or he's color-blind. He attached blue to red. You could hit the stuff with a sledgehammer and nothing would happen."

Scaglione tore along the freeway at 120 mph. He had tossed the transmitter out the window thirty miles back. He slowed down as he approached Brussels. No one had followed him. He drove through Vilvoorde toward Zaventem and parked his car close to the airport. An hour later he was drinking cappuccino at the Brussels South train station. He called the Bruges Police and gave them Nicolai's address.

His next telephone conversation, this time with Herr Witze, took a deal longer.

"The entire operation was botched. The Walloon fucked up, big-time."

"*Ruhig*, Herr Scaglione. Perhaps it's better so."

"Maybe, but I still want my money. My cover has been blown, I've lost my house, and I can kiss good-bye to Belgium."

Witze smiled. He took an expensive cigar from a silver box on his desk and lit it. "I'll give you a hundred thousand marks if you finish the job," he said affably.

Scaglione listened submissively. A hundred thousand Deutsche Marks was a shitload of money.

"On one condition," he said resolutely. "I decide how they die."

"No objection," said Witze. "The Polder Project was doomed to failure, but Fiedle wouldn't listen."

"And I want a new identity and a house on Sicily."

"Consider it taken care of, Herr Scaglione. I'll arrange an escape route via Switzerland. We'll see each other in forty-eight hours. Call me tomorrow. We can't fail."

Witze blew the smoke from his cigar into the light of his desk lamp. Once the gunsmoke over Yugoslavia had cleared, Leitner would be sure to accept his proposal to reconstruct Dubrovnik, he mused. Tourists are capricious creatures. A city bombed flat, rising from its ashes like a phoenix . . . they'll come in their millions. And millions of tourists meant money, big money. *The West is dead*, he thought to himself. *The future's in the East.*

Van In accepted the mayor's congratulations in a resigned mood. Moens made sure to give him a friendly pat on the back for the cameras.

"You've earned this promotion, Pieter, every bit of it," he said with a broad smile.

Hannelore applauded enthusiastically, and everyone followed her example. After the reception at city hall, they hurried back to the Vette Vispoort. Van In unplugged the telephone and disconnected the doorbell. Versavel had been given instructions to leave them alone for three days.

"Now you're a real commissioner," she teased. Van In lay on his back and stared through the window at the ominous clouds.

"I think it's going to rain," he said semi-indifferently.

Hannelore turned on her side and ran her fingers over his chest.

"Next stop: chief commissioner."

"And you, chair of the Court of Appeals."

Van In stretched out his hand, grabbed the bottle of champagne, and filled the glasses to the rim.

"You should be proud. You even made German TV. Everyone's talking about the heroic commissioner who saved Bruges from a terrible catastrophe."

"People have short memories," he said wearily. "Give them twenty-four hours and I'm just another cop."

Hannelore gently massaged his "stomach muscles."

"Don't say that. The people of Bruges will never forget what you did for their city."

"Crap."

"A bet?"

Van In took her hand. "You know the wager," he said with a lecherous grin.

"It's a deal, but I choose the position."

She grabbed the remote and zapped to the local TV station. News bulletins on the half hour. Van In tried to stop her.

"They're still talking about you, I'm certain of it," she stubbornly insisted.

"Give it a rest, Hanne. The whole business is twenty-four hours old."

"Okay, you choose the position," he conceded with a snigger.

Van In let go of her hand and eased his head deep into the cushion.

A commercial break.

"I've been thinking about the Michelangelo," she said.

Van In listened with half an ear.

"Don't you think it's strange that no one seems to be interested in checking out Frenkel's story?"

"Who wants to know the truth at this stage of the game?" Van In sighed.

"Every year, millions of tourists flock to see Michelangelo's *David* in the Uffizi Palace."

"You mean the *copy* of Michelangelo's *David*," she corrected. "The real thing's in a museum nearby."

"Precisely," Van In nodded. "And no one is interested."

"God almighty," she groaned.

"Is something wrong?"

"Jesus H. Christ."

Van In sat up straight and Hannelore gulped at her champagne.

"The city of Bruges is reeling today at the discovery of a horrifying double murder." The newsreader did her best to present the information as serenely as she could. "The judicial police are at a complete loss. The renowned industrialist Georges Vandekerckhove was found dead this afternoon in his villa in Middelkerke. The victim had been tied to his bed." They showed a photo of the villa. "An hour later, they found the remains of Investigating Magistrate Joris Creytens." The newsreader gulped. "Both men died in horrendous circumstances.

The perverted killer garroted his victims and then stuffed a gold chain in their mouths."

Van In grabbed the remote and turned up the volume. "Jesus H. Christ. Who would have thought?"

"Commissioner Croos of the judicial police has denied any connection between the murders and the recent bomb attack. Commissioner Van In was unavailable for comment."

"That's on your conscience, Pieter," she said coolly. "You let the killer go free."

"Can I help it if the scum kill each other? Vandekerckhove and Creytens were responsible for Frenkel's murder, don't forget. And who knows what else they had to answer for."

Hannelore shrugged her shoulders. He was right, of course. Any judge would have acquitted the two men for lack of evidence.

"But don't worry," said Van In. "Before we withdrew into our little nest, an international arrest warrant was issued for Scaglione. That loser has nowhere to go, and if the skin Timperman found under Fiedle's fingernail fits his DNA profile, then we've totally got him by the balls."

Van In threw his arms around her. She put down her glass, closed her eyes, and let him have his way.

"Let's do it missionary style," he said with a wink.

Now wasn't the moment to tell her that he had invented the police report about Vandekerckhove and the hit-and-run on Scaglione's mother. Versavel had banged out the whole thing on his old typewriter and Scaglione had walked right into it. The Belfort had been saved and Hannelore still loved him. What more could a man want?